WAYOB'S REVENGE

Arthur Swan

Wayob's Revenge is a work of fiction. Names, characters, business, events and incidents are either products of the author's imagination or used fictitiously. With the exception of public figures, any resemblance to actual persons, living or dead, is purely coincidental. Any opinions expressed belong to the characters and not the author.

This work is dedicated to the millions who come to Los
Angeles to create,
who believe in LA as an idea,
who believe creativity is not a right but hard work,
the hardest work.
who take risks,
unwilling to compromise their passion,
because passion is life itself.

Where's Wilson?

The door was open. The mattress bare. Aside from the toilet and bunk bolted firmly to the cinderblock wall, the holding cell was empty.

Saul had fucked up, that was clear. How badly depended on who found out that he'd left Rydell in the holding cell instead of booking him into the Metropolitan Detention Center.

But it wasn't just that. It was the way Rydell had begged to be confined with the other inmates. Just like Br'er Rabbit. He should have kept an eye on him instead of going home and lying awake, watching the shadows churn on the ceiling, while a tornado tore through his head.

Who was Wayob? And why would Saroyan, Rydell, and Aleman all claim to be him? How were they connected? Saul looked at Hernandez. She had all but ordered him to book Rydell into the MDC.

Her eyes seemed to darken. She brushed back her shock of white bangs.

"Don't worry," he said. "You're not accountable."

1

"You should've told me he was in the holding cell," she said. "We're supposed to be partners."

"I get it." No point in excuses. If he had any hope of recovering the way she'd seemed to soften toward him, he had to rectify the mistake. Maybe it wasn't as bad as it looked. Maybe someone else had simply moved Rydell or even booked him into the MDC like Saul should have done, which would be embarrassing but soon forgotten.

Saul pulled out his phone. The watch commander would know.

The elevator chimed.

Lieutenant Levy stepped out, her starched shirt strapped down by red suspenders, hair like fluffy curtains flapping against her cheeks as she marched toward them. Levy never left her office. She avoided conflict at all costs. Yet here she was. A soldier marching to the fray.

"Where's Rydell?" Saul asked her. No point in playing dumb.

Levy had the sort of plaster-pale skin that burned from a minute of direct sunlight, which made her flushed cheeks all the more dramatic. Her answer was an octave lower than normal: "The morgue."

The hallway seemed to sway. Saul's legs felt like guacamole. He grabbed the door of the holding cell, the steel cold in his hand.

Hernandez straightened. "Shit. How?"

Levy crossed her arms and stared at Hernandez, her eyes burning with an intensity he hadn't known she possessed. "Strangled himself with his shirt."

"This is on me," Saul said. "Hernandez told me to book him."

"I could have guessed," Levy said. "Wish I could

2

shield her from the blowback."

"What's the big deal?" Hernandez asked. "Rydell could have offed himself in the MDC just as easily."

Good point, Saul thought. To him the big loss was that Rydell had taken the easy way out when he could have led them to Wayob.

Levy explained how Lieutenant Mayfield, commanding officer of the Jail Division in the sheriff's department, was making a big deal about Rydell's suicide in the hopes of sweeping the Saroyan fuckup under the rug.

Hernandez snorted. "Good luck with that."

"Mayfield has friends in top brass," Levy said. "They're looking for blood."

Saul held his wrists out toward Levy. "So, take mine."

Levy wasn't about to stick her neck out for him, nor did he want her to. Despite Saul's seniority, she'd promoted Hernandez to lead detective and then blamed it on politics, as if the decision were above her pay grade. But they both knew she was punishing him, still, because when he'd shot a Black man on her watch, the fallout had stalled her career.

"You'd better hope this doesn't get out in the press." Levy turned toward the elevators. Then added, "I'm putting you on cold cases."

Saul's stomach churned. *Cold cases.*

Hernandez marched after her. "Both of us?"

Levy pressed the up button. "Sorry." The doors opened, and she hustled inside. End of the conversation, as if he could just let it go.

He reached out and blocked the left elevator door from closing as Hernandez grabbed the right. In his haste to reach the back of the elevator, where his belly would be less obtrusive, he bumped her aside. She pretended not to notice.

Instead of standing by the door, she squeezed in beside his plus-sized frame, her compact stature accentuated by his size.

The doors closed. Levy pressed the button for the sixth floor. Saul was already sweating. She pressed it three times and then stared at the numbers above the doors, as if she could ignore him and Hernandez into non-existence.

Saul glanced down at Hernandez. She was looking at him. His fuckup. His chance to justify his actions.

"Rydell wasn't working alone," he said. "If we don't continue the investigation, more people could die."

Levy frowned. No eye contact.

Saul continued, "He knew things he had no way of knowing, like where I was Saturday night."

Levy crossed her arms. "Like that's some kind of a secret."

Saul kept his life at the Magic Castle separate from work—like the Castle itself seemed separate from LA, an alternate world of ornate wood and crystal chandeliers where possibility sparked in the air—but sometimes his enthusiasm boiled over. On multiple occasions, he'd invited Hernandez to join him, though she'd never accepted, and now there was no point in asking again.

"He wasn't at the Magic Castle," Hernandez said. "We were on Olvera."

Levy chuckled. "At the Day of the Dead festival? How many people were there?"

"I doubt Rydell was one of them," Saul said. "Wrong demographic." As a white male, he'd received more than his typical share of odd looks.

"So why were you there?" ·

"Working the case," Hernandez said.

True, technically, though at the time Hernandez had been skeptical. She'd even teased him about inventing the whole thing about tracking Aleman there as an excuse to lure her out for dinner—and with a twinkle in her eye, like it was a good thing, maybe. But now that she'd seen his huge, hairy belly hanging over his too-tight tighty-whities, he could forget all about ever asking her out for real. He'd seen the look of pity in her eyes, and there was no path from pity to love.

The elevator doors opened. Sunlight poured in from the hallway that ran along the outer wall of the glass building. Levy marched out into the brightness, her figure blurred into a silhouette.

Saul motioned for Hernandez to go first, then trailed after.

Bad idea to mention Wayob, Saul knew, but he had no other card to lay down. "Saroyan and Rydell both pretended to be the same person," Saul said to Levy. He pulled out his phone and started the recording he'd made of Rydell. "…your fault that I am here…"

Outside Homicide Special, Levy paused and glanced back.

Saul turned up the volume. "Release me," Rydell was saying, "or I shall have to take revenge." Saul paused the recording.

"It was freaky," Hernandez said. "We've got Saroyan on video acting like that. You should see it."

Levy shrugged. "Weird's not enough." She pushed through the door.

Saul charged after her into the windowless room. As he reached for her shoulder, the half-dozen detectives

5

at their desks fell silent. Saul held back. No hard evidence. No hope of convincing her.

Levy slinked through the desks, slipped into her office, and locked her door with its papered-over window behind her.

Detective Williams smirked up at Saul from his desk. Saul stepped closer and glowered back until Williams looked down at his screen.

Hernandez motioned Saul back to the hallway.

He shut the door behind him. "It's not fair for Levy to punish you too," he said.

"That's not how this works. We're partners." She smiled with her lips but not her eyes.

"I get it. And I'm sorry. But...I can't give up until we catch this Wayob bastard."

"Don't apologize. I'm with you. We have to catch him. Levy might even be grateful once we do and she takes all the credit."

Saul shook his head. If they ignored her orders, Levy would hold a grudge regardless of the outcome. "You've got a big future in the department," he said. "Better if you work the cold cases for now. I've got nothing to lose."

In a couple of years Hernandez's son, Rumi, would be going to college. She needed this job, and so, as the lead detective, she couldn't permit Saul to go off and investigate Wayob. Which meant he'd have to go behind her back, which would probably shred whatever remained of their relationship, but what choice did he have?

Hernandez swallowed. "You go check out Wilson," she said. "I'll keep Levy off our backs."

A current of energy surged through his chest. She was going out on a limb because it was the right thing to do. "Wish you could come with me."

She lifted her head. Her eyes sparkled in the bar of sunlight streaming down the hallway. "You owe me one."

He almost hugged her. "That I do."

—

It was half past eleven by the time Saul turned onto Gray Wilson's street. As he rolled up the hill, he scanned the cars parked along the curb for Wilson's Camry. Not there.

Wilson lived in a single-story Craftsman with pale wood siding. Its driveway was empty. As Saul heaved himself out of the car, a crow squawked from a nearby power line and flew off.

He knocked on the door.

No answer.

He went around the side of the house and unlatched the gate. A narrow path led to a back deck shadowed by a palm. The yard of scraggly grass, surrounded by a tall gray wooden fence, sloped down from the house. He stepped up onto the deck and approached the double sliding doors. Blue sky reflected on the glass. He shielded his eyes and peered through.

Inside, a disarray of toys and magazines lay strewn across the carpet. Beside a couch was a plate of what looked like dried marinara. The house was as still and silent as the aftermath of a storm.

Saul returned to the front yard. Across the street, an elderly gentleman in a brown suit stood on his lawn, hand tented over his eyes.

Saul waved.

The man turned away. Staggered on rickety legs toward his house.

"Wait," Saul yelled. He hurried across the street. Instantly out of breath.

As he pounded up the front walk of the man's home, the man shuffled inside and slammed the door. A solid clap of wood on wood.

Saul lumbered onto the stoop and knocked. "I'm Detective Parker with the LAPD."

No answer.

Saul held his badge to the peephole. "I just want to ask a few questions. It's about your neighbor, Gray Wilson."

"I don't talk to crazies," the old man shouted through the door.

"Smart," Saul said. "I'm trying to stop one the crazies, and I'm hoping you can help me."

There was a long pause. The old man's voice trembled. "You know about the crazies?"

"That's why I'm here," Saul said, unsure if the man was referring to the Wilsons or some product of his own dementia. But he had to find out, unlikely as it was that the old man had seen Wilson do or say anything that would explain why Rydell had been so desperate to follow him. "Mind opening the door?"

The door unlocked. Inched open a crack. Behind it, the old man's eye was open wide above a dark bag of sagging skin. "Gray's not home."

"Any idea when he'll be back?"

"His car was towed."

"When was this?"

The door opened wider. The man's face was sallow, lined with deep crevices. "I'm Charlie Streeter." He held out a hand for Saul to shake then led him into the house. His suit still had the creases from where it had been ironed and it flapped around when he walked, like it was staked up by seven or eight frail bones and nothing else.

They reached a dusty living room with drawn curtains, lit by a table lamp with an incandescent bulb. Streeter sat stiffly in the wingback beside the lamp.

Saul sank into a catty-corner loveseat across from Streeter and waited. Give people silence and they tend to fill it.

Streeter snatched a prescription bottle from the side table. He clawed it open. Emptied two big pills into a trembling palm. "For my back." He dry swallowed. He leaned back. His face slipped into the shadow behind the lamp. "So, what do you want?"

From his coat, Saul pulled a deck of cards and a handkerchief. Magic tended to relax people. Something about the mystery made them want to open up. "Do you like magic?"

"No."

Saul folded the handkerchief around the cards and squeezed them in his fist. With his other hand, he pulled out the handkerchief with a flourish. He opened his palm.

The cards were gone.

No reaction from Streeter. His eyes were glassy, out of focus. Whether or not he'd even seen the trick, Saul had no idea.

"I want to ask about your neighbor, Gray Wilson."

"Good painter," Streeter said. "Sweet little girl."

"Anything unusual?"

Streeter exhaled. "He's not a crazy, if that's what you're asking."

Saul folded the handkerchief and creased it, stretching out the silence for Streeter to fill.

But he said nothing more.

Saul slid the handkerchief into his coat pocket and leaned forward. "I'm just covering the bases, you know? It's probably nothing to do with Wilson, but I've been dealing with these perps—crazies, you might say—who are all connected somehow."

"Crazies." Streeter nodded as if he knew exactly what he meant—how three different people had all acted like Wayob, and all spoken with that maniacal-musical cadence.

"Yeah. Do you know where Gray Wilson is?"

"After his car got towed, he and his wife loaded the kids in the minivan. I'd have told him not to park by the hydrant, if he'd asked me, but some people never learn." Streeter swallowed. "If they don't suffer the consequences." His hands were shaking, perhaps from guilt of not warning Wilson but more likely it was the blue pills.

"What you should be worried about," Streeter continued, "is crazy officers."

"What do you mean?"

"I'm talking about guys who attack people for no reason."

"I hear you."

"Yeah, you hear me, but what are you going to do about it?"

Was he referring to some incident in particular? Now it was Saul's turn to swallow. Had Streeter read about the Brown shooting? Saul never should have confronted him alone, and for that he accepted the consequences, but it had been Brown's play. He was the one who drew what Saul confirmed, after he shot him, was a gun. Saul had followed procedure. The shooting was justified. Not that anyone in the press cared to mention that. They had made it about another

Black man shot by a white officer.

"Do about what?" he asked.

"About the crazies," Streeter growled. "What do you think we're talking about?"

"I work homicides," Saul said. "But I want to help."

"What if you had a body? Then what would you do?"

Saul didn't want to go off on a tangent, but if Streeter had witnessed a crime… "Is this hypothetical? Or—"

"What if someone was killed in an accident caused by a crazy officer?"

"Then I'd call it in, same as with anyone else."

"But the officer might blame someone else. Like an innocent person who was just driving by in his car."

"There would be an investigation. Internal Affairs would jump on something like that."

"With all that bureaucracy, it's a wonder you guys ever solve anything at all."

Saul nodded. "I know what you mean. Did this happen to you, or someone you know?"

Streeter glanced down and to the right, all the wrinkles on his brow clenched together. "Can't a man ask a question?"

"Was Wilson involved?"

"Gray doesn't have anything to do with anything. He's going through a tough time and doesn't need you asking a bunch of questions and making things worse."

"Like what kind of a tough time?"

"How would I know? I only just met him Friday night."

That wasn't too surprising. In LA, neighbors rarely had time to be neighborly. Saul still hadn't met his.

"So, what makes you think he's going through a tough time?"

"Well." Streeter clasped his hands together. They kept shaking. "For one thing, he ran outside in his underwear."

Saul's gut churned. Rydell had forced Saul to strip down to his underwear before taking him hostage. Could this be related?

"Did you see who made him do it?"

"No one made him do it. He was out of his head."

Saul squinted. "So, you're saying Wilson is crazy?"

"Meh." Streeter coughed dryly. "I was married once. There's a reason I'm not now." He looked down, and light glinted on the sparse oily hairs combed across his sun-spotted scalp.

"You think it was an argument with his wife?"

"What else would it be?"

Good question. If Rydell hadn't tried to take Wilson hostage, then maybe this was just a coincidence. Saul was skeptical of coincidences, but the flip side of the coin was the human tendency to invent patterns where there were none. Coincidences *did* happen.

"Where did Wilson go in his underwear?"

"What? No. He went back inside. And don't ask him about it, either. What goes on between a man and his wife is his business. Besides, you only care about homicides."

"I care about all crimes. It's just a matter of priority. Did anyone else witness Wilson's unusual behavior?"

"In this neighborhood? Of course not. If a jetliner landed in the street, no one would notice unless they saw it on their phone."

"It's great you're here, then, to keep an eye on things."

"Meh. If they knew anything about anything, they would setup a neighborhood watch. I don't even live here. I'm just staying while my daughter is out of town." Streeter eased himself up out of the wingback. "Now, you'll have to excuse me."

Was Streeter holding back? Or was this feeling in Saul's gut just his own desperation to know why Rydell had been following Wilson?

Saul heaved himself up. "Where you headed?"

"Why would I be going somewhere?"

"You're all dressed up."

"Grand Park." He pointed at his eyes with his index and middle fingers, and then at Saul. "That place is swarming with crazies."

"Keep an eye on them. Good idea." Saul snapped his fingers and revealed a business card as if it had appeared out of the air. "Give me a call if anything else comes to mind about Wilson."

Streeter blinked, back hunched, but did not reach for the card. His arms seemed lost in the loose sleeves of his coat.

Saul placed the card on the side table beside the pills. "Don't worry," he said on his way out. "I'll do my best to stop the crazies."

No Such Thing

No sign of the marine layer. Not a wisp of cloud.
Nothing. Just the giant ball of burning hydrogen stuck
stubbornly above the horizon, its heat amplified by the
windshield.

Saul was desperate for AC, but that required
starting the car, and the kick of the engine would
almost certainly draw Wilson's attention.

Finding him had been easy. He'd pulled up Wilson's
LinkedIn profile and found his current employer,
Intrepid Solutions, right at the top. After driving to the
office, a tower in West LA, he found Wilson's Camry
in the lot and waited nearby. Having an officer show
up at work tended to put people on edge.

At three thirty, Wilson emerged from the stairwell
and approached his vehicle. He had a determined,
maybe even desperate, look on his face. Saul decided
to follow him. Maybe a domestic dispute was the
reason Wilson had run out of his house half-naked, but
what if it was something more?

Wilson drove to a residential street in Beverly Hills,

parked, and then just sat alone in his car. Saul parked a hundred yards behind him and waited. Was he meeting someone? Stalking someone in one of these multimillion-dollar houses? Ahead of the Camry, the street widened into a cul-de-sac where a formidable gate restricted entry to the exclusive neighborhood of Beverly Park.

As Saul waited, people returned to the other parked cars and departed, along with the shadow of the eucalyptus tree, which had provided some respite from being cooked in the heat. He sloughed off his jacket, took out his cards, and began shuffling.

Now that Rydell had offed himself, Saul's only hope of finding the truth was if Wilson knew something about him. It was hard to imagine what Rydell would have wanted with a software engineer, but then it was also hard to imagine how he'd have gotten tangled up with Saroyan and Wayob. If Wilson was involved too, would he admit it? That was the question.

Perhaps he'd just happened to be there when Rydell sped through that red light.

Since Wilson was Saul's only lead—besides the Lunas, who were stonewalling him—he wasn't ready to blow his cover just yet. Not until he knew what Wilson was up to.

He pulled out his phone and called Hernandez. After everything that had happened, he'd neglected to tell her that the Lunas never came home Saturday night and that Rosa claimed they had stayed with a friend—one she refused to identify.

Hernandez seemed unfazed. "Maybe their friend is illegal as well."

"It's more than that. They're hiding something. You saw how Rosa's grandmother acted at the death notification."

"Maybe, but we can't make them tell us, and it's probably unrelated. Let them mourn in peace."

"Maybe if you talked to them without me around, they'd open up? Use your Spanish powers."

Hernandez sighed. "They'll never trust me. I'm a cop."

"Just try," Saul said. "Please. I'll owe you one."

"You already owe me for covering for you on the cold cases."

"Indeed, I do. And now I owe you two."

"I charge interest."

"I'd expect nothing less."

After ending the call, he reclined his seat and prayed for the marine layer to roll over the city and cool things off. He squinted through the glare on the windshield at the dark shape of Wilson in his car.

The boom of an engine woke him. He'd dozed off with his mouth hanging open. He sat up, wiping the drool from his chin, just in time to see a black Maserati, the gate closing in its wake. The Maserati squealed as it hot-dogged down the hill.

Wilson's ignition kicked. As he U-turned, Saul slouched down and waited for him to pass. Then he started his own car and followed at a distance.

At Sunset, Wilson turned east toward his house in Silver Lake. Traffic was heavy. Saul closed the gap. They inched forward. Gridlock. Low clouds rolled across the sky: the marine layer, at last. The temperature dropped, and Saul opened all the windows and inhaled the moist, coastal air. It felt good.

After half an hour of stop-and-go grind, they reached Hollywood as the sun pierced the clouds on the horizon. Wilson turned right on Highland and parked a few blocks down. Saul cruised past. In the rearview, he watched Wilson enter The Woods, a dive bar with a stone and wood facade sandwiched between a liquor store and a Middle Eastern joint. Saul circled back, found a parking spot two spaces behind the Camry, and walked to the bar.

He opened the door to darkness. Peering inside was like looking into a cave. The Woods was the trendy sort of establishment that would be packed by midnight, but as his eyes adjusted he saw that right now there were only three patrons, including Wilson. All men, all at the bar, all turning toward Saul in the doorway.

He pretended to receive a call and retreated.

He understood the allure of booze. He'd tried on drinking after his marriage ended, but all he found at the bottom of the bottle was more misery and exhaustion. And despite eating less, he'd gained weight. After depositing countless paychecks into the Castle bar, it got to the point where he couldn't follow even basic sleight of hand, and that's when he finally gave up the booze. Because he lived for magic. Not to be fooled by it but to understand it. To learn the method because there was always a method.

But there was no such thing as real magic. No such thing as Wayob remotely controlling someone else.

The bottom dropped out of his stomach. He needed a snack. Wilson might leave while he was gone. This was a test, an opportunity to finally start his diet. His stomach would just have to wait. Maybe burn some of the excess baggage he was wearing.

Then, as if to try his resolve, a burger truck rolled to a stop in front of him. The Patty Wagon, its name decaled in a loopy cursive, hit reverse and wedged into the gap between his plain wrap and Wilson's Camry.

A line of customers materialized along with the smell of the grill. Saul swallowed. He could almost taste the fries. Sprinkled with bits of bacon and malt vinegar. Smothered with ketchup. Gourmet buns brushed with butter, toasted on the grill. Cheddar cheese melted over grass-fed beef, medium-rare.

More people got in line. They blocked his view of The Woods. So he basically had no choice. The only way to keep an eye out for Wilson's exit was to get in line. And if he got in line then he had to order.

Distance

Outside his front door, Gray paused. On Saturday, he'd parked in front of Charlie's house—he was quite sure—and Claire never drove his car. So the fact that it had been moved, and not only moved but parked in front of a hydrant, which he'd never do, meant that yesterday while he was in Ashley's body, someone else had been in his.

He took a deep breath. If he was going to find out what had happened with his body, he had to tell Claire the whole story.

Inside, it was dark. The TV illuminated the living room with a dancing tampon commercial. Claire was on the couch, hunched over her phone as usual, in her usual sweatpants and the green sports tee whose white letters had mostly peeled off after so many washes.

He stood in front of the TV until she noticed him.

"Where were you?" she said without looking up.

"Had to stay late," he lied. Though he might as well have worked late. Leaving early had hardly helped him come to terms with the insanity of spending a day in another person's body, and the three drinks had done little to prepare him to tell Claire.

As she glared up at him, her eyes sparked in the blue light of the TV. At the beginning of their relationship, her unfathomable gaze had made him feel drunk. They had spent hours staring into each other. A turn on, a dare. Who could last longest before diving into the other, before tearing off their clothes? But as the years slogged by, the charge in her eyes when she looked at him had changed. It felt dangerous.

She raised her brows. "Really."

Did she think he wanted to stay late?

"You heard Brad this morning," he said. She'd been in the car when he called his supervisor to say he'd be late since his car had been towed to Pomona. Brad had given him a guilt trip about the big sprint for the deadline on Wednesday—a deadline invented by Brad.

Her nostrils flared. "Were you actually doing something or just avoiding me?"

"I wasn't avoiding you…" But he had been, at least in part. He forced himself to hold her gaze, like a soldier under fire, as she pressed her lips together and waited for him to speak. "It's just…" He had to tell her the truth, the whole truth, or as much as he knew. "Mind if I sit down?"

"Just tell me," she said.

How could he say he'd been Ashley York without sounding ridiculous? "So, yesterday—"

"I called your office. And your supervisor said you left early *again*."

"Yeah, well, Brad thinks leaving before nine is

leaving early."

Claire crossed her arms. "I called at like four thirty."

"I was just driving around, okay? The point is—"

"You were just driving around? Every single night? You expect me to believe that?"

It was a double standard. She'd disappeared all night once, and here he was just a few hours late. "You expect me to believe you about your little drive."

Her eyes darkened. "That was college. You want to go *there*?"

"You want to tell me where you went?"

She rifled through the magazines on the coffee table and dug out the remote. "I'm watching my show." She ramped up the volume. A hardness came into her face.

Gray clenched his teeth. They were too charged up to talk. No sense in trying.

—

In the kitchen, he jerked open the fridge. Bottles of condiments clanked in the door. There on the center shelf was a bag from Sharky's, his favorite. He stared in disbelief. Claire rarely ordered delivery, and when she did it was Noodle World, never Sharky's.

He took out the bag and opened it up. It contained chips, salsa, and a giant burrito wrapped in foil. A Fiesta burrito, his favorite.

He stood over the sink and devoured it. Outside the window, fog drifted through the beam of the streetlight. Maybe he should quit worrying about whatever had happened yesterday—it wasn't like it changed anything now. He should focus on the future. If anything, he felt more confident than ever about quitting his job. He decided to give notice tomorrow. Only, he really should tell Claire first.

He chased the burrito with tap water and then

checked the pantry where Claire stashed chocolate behind a box of old orzo. A single square of Special Dark remained. Tempting, but he couldn't eat the last of her supply. He should get some Godivas, like the ones Ashley had had, and hide them here for Claire to find, as a peace offering.

He balled up the burrito wrapper and opened the cabinet to the trash can. When he saw what was inside, his pulse quickened. It couldn't be—but there it was, right on top, half-covered with wilted lettuce. The charm. What the hell? He snatched the stone from the trash and examined it. Aside from some oily substance that might have seeped into the little holes on the bottom, it appeared intact.

He marched back to the living room. In flickering blue light, he held the stone out toward Claire's face, which remained an expressionless mask.

"Why would you throw it away?"

"That thing almost sliced Mindy's hand open," she said. "You smell like alcohol, by the way."

Gray glanced toward the hallway. Mindy's door was closed.

As he rushed down the hall, Claire called after him, "Don't you dare wake her up."

Gray flung open the door. *Please, be Mindy.* Her bedroom was dark, except for the spinning moons and stars on the ceiling projected from the nightlight. She was swaddled under pink covers, lying on her back. *Please be Mindy. Please be Mindy.*

He flicked on the overhead light and kneeled beside her bed.

Her eyes came open.

"Mindy?"

"What's the matter, Daddy?" The inflection of

concern in her voice, the innocence in her eyes. *It was her. Had to be her. His Mindy.*

He threw off the covers, drew her up into his arms, and hugged her. Tears welled in his eyes. *Thank god.* "Were you asleep?"

"It bit me." She was looking at the charm, which he'd dropped on her bed. She showed him the pink Band-Aid, with a cartoon princess, on her palm.

He brought her hand to his lips and kissed it. "What happened?"

She shook her head. "I didn't do anything."

He picked up the stone, avoiding the oil on the bottom. The head of the obsidian snake faced him. The tail was aligned with the flattened area on top, at what he thought of as the six o'clock position, just as he'd left it this morning. On Saturday, when he dialed the snake to the twelve, something inside the stone had pricked him.

He glanced at Mindy. She was staring at the stone in his hand. Her eyes were wide.

He asked her, "Did you turn the snake?"

She looked down. "No."

She was lying, obviously, but why? "It's okay if you did. I just want to know."

"What difference does it make?" Claire was in the doorway, glowering, her arms crossed.

It made all the difference in the world. But Gray couldn't explain it right now. Mindy was scared enough. Since the snake was still at the six, she should be safe from waking up in the body of a stranger.

But...how could he be sure?

And the snake, perched on the porous white stone, its mouth half-open, forked tongue lashing out beneath the fangs, seemed to mock him. Its beady eyes looked malicious. Hard to believe that turning the snake had caused him to spend a day in Ashley's body —but it must have. The way the fortune-teller had refused to touch it after she gave it to him, like she had finally rid herself of some great burden she could no longer bear, made him suspect it only worked on one person at a time. And her granddaughter seemed to reinforce the idea. "It is yours now," she had said. After all, if it worked on multiple people at once then why was he the only one who could destroy it? So he had to make sure it was still his, for Mindy's sake. He gripped the stone in his left hand, avoiding the spot at the bottom where it had pricked his palm, and rotated the snake. *For Mindy*, he thought as he flicked it to twelve o'clock.

It stabbed him anyway—what felt like a needle pierced the flap of skin between his thumb and forefinger. He yelped and dropped it on the bed. But whatever had stabbed him had already retracted into one of the stone's many pin-sized holes.

Mindy scooted away from the charm on her bed. "That's what happened to me!" She hugged a pillow in her lap.

Gray sucked the wound. Beneath the iron in his blood, he tasted something sour, something foreign. He examined the spot. A dot of red the size of a pinprick. It had stopped bleeding.

"Can you come out here, Gray?" Claire, still in the doorway, had that look in her eyes. "It's past bedtime."

Gray gingerly moved the charm from the bed to the bookshelf and helped Mindy under the covers. She stared at the stone.

"Think you can go to sleep?" he asked.

"If it stays quiet."

No doubt she was well aware of the impending argument between him and Claire. "It'll be okay." Gray stroked her hair and kissed her.

He picked up the stone and turned out the overhead light. In the softer light of the stars spinning on the walls and ceiling, Mindy's face relaxed.

He closed the door behind him as he stepped out into the hallway and whispered at Claire, "Why would you let her play with it?"

"I didn't let her play with shit."

Too loud. He motioned her toward the living room. And now he remembered that when he was hiding the charm, Mindy had asked what he was doing.

At the end of the hallway, Claire spun to face him. "Why would you leave it out where she could find it?"

"I can't believe you threw it away."

"How much did it cost?"

"Nothing." He smelled the greasy spot on the bottom. Olive oil, stale cheese.

"You mean you stole it?"

"No."

Claire snatched it from his hand and marched toward the flickering light of the TV.

"Careful." He launched after her. "There's something sharp in there."

"Yeah, no shit." With her shirt, she cleaned off the goo. "So, what is it?" She held up the stone and examined it.

"I don't know." He wasn't sure how to explain and didn't know *if* he still wanted to. Would she believe that it had somehow transported him into the body of Ashley York?

"Then why do you have it?"

Gray shrugged. "A fortune-teller gave it to me."

Claire rolled her eyes. "Please don't tell me that all these nights you've been seeing a fortune-teller."

He shook his head. "At Dia De Los Muertos, there was a long line for the bathroom. She was right there and insisted I take it."

"So, wait. You were in line, and she came along and gave this to you?" Claire shook the stone. The flattened head of the chiseled snake seemed ready to strike.

"No. I got distracted." He reached for the charm.

She snatched it away. "Right. So while I was waiting for you, you went off and did your own thing, like you've been doing every single night." She collapsed on the couch, closed her eyes, and exhaled.

He sat, leaving a cushion of space between them. What could he say? "Have you ever wished you could wake up as someone else?"

"What are you talking about?"

"What if you could wake up with a totally different life?"

"Like?" Her voice softened. "How?"

"That actually happened to me yesterday."

"If you're talking about the sex, I don't want to talk about it."

Sex? Gray felt like he was falling. It had been months since that morning when he and Claire had managed to find each other in the pre-dawn darkness —the warmth of her body under the covers when, almost the instant they started touching, Tyler had started crying. Claire had launched out of bed, and Gray had waited an hour, maybe two. He'd watched a beam of sunlight coming through a crack in the curtains as it worked its way down the wall. She never came back to bed, and nothing had happened since. Neither of them had even mentioned it.

And now he was jealous. Jealous of what his own body had gone and done without him. He reached for his drink. But on the side table was only the baby monitor and a pile of Claire's magazines.

Almost on cue, Tyler started wailing.

"I'll go," Gray said.

Claire groaned. "I'll be faster." Which was true—she could change a diaper in two minutes flat—but Tyler was wailing. It might take an hour to calm him down. She heaved herself up from the couch and shot him a look like a cold stake in his heart. "You wait here." She dropped the charm in his lap and scuffed her feet as she trudged down the hall.

Gray again reached for the phantom Scotch on the side table. He needed it to be real.

—

In the garage, Gray ripped the top from the Dewar's and tilted back the bottle, longing for the burn in his throat. But, thanks to his earlier drinks, he was too dehydrated and too numb, and now no amount of alcohol would bring back the buzz. He needed to escape, and the truth was that he only ever really lost himself while painting.

Recalling the passion that had surged through him on Saturday when he'd envisioned his painting of Charlie, he uncovered the canvas. The sketch hardly looked like Charlie at all. He looked sinister, silhouetted by sunlight from behind. Gray grimaced. No point in finishing the painting. The idea seemed meaningless now.

He removed the canvas from the easel and added it to his collection of unfinished works, which he kept hidden below the workbench, tucked behind some boxes.

Maybe if he painted the fortune-teller, he could grasp her reason for both giving him the charm and then insisting he destroy it. He recalled the way her tears had flowed into the deep crevices on her face. Perhaps she'd given it to him for his own good. After living for a day as Ashley York, he felt even more unsatisfied with his life than before.

He slapped a fresh canvas on the easel, selected a Vienna Taklon brush, and dabbed it in some black acrylic. As he blocked in the underpainting, the fortune-teller's face faded into darkness in his mind's eye. He fought to recall the way she'd looked in the candlelight, the backdrop of black curtains and the marigolds.

When he focused on the canvas again, he saw he'd painted a black, spiraling blotch of nothing. He tried again, and again, but still he painted only a sickening swirl of blackness, as if this was all he could paint now. How in the hell was he going to make it as an artist if he'd lost all control over his brush?

He'd lost control at Ashley's yesterday, too, but at least then he'd managed to paint a portrait: a man with a head like a boulder atop a mountain of trench coat. The amazing realism with which he'd painted this man, who he'd no recollection of ever seeing in real life, and who had seemed to appear on the canvas from some deep recess of his imagination, proved Gray could paint as well as he always knew he could. Painting was woven into the fabric of his soul. It was very core of his being.

Perhaps the fortune-teller was the problem. Maybe she was somehow impossible to paint? To test this new theory, Gray tried sketching the Dewar's bottle on the workbench... Another damn swirl. It was as if his hand could only draw a swirl now. What was wrong with him? Artist's block? Beside the Dewar's, the flattened head of the obsidian snake seemed to sneer.

He snatched up the charm and looked for a place to hide it. He wanted the thing as far from his paintings as possible. To reach the shelves on the opposite side of the garage, where he knew Claire never looked, he'd have to clear a path through the bins, boxes and junk they were too lazy to get rid of.

The kitchen doorknob rattled. Gray lunged to block the view of the easel.

28

The door swung open. She squinted in the fluorescent light, an empty Snapple in her hand. "What are you doing?"

What could he say? The cover was off the canvas, and the acrylics were out. "I'm just cleaning up."

Her face soured as she glared at the Dewar's on the workbench. Which was fine, for now. Better if she focused on the Scotch than on the sloppy spirals on the canvas behind him, which would undermine his case for quitting his job to become an artist. She would laugh in his face. *You and Mindy can open a gallery together.*

"I'll be there in a second," he said.

She dropped the Snapple in the recycle bin. "Whatever. Just don't interrupt my show."

They had said enough for one night, and they both knew it. She turned out the light and shut the door.

"I'm still in here," he said to the darkness.

He found his way the stool by the workbench, sat down, and slumped. The stone was still in his hand. He ran his finger over the pores.

What if, yesterday, his body wasn't on autopilot and someone else—Ashley?—had been driving it? What if she'd had sex with Claire? Would Ashley have wanted sex with Claire? While in Ashley's body, he'd only declined August Grant's attempt because August held no attraction for Gray.

He sighed. He could drive himself crazy trying to get the details out of Claire. When it came to answers she didn't want to give, he was better off asking a brick wall. Maybe next time she prodded about where he'd been going, he'd stonewall her, let her see what it was like. Because he knew how ridiculous it would sound if he said he was going to bars, not just for drinking—though he was drinking, probably more than he should—but to scope out some way to support her and the kids while at the same time supporting his art.

Art? She would laugh. And without any worthwhile pieces to prove his potential, he'd deserve it.

His thoughts were fuzzed from the Scotch. He should just go to sleep.

He found his way to the light and flicked it on. In his

hand, the snake was still at the twelve. Mindy was safe now. He should just dial it back to the six.

He should.

He returned the canvas. Took a nip off the Scotch—just one more, to take the edge off the awful black swirl, to still the fear spinning through his head so he'd have some chance of falling asleep. This weekend, if he could just get a few hours to himself, he'd paint something spectacular.

But would he?

He slammed the stone down on the workbench, harder than he'd meant to, and instead of corking the Scotch, he decided to treat himself. He tilted the bottle back. *No time to get anywhere, and there never will be, will there?* All his life, he'd played it safe, and where had it gotten him? *Right here.* Boxed in. Drinking in a garage with an obsidian snake, its tongue out, mocking his sad attempt at a painting, his attempt to develop a skill with only two hours to paint every other weekend.

With his fingers, he smeared the paint across the canvas. "What did you expect?"

He tilted back the bottle. Gulped hard, and this time he felt the burn.

"Yeah, I know—no one ever gets anywhere by following the rules."

He wiped his hand on his jeans, yanked the phone from his pocket, opened Google Chat and started a new conversation.

Gray:
Dear Brad,
I quit.

He swirled his finger toward the little green icon for send. The message *swooshed* out of his phone and into the ether. *No taking it back, now.* Gray suddenly felt sick.

He leaned down and stared into the snake's eyes, which were really just gouges in the obsidian. "You happy now?"

But the obsidian snake had nothing to say.

As Gray tilted the bottle, he imagined Brad's panic as he

read Gray's resignation. He slammed the bottle down and swallowed. He felt better. He felt free. Free for the first time since...since when? But he did feel free. He'd taken the first step, and the first step was the hardest. Now it was behind him. Now he was moving, gliding on the momentum from the change he'd set in motion. Keep flying or fall out of the sky.

He grabbed the bottle and tilted his head back, longing for the bite, the smoky liquid on his tongue, the burn from his throat down to his belly, the rush...

But got nothing.

The bottle was empty, and he had no memory of finishing it.

He reached toward the chiseled head of the snake. "It was you. You drank it. Didn't you?"

But the snake suddenly seemed, somehow, out of reach.

"What?" Gray tilted his head. The snake blurred. Now it was two snakes.

He rubbed his eyes and blinked the two snakes back into one.

And how are you going to support yourself? What about Mindy, Tyler, and Claire?

Gray stood, and the room spun. His pocket buzzed. The garage jolted into focus, the terrible black swirl on the canvas.

He knew it was Brad. He almost ripped his pocket yanking the phone out. He squinted at the screen.

Brad:
Thanks for the two weeks' notice.
Hope you don't need a recommendation.

Idiot, Gray thought. Like he cared about the opinion of a middle manager at a second-tier tech company. Brad's opinion was worthless now that Gray was an artist. But Ashley York, an endorsement from her—now that would count for something.

And Gray could get that, couldn't he? Maybe the fortune-teller had given him the charm for a reason. Maybe she'd sensed his desperation. Maybe she knew that by telling him not to turn the snake, he would.

Anyone would. Of course they would.

Gray had read in Evan York's biography how he'd clawed his way to the top by exploiting every opportunity he was given. All his decisions were made from the gut. Overthinking creates hesitation. Hesitation leads to failure. And right now, Gray's gut was saying, *Leave the snake at the twelve.*

Maybe nothing would happen, but what if? What if he woke up as Ashley York? Then, well, he could help himself.

He stumbled through the kitchen to the living room, which was filled with a jarring cacophony of light. The TV was muted, and Claire must have gone to bed. If he weren't so tired, he'd have turned the TV off, but fighting his way through the frenetic light to the button required more effort than he could muster. Besides, his sense of balance was lacking, and the remote was lost beneath Claire's magazine pile.

He half-stumbled, half-fell onto the couch, rolled onto his back, and tried to focus on the swirling people flashing on the screen. *What are they doing?*

He rubbed his temple. He felt hungover. If Claire thought he smelled like alcohol before, there was no way he could lie down next to her now.

On the screen was a close-up of a woman, blonde hair curtained across her face. She pulled it back—Laura. It's Laura. Her doe eyes and broad cheeks. Laura after their sophomore year when they went to Paris for the summer, when they thought they'd be together forever.

A roll of paper towels replaced the woman on the screen. She must not have been Laura. Of course not. Though now Gray pictured Laura perfectly in his mind. The tortured look in her eyes when she broke up with him. Living together, isolated in a foreign country, had strained their relationship. At the end, they had hardly gotten along.

Afterward, to stop himself from breaking down—to stop himself from begging her to come back—Gray had pursued other girls. Girls more mysterious than Laura. Girls like

Claire. But, as he later came to learn, Laura's optimistic outlook outshone them all.

What if Gray could experience her life now, the older-but-still-smiling Laura who rarely posted on Facebook. Maybe, thanks to the charm, tomorrow he'd wake up in the body of her husband, who was probably even more miserable than Gray. He probably worked at some Midwestern insurance agency, adding weight as his hair thinned away.

Laura might have changed since college, but so had Gray. Her life might not be so different from his. Maybe if he just messaged her, he could stop thinking about her all the time. But he knew her reply—if she replied at all—would be some meaningless platitude, a half-sentence at most.

Pulsing light from the TV penetrated his eyelids. When had he closed them? The light made him nauseous. He rolled his head on the throw pillow.

Why Ashley York? If it weren't for Claire following Ashley's every action on Instagram, he'd hardly have known who she was when he woke up in her castle on the hill yesterday. Her isolated life had held a certain thrill. To be a woman, rich and young...

Drifting across the threshold of sleep, he was pulled back by a burning sensation in the skin between his thumb and forefinger where the charm had pricked him. He groaned. He should put something on it. But if he got up now, he'd never get back to sleep. His head throbbed. The Scotch had left him strung out, his mouth dry as sage in the sun. His brain shriveled in his skull.

Should have drunk water, not Scotch. He needed water now. But from the back of his mind, a whisper insisted, *Better to sleep... Everything shall all be better...once you sleep... Sleep...*

Sleeeeeep.

From Out of the Fog

Startled from slumber, Saul's head knocked against the driver's side window. He glanced around.

Fog.

Across the street, the Wilsons' house was a dark blur in the fog.

Saul had followed Gray Wilson, who had left work early to go to a bar. If he had any idea that yesterday a maniac kidnapper and murderer had been following him, he showed no sign of concern.

Saul reviewed the facts again, trying to piece together the motive. Three people had claimed to be Wayob: First Saroyan, who murdered Luis Luna but who then, after provoking a fight in MDC that landed him in the hospital, denied all responsibility—despite admitting it had been his hands swinging the bat. Then Aleman, a guard at the MDC, who claimed to be Wayob while threatening to kill someone but later denied the whole thing. Last, Rydell, who claimed to be Wayob when he kidnapped and eventually killed Bob Jaggar. The question was, why?

Now that Rydell had killed himself, Saul feared he might never learn.

Fatigue burned in his eyes. He cracked open the window and rubbed them. If Hernandez were here, he wouldn't be dozing off. His heart fluttered whenever she was near. He could call her, but not this late at night.

Hernandez was not easily riled, but somehow Rydell had gotten under her skin. Maybe, once Saul solved this thing, it would bring them closer together. Maybe she'd forget all about how pathetic he looked in his tighty-whities. Once he was thin, it wouldn't matter what she'd seen before because that was a different person. He had to get thin.

His belly filled the space below the wheel. He sucked in and tightened his trench coat. *Get thin*.

The fog was thinning. Streeter, whose house Saul was parked outside, appeared in an upstairs window. He switched off the light and vanished in the shadow behind the glass. A minute later, the downstairs lights went out. By the front door, a curtain moved.

However, all remained still and quiet at the Wilsons'.

Saul's eyes began closing of their own accord. Only the vast hollowness in his stomach kept him from drifting off. He shook his head and started the car. Tomorrow morning he'd return to question Wilson.

As he drove up the hill, he pictured the steak at the Castle, a baked potato stuffed with cheddar, butter and bacon on the side. After the burger he'd eaten earlier, he shouldn't be hungry. But he was. And a starchy potato would help him sleep. Maybe, instead of the steak, he should just have a potato or fries—just a half order. The Castle didn't offer a half order, so he'd just eat half.

The fog thickened. The road narrowed and wound like a maze walled by darkened houses set close to the curb. No sign of an on-ramp. No sign of the 101 at all. He reached for his phone to check the map.

Hair stiffened on the back of his neck, like there was someone behind him.

He adjusted the mirror.

A cloud of solid gray closed in on his wake. Ahead, through the fog and the glare of his headlights, the blacktop faded away. He sped through the curves. At a random intersection, he turned right.

Saul knew his fear of being followed was irrational, but that did little to ebb his apprehension. This feeling he'd almost forgotten: the fear of a child.

In the headlights, fog swirled, made one last final barrage against the windshield, then abated. The road descended toward an intersection with a two-lane. A stoplight and a sign. Griffith Park Blvd.

Then he saw a girl, probably a teenager, standing in the road. Her hands swallowed in the sleeves of a plaid button-down. Black hair curtained the thin oval of her face.

He slammed the brakes. The asphalt was wet and oily. The descent, steep. And she just stood there in the street as the car skidded toward her, glaring at him. As if expecting him to mow her down.

Expecting *him*.

Andrea Won't Stay

Ashley stood in her driveway and watched Jonah seal himself in his cherry-red Maserati. He had made her repeat each line a hundred times, enunciating each word differently, until she had no idea how they should sound. And when she asked which way was right, all he said was "Whatever feels right to you."

Right. It all felt so forced and fake.

He extended his arm out the window and gave her a big thumbs-up, as if she'd actually learned something from all his classical training as an actor, as if he thought she actually had talent and might still think so without all the money she had paid him.

"I could *kill* him," she said to herself as he sped up her driveway and disappeared into the fog and the darkness. "I *could* kill him."

She felt even less confident now than before he had arrived. Tomorrow, at the screen test, Sean Penn was going to see she had no talent. No talent at all. She was going to embarrass herself. She had no idea how to *act*. The more she tried, the less she knew. And what for?

She only wanted to be an actress because that was what the world seemed to expect. It was so hard to get anywhere. Rejection after rejection. Hard to get up in the morning and try again.

Maybe she'd feel more confident if Jonah hadn't made it all about himself, taking selfies of them together, fishing for quotes from her to put on his website. The way he kept name-dropping Jennifer Lawrence—*Jen* this and *Jen* that, all the spiff work they had done together. Like Jennifer Lawrence mattered more than anyone else.

And he kept wanting to rehearse the romantic scene with Ashley, saying she was *amazing,* like that would get him in her pants when he'd all but said the role was out of her league.

She returned to the house. She realized that, without Jonah's weird vibe to contend with, her fear was not all about the screen test. It was becoming harder and harder to pretend that yesterday—that feeling of appearing to be someone other than herself, being trapped and alone with no one believing who she is—was a dream.

Alone in the parlor, she watched the fog descend over the windows and snuff out her view of LA. She turned on the outside lights. The fog walled up the windows, solid white.

"Good night, Ms. Ashley."

Ashley jumped at the sound of Andrea's voice almost right behind her. She whirled around.

"Didn't mean to scare you." Andrea released her hair from the ponytail and draped it over her shoulders.

Ashley crossed her arms. "You're leaving?"

"Your dinner is in the kitchen. I'll wash the dishes

tomorrow."

Ashley couldn't bear the thought of being alone in the house. Not tonight, not with Sammy, the only security guard she trusted, going off shift at eleven. And the portrait she couldn't explain shut up in the office. When Ashley told Andrea not to clean in there, Andrea had shrugged it off as though it made total sense to her, and now Ashley wasn't sure how to ask without sounding crazy.

"Ever get tired of the commute?" Ashley asked.

"I don't mind. Good night." Andrea turned to leave.

"Wait. Stay here."

Andrea turned back. "What?"

"I mean, you should move in here." Ashley couldn't believe what she was saying. Andrea did sloppy work, and now she was begging her to stay?

"I...don't know," Andrea said.

"It's silly for you to keep driving back and forth every day. You can have the guest studio. You clean it twice a week and no one ever stays up there." Ashley took both Andrea's hands in hers. "You don't have to pay rent or anything."

Andrea pulled her hands back. "Maybe. I'll sleep on it. Okay?"

"Sleep on it here." Ashley shrugged as if this were only some minor favor she was offering, as if she weren't afraid of being alone in her house. Because ordinarily she wasn't, and she didn't like the way Andrea called her *Ms. Ashley*, the way she always arranged things not quite the way Ashley had asked. But maybe the problem was that Andrea wasn't suited for a housekeeper. She didn't have any prior experience when Ashley offered her the gig. So maybe they could just be friends? From now on, Ashley only had room in her life for people who were genuine.

"I don't have any clothes for tomorrow," Andrea said.

"Okay." Ashley turned toward the kitchen. "Let's talk tomorrow."

Ashley's Assets

The Pacific Design Center was all lit up as August cruised past. The primary colors and rectangular shapes reminded him of the graphics in retro games. The colors were cool, though. Other buildings in LA should take note.

An Ariana Grande tune, "Dangerous Woman," sparked up on his phone. It was Raquel calling. She had totally played him. She had stepped out of her panties and led him into the dressing room, where he hiked her skirt up and pressed her against the wall. The things she did—*oh man*—too good to ask for. Then, afterward, she'd acted like she wanted more, but, of course, she knew he couldn't come two times in a row, which had made it a matter of pride for him. He'd had to force himself just to prove that he could.

Yeah, Raquel was good. Damn good. August wished that he *could* cast her, but the director, Sergei, wanted someone hotter and younger. Still, he'd call Sergei right in front of Raquel and beg him to cast her. Hopefully that would be enough to make her chill out.

He had made an effort. No need to blackmail him.

He let the call go to voicemail, but if she figured out he was ghosting her, she might tell Ashley about the hook-up.

He turned left on Sunset, slammed his fist on the wheel, and called her back.

She answered right away. "Where you headed?" She must have heard the engine of his Porsche.

"Just driving around," August lied. He was headed to Ashley's, two dozen roses riding shotgun, which he hoped would patch things up.

"Want to stop by?" Raquel said lasciviously.

"Can't. I've got my insanity workout."

"At seven o'clock at night?"

"Uh, yeah, it gets me juiced up for the club."

"What club?"

"Don't know. Got to talk to the guys." In truth, it was up to him and he'd already decided. They were going to The Standard.

"The Standard?" Raquel guessed.

"Maybe."

"Ashley going to be there?"

"Probably." *Hopefully*.

Why the fuck did he tell Ashley he was too busy with *Quantum-Man*? Such an obvious lie.

It was just, no one had ever broken up with him before. So yesterday, when Ashley tried to break it off, he'd panicked and broke up with her first. No one breaks up with August.

Come on. As if Ashley really needed to focus on acting all of a sudden. *No way*. She was just overreacting because he'd wanted a BJ last night and then stormed out when she wasn't into it. It should have been a relief to him; he'd been exhausted from doing Raquel twice, and if he really wanted his dick sucked, he could have let Andrea go to town, like she'd tried to, with Ashley right there in the other room. He shouldn't have walked out on Ashley just because she wasn't into it.

The problem was that sex with Ashley no longer interested him, and he wasn't sure if it ever had. He'd only hooked up with her because the guys in his entourage all wished they could. And then he had to keep it going because dating was a prerequisite for marriage, and marriage was probably his only way to tap into her assets. He couldn't afford his lifestyle much longer. His accountant had taken to calling almost every day in a panic.

The main reason August had landed the starring role in *Quantum-Man* was his willingness to work for next to nothing. His agent, sworn to secrecy on the disheartening sum, had tried to negotiate based on the massive box office of similar releases, but the producers were hedging their bets. Who knew if it would be a success at all? What choice did August have? If they wanted to pay some big fee, they would hire a big-name actor. To them, acting was less important than fight scenes and explosions, and August was pretty face among many who would have signed on for even less than he had.

Yet, he was spending like a billionaire. You have to fake it until you make it, and August Grant was going to make it. He was on the way up, spending more on A-list parties than the richest actors in Hollywood. Plus, he was supporting his entourage, and the house in Malibu, which they hardly ever used, cost even more than his house in Beverly Hills.

So he had to get back together with Ashley. She was

his ticket out of debt, and dating her had propelled his notoriety even higher.

"Hello?" Raquel said.

"Bad reception," he said. "I'm in the hills." He wasn't, but soon he would be. "See you later." He ended the call.

She was obviously going to show up at The Standard, whether he wanted her there or not, but so what? By then, Ashley would be back at his side. And if Raquel wanted any more favors from him, she'd keep her mouth shut.

In the Fog

Ashley ate dinner while watching the third season of *30 Rock*, a show that Raquel thought was uncool, which made Ashley enjoy it even more because she was done with Raquel. She no longer had room in her life for people who only gave a damn about what they could get from her. Aside from her dad, Sammy might be the only person in her life who truly cared about her. The way he smiled at her made her feel warm inside, which made her feel awkward for being his boss.

She turned up the volume on the TV. What she needed was a laugh.

Headlights raked the wall.

Probably August. Anyone else and Sammy would have called before opening the gate, but August made a sport out of sneaking into her house without any kind of a warning, as though he lived here too. She should have told Sammy they had broken up. And she should have been more forceful with August. Instead of saying she needed to focus on acting, she should have told him she simply didn't want to see him anymore.

She peeked out the front door. August's Porsche was in the driveway. As she stepped outside, he popped out of his car and flashed that charming smile of his that melted hearts around the world. But now she found it kind of creepy. He had brought her red roses. She loved roses. Clearly, she had been too soft. He wasn't taking her seriously.

"Nice touch," she said. "But I can't take those."

He held them out, his smile unbroken. "I'll just throw them away otherwise."

She took them. His fault for buying them. As she smelled them, he raised one eyebrow, his eyes smoldering in the floodlights. The fog behind him seemed to glow.

"Alright, well, I'll call you tomorrow." Now wasn't the time to have it out with him. She glanced over her shoulder toward the house, and when she looked back, he'd moved into her personal space.

"Let's take back what we said earlier," he said. "A relationship doesn't have to take a bunch of time, and we can help each other. Who's directing your screen test? I'll call him. No one says *no* to August Grant."

She shook her head. His oversized ego would only hurt her chances. Besides, she wanted to do this on her own.

"Nice speech." She clapped. "Too bad you hooked up with Raquel."

His eyes widened. "She told you that? Fucking bitch."

"You're saying it's not true?"

He grimaced. "No."

Ashley dropped the roses in the driveway and

turned toward the house.

"Wait," he yelled. "It meant nothing."

She whirled around. "What about with me? Was that nothing too?"

He raised his one eyebrow again, the other squinted down. "With you it was everything."

Behind him, the fog was like cotton in the floodlights. A dark figure marched toward them.

Without thinking, she took a step closer to August. Primeval instinct. Safety in numbers.

He pulled her into an embrace.

As she struggled free from his arms, she heard what the dark figure was whistling: the *Mission Impossible* theme song. Relief surged through her.

Sammy emerged from the cloud and flashed his Cheshire smile. "Everything cool?"

"All good, Sammy," August said.

Sammy ignored August. He was looking at her. In his hand was a leash, and beside him, the black dog he'd promised to get rid of.

"Why is the dog still here?" she asked.

Sammy's brows furrowed. "Yesterday, you said to keep her."

A chill ran down her neck. "Seriously?"

"You don't remember?" Sammy squatted down and stroked the dog's head. "You said if anyone could give her a good home, we could."

The portrait in the office was one thing. By avoiding it, she'd been able to get through the day, but now there was no denying it: someone else was in her body yesterday. "You okay?" Sammy asked. Near his hand, a wisp of fur floated in the air.

"It's going to shed all over everything," she said. "We don't even know where it came from. It might have some disease."

"Don't worry," Sammy said. "I got Shera a vet appointment tomorrow."

"You named her?" She meant to sound angry, but it was kind of cute.

"Way out of line," August said. "Not cool."

"It's time for you to go," Ashley said to August.

"Let's talk inside." He grabbed her arm. "Just for a minute."

Sammy abruptly stood and moved closer.

Ashley jerked her arm free. "Not tonight," she said to August. Then, to Sammy, "I'll pay for whatever Shera needs, okay? But find her a new home. Somewhere nice."

"You got it," Sammy said with his big white grin. He turned to August. "Later, man." He clicked his tongue against his teeth.

Shera growled and lunged at August, but Sammy held her at bay.

August slunk into his Porsche and made one last attempt with the brows and the smile before he finally drove away.

—

In Ashley's bedroom, fog pressed against the windows and the skylight like it might crush through, pour in, and drown her.

"It's just a cloud," she said to herself. Using the app on her phone, she closed the electric shades. *Out of sight, out of mind.*

But the room seemed too empty. Too big.

Too still.

She went to the window by the bed and peeked around the shade. Someone could be right below standing on the lawn, and they would be invisible in the fog.

She called the guard booth.

Sammy answered right away. "Ashley. What can I do for you?"

Her throat tightened. "Thanks." She swallowed. "That's all. I just wanted to say thanks."

"For what?"

"August." She wished she could talk to Sammy— really talk to him—and have him believe her that yesterday she'd been trapped in the body of this random guy, Gray. So whatever she'd said yesterday was really someone else—most likely Gray.

"That was my bad," Sammy said. "He fed me some bullshit about wanting to surprise you. Don't worry, I'll call ahead next time."

"Actually, next time, don't let him in."

"You got it," Sammy said. "I know it's none of my business, but did you two break up?"

Was that eagerness in his voice or just her own wishful thinking? "I'm not even sure we were together."

He laughed. "I know what you mean."

His easy laugh made her feel better, safer, just knowing he was here. She wished she could be more easy-going like him. "Actually, do you mind staying tonight instead of Franco?"

"You mean work a double?"

She chewed the knuckle on her thumb where the skin was raw from nibbling at it all day. She should ask Sammy to live in the guest studio instead of Andrea. She wanted him on site 24/7.

"I'll pay double."

"I'd better check with the wife," he said.

Wife. Ashley had almost forgotten she existed. What

was she thinking?

"You know what?" he said. "I'll do it."

She sat on the bed. "Really?"

"Of course," he said without hesitation, like she could ask for a whole lot more, like maybe he wanted her to. In fact, she knew he did. The way he lingered around her, always smiling, his eyes searching.

"I owe you one," she said.

Hooking up with Sammy was a bad idea on so many levels. She pushed the thought from her mind, just like she was pushing away the question of how in the hell she'd ended up spending a day in someone else's body…because what could she do about it anyway? Right now, she needed to stay focused. If she could land the role tomorrow, it would be epic. She would almost certainly win an award.

"You don't owe me anything," Sammy said, and she knew that he meant it. He'd have stayed even if she didn't pay him.

After ending the call, tension clamped down on her shoulders.

She kneeled on the floor, stretched her arms into an extended puppy pose, and held it for a couple minutes.

She moved the throw pillows from the bed to the basket beside it, stacking them neatly, the corners aligned. She turned down the covers and went to the bathroom where she brushed her teeth and her hair.

Then, she turned off all the lights and climbed under her fluffy comforter.

And lay there, awake. On the nightstand, the pink glowing dials of the clock seemed stuck at twelve past eleven. She checked her phone. 11:12.

Her eyelids grew heavy with sleep. Although she

wanted to be pissed the black dog was still here, it was sort of cute, and she liked the name Shera.

Her eyes popped open. Shera had slipped past Sammy. What if a person could, as well? What if someone had? What if someone was outside her house, right now?

And yesterday… What if it happened again?

She couldn't stay up for the rest of her life. But at least she could memorize a few phone numbers, starting with her own. She picked up her phone and opened her contact list. After committing her own number to memory, she memorized her dad's. Strange that he still hadn't called her back. Although it was sort of late, she tried calling him again anyway.

After several rings, she got his voicemail instead of Niles. She left a message for him to call her just in case Niles hadn't relayed her message from earlier.

As she scrolled through her contacts, she was struck by the lack of real friends in her life. Although she could count on Sammy and Don for some things, they hadn't believed her yesterday, so there was little hope they would believe her if it happened again. And forget about Raquel. Ashley had ended their relationship. Same with August, and after the creep-fest tonight, he was the last person she wanted to call. She climbed out of bed, plodded into the bathroom, and turned on the light. The medicine cabinet was jammed full of prescriptions from the shrink Raquel recommended. He'd scribbled them out before she'd even started talking, like he already knew everything she was going to say, like her feeling of isolation was due to a lack of pills.

She reached toward the Ambien, which would knock her out…but then waking up the next day always felt impossible. It left a fog in her head way worse than weed, which knocked her out just as well but also gave her amazing dreams. She left the Ambien on the shelf, took out a vape pen, and shoved in a cartridge.

She returned to bed and took a long hit. Stretched out her arms...and was floating, the bed a feathery ocean. She closed her eyes and drifted up into the sky through vast, multicolored clouds.

Wayob Versus Parker

Wayob wakes in a room of gray shapes. From a dim light outside the window, he can make out a desk, a chair covered with clothes, walls postered with pictures too dark to see. Beside him sleeps a man, a very young man who, beneath a tangle of sheets, appears to be naked. Disgusting.

What went wrong—way, way horribly wrong—with Wayob's plan? In order to escape the wrongful imprisonment Parker inflicted upon him, Wayob had to kill himself. Had to endure the agony of dying. He should have awakened in a new vessel, but instead he had been pulled back into the blackness, the torture of total nothingness, the Encanto. Helpless. How long had he been there? Days probably, not years. But too long—too long to endure. And yet he had had to. Thanks to Parker, he had suffered.

Alone in the darkness of the Encanto, a new thought had dawned on Wayob: he cannot end his own life. That priest, that fucking priest, had taken even this basic human right away from Wayob.

Immortality is a curse when living is suffering, another curse Wayob must endure. Yet another unjust punishment inflicted by the wretched priest.

At least now Wayob is free. No thanks to that little girl, who shall suffer for refusing to free him. She shall learn the Encanto is no toy when Wayob kills her father, for her father is again the one who holds the Encanto. His mind is even easier than before for Wayob to reach out to, to tempt into acting on his desire to become someone better than himself. Yes, he who holds the Encanto must be in someone else's body now because Wayob is free. Wayob would rather not end his life. But after all Wayob has suffered, does he not deserve freedom? Although Wayob's hand may do the killing, responsibility lies with the priest.

Wayob will not go back to the Encanto. Will not. Not. Not! So, he who has the Encanto *must* die.

Who is this boy-man asleep on the mattress beside Wayob? So far away from he who holds the Encanto. No end to this torture. Odious priest.

While distracted in thought, Wayob's host body, a girl-woman this time, starts putting on a pair of jeans. Habit is strong. A lower part of the mind—powerful.

Let her dress. Keep her distracted as he digs through her mind and masters it.

The first and most important question is, where is he who has the Encanto? The window looks out on a hillside of houses which descend into cheap stucco storefronts. Squeezed between the buildings, desert palms rise like pillars into the clouds snaking over the hill: Los Angeles again. Must be, for the only thing Wayob can count on is to awaken within some proximity of the one who holds the Encanto, whose location Wayob shall meditate to find.

Before leaving the house, there is *something*—a weapon. The body he now possesses, Sadie—her mind in a panic, muffled to a dull soundless scream by his own mind—she knows, and so now he knows: the gun her father keeps hidden in the back of the downstairs closet. She had found it one rainy day while her parents were out, wrapped there in an old rag, but she knows not how to use it. Nor does Wayob. But he shall. Soon, he shall.

He descends the stairs. In the closet, he finds a bag and throws in the gun.

He exits through the front door. Walks to the road. Feeling a sense of urgency, he runs down the hill.

Stops in the intersection, bewildered. Where is he? He must meditate. Find the mind of he who has the Encanto.

A car approaches, descending the steep grade. The lights blind him. The car is not braking—it is going to hit him. And for a moment, he hopes it will. If he concentrates as he dies, he will find a new vessel closer to the Encanto. The car stops. And over the headlights, Wayob can now see the driver, a wide, wide man filling up the front of the car. Parker.

Of course.

Parker had been on Wayob's mind when he committed suicide while in Rydell's body. It was Parker who had locked him there in that cell, Parker who ruined any chance Wayob had of finding peace in the darkness of the Encanto. So, Wayob had awakened near Parker.

Just like Guatemala City, when the chief of police hunted Wayob like a dog, and each time Wayob died, he would awaken in a new vessel close to the chief instead of close to he who held the Encanto. So the chief had to die.

How does this all work? How should Wayob know? That priest. That fucking priest. He had damned Wayob to eternal darkness with no explanation, thinking Wayob would never be free from the Encanto. Soon Wayob would show the long dead barbaric priest. Soon Wayob will free himself. Forever.

Wayob would be closer to the Encanto now, so much closer, if Parker had not invaded his thoughts. Wayob cannot—will not—stand for this. Parker shall not ruin what Wayob must do.

Wayob must stop Parker. Yes, Parker must pay.

Of course, Parker halts his car. He would not run down a defenseless girl. But Wayob is not defenseless. He reaches into the bag. Curls his fingers around the cold steel of the weapon.

—

As Saul slammed the car into park, the girl clutched her tote like a shield. From between long curtains of Asian hair, she stared back at him. Her expression changed from confusion to laughter, maniacal laughter, as though she found it hilarious that he nearly ran her over.

He climbed out. "Are you okay?"

She tossed her hair back over her shoulder and spread her feet as if daring him to fight her, despite that he was three hundred pounds—though hopefully less since he skipped lunch—and she was a waif in an oversized plaid flannel. Where had she come from? The houses lined along the street were all dark and closed. And it was too cold for the shirt to be unbuttoned.

"Parker," she snarled.

Saul frowned. Had he met her before? No, he

hadn't. He was quite sure.

He moved toward her, extending his arm to usher her out of the street.

Her body tensed. She backed away. "Parker," she sang in a sinister tone that clawed into Saul's stomach with talons of ice and squeezed.

Impossible. It could not be...

"Parker-Parker-Parker-Parker," she said.

"Who are you?"

"You know who I am. Par-ker?"

He lunged and tried to grab her by the wrist, but she snatched her hand away.

"I'm a victim, like you, Parker."

She enunciated words the same way Wayob did. The impossibility angered Saul more than the threat. "I'm no victim."

"Not yet," she said.

"You don't know me."

"I'm sorry, Parker, to have to do this. I prefer to take revenge in equal measure. But you keep getting in my way, you see?"

The leather tote fell to the ground, revealing the pistol in her hand. A Smith and Wesson 45. A 1911, probably. Held loose in slender fingers, as if the weapon were a toy.

As she raised the gun, aiming at him, he stepped forward, grabbing for it. She jerked the barrel up toward his face. But too late—he gripped her arm below the wrist and, before she could pull the trigger, he twisted, aiming the barrel up and away from himself.

She was stronger than she should have been. Leveraging his momentum, she continued twisting her arm up, around, and down. He did not suspect she would turn the gun on herself, and by the time he realized what was happening, it was too late.

She laughed and pulled the trigger. The bullet entered her mouth, spraying blood and brain and bone behind her on the street.

Her body dropped. Leaving Saul holding her by one arm, like a limp doll of a girl he'd dragged into the street. The gun fell from her hand.

That final laugh had been a mask, he thought, and not enough to hide her fear—her pain. In that moment as she pulled the trigger, she'd clenched, a brief but intense hesitation before giving in. She hadn't wanted to die. She had done it, but it was not so easy for her as Wayob seemingly wanted Saul to believe.

Saul was sure Wayob was responsible—had never been more sure of anything in his life. Whatever sick form of hypnosis he was using could not be permitted to continue. Not on Saul's watch. Saul would find Wayob and Wayob would answer for forcing this innocent girl to turn the gun on herself—

He laid her body on the damp road.

No witnesses. He hated himself for thinking that, for considering that if he wanted to catch Wayob, his best option was to abandon this dead girl, leave her alone in the road, and avoid getting caught up in the inevitable investigation by Internal Affairs, who inevitably would put him on suspension.

But he couldn't leave her here. Not like this. Not with blood pooled around her head. Soaking her blouse, congealing in her hair. He had to shut her eyes at least, move her out of the street. But any evidence he left would cost him his badge, maybe worse. No, he had to call it in.

He called dispatch and ordered the parade: fire

truck, ambulance, squad car—the minimum for a suicide. Neglected to mention his involvement.

He leaned into his car, turned on the strobes in his grill, and retrieved his coat. He wanted to lay it over her. *Screw the crime scene.* He would have, if he thought it would bring her any form of peace. Instead, he stood there holding his coat like a reluctant toreador, prepared to obscure her from any passersby.

The siren of the first responding officer approached from the south. As the patrol car sped through a red light and up the hill, blue lights spun across the night.

When it pulled up, the uniform cut the siren and leaped from the car. He was clean shaven with red cheeks, probably fresh out of the academy.

Saul marched toward him. "What's with the siren? This is code two."

"You've got shots fired and a body," said the uniform, J. Scott according to his name tag. "That's a code three. Figured you might need help."

"Get the scene cordoned off," Saul said. "And we'll need more uniforms."

Scott stared at the girl's body. She lay on her arm, her head at an unnatural angle.

"You get that?" Saul asked. "You woke the neighborhood. We need a perimeter."

Scott's gaze leaped to the blood on Saul's shirt. "What about the shooter?"

At this point, it was in Saul's best interest to say as little as possible. He grimaced. "She shot herself."

Yet it was not a suicide. This was a murder scene.

"Let me speak with my lieutenant before you report anything, okay? I'm thinking we'll handle the investigation."

When the ambo arrived, Saul moved his car down

to the intersection. He ushered the firetruck to park diagonally, blocking access to the scene.

Levy didn't answer his call, so he left her a message explaining that although it would look like a suicide, the girl's death was a murder. However, afraid she might not buy that he'd just happened upon her at that moment, he didn't mention the connection to Wayob. He decided to save that for later.

He hiked back up to where the girl lay sprawled in the road, donned a pair of latex gloves, and checked her bag for ID. It was empty.

More uniforms arrived. As Saul returned to his car to call Hernandez, an unmarked cruiser backed up to his front bumper—Arcos and Carter from IA. They pinned him in, as if he needed their permission to leave. Technically, he probably did.

Saul would take anyone over Arcos and Carter. They seemed to have a fetish for blockading true detective work by pulling good officers out of action. They had arrived in record time, as if they had been circling, like vultures starved for fresh kill.

Although it was standard procedure for IA to investigate an officer involved shooting, he wondered who had called them: Scott or Levy?

He approached the passenger side of their car, where Carter sat looking down at his phone. He knocked on the window, smiled, and waved.

They leaped out in unison. Arcos's cranium was freshly shaved to match Carter's. Carter, the trendsetter as well as the alpha of the duo, had a mustache like a chunk of dark, wiry carpet. It twitched on his lip when he spoke. "We'll be needing your badge and your gun."

"If I'm suspended," Saul said, "that means you

completed all paperwork and got it signed off without even bothering to learn the details. Good police work."

"It's just a matter of time."

"I'll take all the time I can get."

"Things will go a lot smoother for you if you play like we're on the same team."

"I'm on the team trying to stop a murderer," Saul said. "Don't know about you guys."

"Who's the girl?" Arcos asked.

Saul wondered if Arcos couldn't grow a mustache or if Carter had ordered him not to. He explained his theory that the girl, who was unidentified, may have been under hypnoses when she attempted to shoot him before committing suicide. He did not mention Wayob.

"Sounds like a load of bullshit," Carter said.

"Big steaming stinking pile," Arcos agreed.

Saul couldn't disagree, but they hadn't been there. They hadn't seen the conflicted look of fear on her face, the way she'd forced herself to laugh as she pulled the trigger.

"I'll start knocking on doors," Saul said. "She must have lived close by."

"You'll do no such thing," Carter said. "You're on the bench. This is our investigation."

An investigation they would surely botch by focusing on Saul and dismissing all other more relevant details. "I was there when she died. I should be the one to tell her family."

"Do we have to wake up command staff to get this into your fat head?"

Saul stomach constricted. The last thing he needed was the wrath of some commander pulled out of bed. The best he could do for now was to go. So he climbed

61

into his plain wrap, ignoring their orders to the contrary, and sparked the ignition.

Arcos reached for his sidearm, and panic straightened Saul's spine. If he drew the Glock 22 in his shoulder holster, he might have to shoot it. But if Arcos drew on him first, then maybe Saul could have them both removed from the case. Drawing on a fellow officer came with consequences.

Carter grabbed Arcos's arm, and Arcos froze, his hand on the holster. He looked at Carter. With a shake of Carter's head, Arcos, the bulldog, was held at bay. Saul hoped to avoid ever encountering Arcos alone.

He hit reverse and worked his car out by backing up and pulling forward in short bursts until he was finally clear. Arcos and Carter just stood on the sidewalk, arms crossed, shaking their heads like synchronized puppets.

Go ahead, Saul thought as he drove away. *Report me for leaving the crime scene.*

Suspended

Later that night, in the Owl Bar at the Castle, Saul stirred a dry salad in the dim orange light. Behind him, the vacant grand piano played Chopin's Prelude in E Minor. A clever illusion. According to Castle legend it was the talented but invisible ghost of Irma playing the piano, and she appreciated real tips. The descending notes hit a chord in Saul's heart and pulled him down.

Pete, the bartender, was an average guy. Not tall or short. Not fat or thin. His nose was normal. His hair average brown. He was average in every way, with one exception: a continuous strip of hair ran across his brow, no discernible separation between left and right. Anyone else, especially in LA, would have shaved in a part above the nose, but not Pete. Saul suspected it was more irony than laziness that inspired Pete's unibrow, which he raised at Saul as he held up the bottle of blue cheese dressing.

Saul shrugged, like he might not smother his salad. Might not open the bottle at all.

Pete slid the bottle across the bar. Saul decided to live a little. After all he'd been through, he deserved more than just salad. Plus, he needed fuel to take down Wayob.

Saul loaded his fork with cheese. From above the bar, the stuffed owl seemed to glower. He added a piece of lettuce.

When Saul had called Scott to check on the scene, he'd learned the girl's name was Sadie Wu. She must have been sent by Wayob, but how? How could she possibly have known he'd be driving down that road at that time?

And then, after failing to kill him, why turn the gun on herself?

Wayob was growing more deadly by the day. Saul had to find him.

Pete planted a foot-high stalk of mint in a glass of ice and gin. Placed the glass on a napkin, and delivered it to the guy in a black suit at the end of the bar. He had a receding horseshoe of hair. He sipped his drink and summoned a flame from his hand.

Pete returned to Saul. "You performing tonight?"

Saul hadn't performed in over a year, but he appreciated Pete's persistence. "Someday, Pete. Someday."

"You're going to let me in on the Table of Death, right?"

"Next time I'm up."

"Just don't let me miss it." Pete, like Saul, liked to be in the know.

"I think I'll have those fries after all," Saul said. "A double order. And a slice of apple pie."

After the fries arrived, Saul covered them with salt and ketchup, and shoveled one after another into his mouth. As he glanced up the owl, he caught his reflection in the mirror. And was disgusted by what he saw. Then embarrassed. Here he was—cheeks so stuffed he could hardly chew—and Hernandez slid onto the stool beside him. Her raven hair, with the shock of white bangs combed back, flowed over her black leather jacket, the hair that in his dreams fanned out around her on the pillow as they made love, with him thin enough to lie on top and look into her eyes.

She sat erect, faced ahead, and said nothing. The silence was her way of pointing out that he'd screwed up again.

Yet, she was sitting so close they were practically touching, and she'd appeared so suddenly, so unexpectedly, like an illusion come to life. Saul felt hopeful, young, alive.

He swallowed.

The fries caught in his throat.

He reached for the water. Gulped it down. Turned toward her, her beauty, her intelligence. "Up late?" he asked. *Dumb question.*

Although she seemed determined not to look at him, the corners of her mouth seemed to soften. "Thanks to you."

If only he could tell her how much it meant to him having her here at the Castle. If only he could say all the things he'd rehearsed a thousand times in his mind. There was so much to tell her. But this was not the time, clearly.

"Let's grab a table," he said. The two-topper by Irma was open.

Hernandez squeezed his arm, the thick layer of fat above his elbow. "I just came to make sure you're okay."

He sank into the stool. She patted his shoulder as if consoling a child, transforming the scene from a fantasy into a nightmare. She pitied him—and there was no path from pity to love.

His appetite had evaporated, yet he still yearned for the apple pie. He glanced at the ketchup. Fought his compulsion to cram all the fries in his mouth, to shred what little respect he had left.

Once he took down Wayob, maybe then she'd respect him. Hard to feel sorry for someone you respect.

"Thanks for coming," he said.

"Wish it was under better circumstances."

"What did they tell you?"

"A girl shot herself. IA is investigating your involvement."

"Sadie," Saul said. "Her name was Sadie Wu, and she was murdered."

Hernandez's eyes widened. "How?"

"I'm trying to figure that out." He told her how, after he prevented Sadie from shooting him, she turned the gun on herself.

"So, wait," Hernandez said, "how is that a murder?"

Parker-Parker-Parker.

Saul shoved the fries aside and squared Hernandez in the eye. "It was Wayob. He's hypnotizing them somehow. That's why Saroyan and Aleman can't remember. Probably why Rydell offed himself as well."

Hernandez blinked rapidly. "Hypnotizing someone to commit suicide? And murder? Is that even possible?"

Saul shrugged. "Susan Atkins claimed it was

Charles Manson's 'hypnotic spell' that had compelled her to commit murder." *Not that it held up in court.*

Hernandez studied her hands. "I'm worried about you."

She didn't get it. If she could have heard the way Sadie was speaking, if she'd seen the fear behind the laughter as she was forced to eat the gun. "If you had been there—"

"Parker," Hernandez said harshly. Then started over, her voice thick with tenderness, like speaking to a child. "Saul, take it easy, okay? I'm just worried you're reading something into this that wasn't there. I know how obsessed you get."

This was the first time she'd ever used his first name. He'd always imagined that using first names would bring them closer together, but she'd said it in a way that actually increased the distance between them. He stared at the fries. More than anything, he wanted to stuff his face with fries and pie like the fatty he was.

She continued, "I believe you. It's just...it's a lot to take in right now."

"She knew me," he said. "She knew my name."

Hernandez smoothed back her shock of white, which hadn't fallen out of place. "This keeps getting crazier. Do you think she knew you'd be there?"

Saul inhaled deeply. Avoided staring at his food. "She couldn't have. To be honest, I was a little lost."

"Crazier and crazier," she said. "They must be tracking your phone."

It was possible. But how could *they* have predicted his route? Had they sent someone to intercept him at all possible routes? And why? This was more than a conspiracy.

If only Hernandez had seen Sadie's face. "She was hypnotized."

Hernandez raised her brows. *"It is a capital mistake to theorize before one has data."*

"Sherlock Holmes?"

"Arthur Conan Doyle, technically, but yeah."

"You're right," he said. "We need to know more. No assumptions."

"What did you tell Arcos and Carter?"

"Nothing."

"Well, they got you suspended."

"I figured."

Typically, an officer involved in a shooting went on paid administrative leave while the shooting was investigated, but Arcos and Carter had, of course, pushed for more punitive measures and succeeded because of Saul's history.

"I'm supposed to take your badge and your gun."

Saul's heart sank. So, she hadn't come here of her own accord. "Levy sent you?"

Hernandez nodded. "I nearly told her to fuck off but then I figured better me than someone else, right?"

"You can take my badge but there's no reason to believe Wayob's killing spree is over. I can't just sit on my hands." He didn't mean to sound bitter but what *did* she expect?

She winked. "Maybe I couldn't find you."

Although her wink was playful, Saul knew, she meant what she said. Stopping Wayob trumped LAPD protocol. He wanted to hug her.

Someone at the table behind them shouted at the empty bench behind the piano, "Bewitched!" Irma jumped into the tune.

"Think Levy will buy it?" he asked.

"She has to. She's too chickenshit to do her own dirty work."

Saul laughed and nearly reached for her, despite that she might think it was inappropriate.

Then *she* hugged *him*. "Be careful, okay?" As she pulled back from the embrace, her hands remained on his upper arms. She looked him in the eye. "You have to be careful. If something else goes wrong..." She didn't have to say it—one more misstep and his badge was gone for good.

"Don't worry," he said.

Her eyes darted around the dining area. Was she concerned someone had seen her hug him? *What happens in the Castle stays in the Castle.* But if he said that out loud, it would be like admitting he thought she was embarrassed, which would garner pity.

"So, you came here to find me and tell me you're going to say you couldn't find me. I'm touched."

"That's not the only reason."

Saul's heart fluttered. She wouldn't come here at midnight out of pity. He studied her face.

A slight smile traced the corner of her mouth. "Wayob's not a common name," she said. "I'd never even heard it before."

His heart fell into the acid of his stomach, and he looked away. In the dining area, the guy with the horseshoe hairline was performing rope tricks, the Impossible Knot, for a couple drinking cocktails.

"I checked NCIC," he said. "If Wayob's a real name, he doesn't have a record."

"But he does on Facebook," Hernandez said. "I found a bartender at Versailles who says Wayob was an urban legend in Guatemala City. Twenty years ago, a string of murder-suicides were attributed to him."

A spike of energy surged through Saul's gut. "Suicides? What kind of suicides?"

"I don't know. Right now it's just a rumor, the bartender doesn't remember much because he was a kid when this all happened. This Wayob was never caught, and apparently no one even saw him in person."

"Seems like an obscure inspiration for a copycat in LA?"

"Maybe it's the same person. I'm going to make some calls to Guatemala City, see if I can find someone who was around back then."

"This could have something to do with what Mrs. Luna was hiding. Were you able to get hold of them?"

"They're not answering my calls. I'll stop by their place tomorrow morning." Hernandez sighed and got to her feet.

"Hang out," Saul said. He nodded toward the guy with the horseshoe hairline. He had just turned a man's drink into a cup full of coins.

She pointed at Saul's chest. "Maybe some other night? I have to get up early if I'm going to drive to all the way to El Monte and question the Lunas before work."

As she left, making her way between the tables, her hips swayed against the hem of her jacket. Saul imagined those hips in his hands and sighed.

"Everything alright?" From behind the bar, Pete was leaning toward him.

"I do not know. But keep her on the guest list. Every night."

Saul reached for the pie. It was cold now and that was fine. He was only having one bite, one big bite, as much as would fit on his spoon.

He left the remaining fries along with a twenty-dollar tip for Pete and Irma.

He followed the hallway of dim chandeliers and plush carpet past the Parlor of Prestidigitation, past the homage to Die-Vernon and the signed posters of Harry Houdini. He grabbed hold of the dragon banister and heaved himself up the stairs. The stairs turned a corner, narrowed, and dead-ended into a shelf of ancient hardbacks. He twisted the candelabra on the wall. The bookcase slid open.

Outside, fog had closed in. The valet stand was unattended. Beyond it, the hill dropped into the mist, which reduced the streetlights below into white globs wavering in the grayness. The two blocks to Hollywood Boulevard seemed more like a million miles.

Saul wasn't paranoid, ordinarily, but what if *they* were tracking his phone? Going home would put his landlord Marla in danger. Besides, after all he'd been through, he deserved a peaceful night's sleep, and if she saw him, she'd rope him into whatever latest house project she'd dreamed up. Plus room service—pepperoni pizza (just a small or maybe a medium) folded like a taco and eaten in bed.

He decided to stay at the Roosevelt—good luck finding him there—and just to be safe, he parked next door at the Ace and left his phone in the car.

Ashley's Nightmare

That night, Ashley slept in fits and starts before finally drifting down far enough to dream…

She is a child again, locked in her room by Shayla, the mean nanny, who orders her to be quiet if she ever wants to get out. Then she hears Shayla moaning, the sounds coming from her dad's room down the hall. Is he home? What happened to Shayla?

Groans. It's her dad groaning loud and long. Shayla is hurting him. Ashley screams.

And keeps screaming. Her dad opens her door and hugs her to him, wipes the tears from her cheeks. "What's wrong?" He's smiling.

Unable to speak, she burrows into the folds of his flannel.

Later, Shayla serves dinner as if nothing happened, speaking all sweet to Ashley. So obviously fake, and her dad doesn't even notice. He's focused on the work papers he brought to the table.

"Guess what's for dessert," Shayla sings.

Ashley glares at her. Shayla winks.

Ashley won't stand for this. Shayla has got to go. Ashley will show her dad how bad Shayla is. He has to see. Ashley throws back her chair, but...Shayla's face has changed. She is not Shayla at all anymore... She's Ashley, her adult self.

Startled awake.

In the moonlight streaming through the window, someone leans over her in the bed... August.

The blade of his knife glints in the silvery light. He throws back his head and laughs. Hair unfurls over his shoulders—not his hair. Her hair. It's not August anymore. It is her. Her body anyway, but someone else inside it.

Like a snake striking, an arm streaks toward her. She opens her mouth to scream—but cannot. She gasps but cannot breathe. Her throat is sliced open.

She clutches her throat and leaps from the bed.

There is no blood. She must be awake now, for real. She stumbles for the bathroom, tripping over clothes on the floor.

In the bathroom, in the eerie moonlight pouring in, she checks the mirror. Gray's face looks back.

Ashley gasps. *No.* She is still dreaming. Has to be. She splashes cold water on her face.

She flips on the light...

Gray Wilson stares at her from the mirror.

No. It can't be. She shuts her eyes and squeezes them tight, rubs her hands frantically over the face that isn't hers. But it doesn't wipe away.

Now she remembers the clothes on the floor on the way to the bathroom; she never leaves her clothes on the floor. This bathroom that isn't hers at all. It's Gray's. She's back in his house. She is Gray. Again.

Claire appears in the doorway. "What's wrong?"

What's wrong? Ashley pushes past her.

In the bedroom, the nightstand is empty. There should be a phone. She wants to just curl up under the covers and close her eyes. This can't be happening. She's still in her house, in *her* bed. This is just a nightmare. All she needs to do is wake up.

It's useless. She knows what she has to do. She has to confront this thing head on.

She turns to find Claire almost right on top of her. "What are you doing?" Claire asks.

"Where's my phone?"

Claire rolls her eyes. "You lost it again?"

When Ashley tries to step around her, Claire blocks her. Ashley grabs her arms, moves her aside, and ignores her protests.

She goes to the living room and, by the silvery light coming through the sliding glass doors, she digs through the clutter on the coffee table. Amazingly, she manages to excavate Gray's iPhone.

Claire and Mindy emerge from the hallway. Mindy's wrinkled pink dress looks as though she slept in it. She holds out a drawing for Ashley with an eagerness that stirs Ashley's heart.

She squats and hugs Mindy, then stands again and pushes her way past Claire.

"What the hell?" Claire says.

Ashley locks herself in the bathroom and turns on the fan to muffle the call she's about to make. Good thing she took the time to memorize her number last night.

As it rings, she grinds her teeth and looks away from the mirror.

"Hel-lo?"

It's her voice. Her voice! But not at all the way she'd

answer, if the mood actually struck her to pick up a call from an unknown number. But then again, this number might be familiar to the person who just answered.

"Gray?" she asks.

"Yes?"

"What the fuck are you doing in my body?" The anger leaps out of her. He must have been in her body on Sunday too, and he didn't even try to reach out.

"This is so weird," he says. "And, I know this is all kinds of messed up for both of us right now, but I need a favor from you before we talk about anything else. Wake Mindy and make sure she answers to her name. Ask her where we went on Friday night."

"You mean, like, you think she's not in her body either?"

"That's what I'm worried about."

"Unless she traded places with some other little girl who likes pink dresses and drawings, you don't need to worry about her right now. Where did you hide the artifact?"

"You mean the charm?"

"The stone thing with the snake on it. That's how we switch back, right?"

The line goes silent for a moment, then Gray swallows. "Did you sleep with Claire?"

Ashley inhales. She wants to pull out her hair, which would be Gray's hair—even better. "What's the big deal?" she says. "You stole my life."

"Not on purpose."

She exhales. *Is this happening randomly? Is he just as helpless as her?* In the mirror, somehow her frustration looks kinder on Gray's face than it ever would on hers. She speaks softer, sounding as nice as she can. "Please.

Tell me where it is."

Silence.

Ashley looks at the phone. He's still on the line.

"I need the rest of the day," he says.

"Seriously? No." A sob wells in her throat, but she chokes it back. "I've got a screen test today. We have to change back now."

He inhales.

She has to convince him. That's all that matters now. "Look, I get it," she says. "Just tell me what you want. Just name it."

"How do I know you'll follow through?"

"I can give you the money, now. I'll tell you how to access my accounts."

"That sounds great and all, but you had sex with my wife."

"No!" If she tries to explain how this is the biggest opportunity she's ever had, she knows she'll start crying. "You can't fucking do this to me!"

Gray hangs up.

She calls back, but he doesn't answer.

Ashley tries her dad, who of course won't to answer an unknown number. His voicemail picks up.

"Dad. It's Ashley…" She falls back against the wall, slides to the floor, and now there's no stopping her tears.

He'll never believe it's her anyway. Or would he? What if he knows what the artifact does? It looks sort of like the cave painting he showed her on his phone of the one he's been searching for. The voicemail runs out of time.

She presses the pound button to re-record. "Mr. York, I'm calling on behalf of your daughter. Ashley needs your urgent help. Call me at this number, please. I've found an artifact. It's a black snake mounted on a round, white stone. It's what you've been looking for, and guess what happens when you turn it?"

"When Ashley was a little girl, she started a fire in her playhouse. I'm telling you this so you know I'm not just some random stranger. You really need to call me back. And call me, not her. Please. Ashley loves you."

She ends the recording, gets to her feet, and turns on the sink. It's Gray's stubbled face in the mirror, but the tears...the tears are her own. She washes them away.

Dad is the only one I can count on. Until he calls, she'll deal with this herself.

Sleepdriving

Saul woke up. He was behind the wheel of his plain wrap. Parked on unfamiliar street. But he'd gone to bed at the Roosevelt. How in the hell did he get here?

His legs ached, and his arm hurt. He slid back his sleeve. Scratches, four of them, gouged the skin from his wrist to his elbow. Thorns or fingernails?

He squeezed himself out of the car and looked around. The sidewalk was uneven and cracked by the roots of the olive trees that lined the street. He was on Berryman, in Mar Vista. But he had no reason to be here.

The three-story apartment building beside him triggered a dim sense of déjà vu. Above the entrance, faded cursive cutouts spelled *The Palms*. The *l* and *s* had fallen out, revealing a lighter shade of stucco outlined in dirt. The building appeared to rise into the line of sunlight along the top wall.

He rubbed his forehead and climbed back in the car. His phone was right where he had left it last night, in the glovebox. It was 7:15. If he hurried, he could make it to Silver Lake before Gray Wilson left for work.

Morning commuters had already clogged up the 10. Saul racked his brain but couldn't recall what happened the night before, aside from a vague dream perhaps of driving in darkness...fog and stoplights, and the low hum of his engine going slow.

He'd read about how Kenneth Parks drove fourteen miles in his sleep and then killed his mother-in-law. But Saul had never suffered from somnambulism. At least, not until today. Must be stress. The memory of Sadie Wu swallowing the gun mere inches from his face still haunted him.

It was almost eight thirty by the time he reached Silver Lake. As he turned onto Wilson's street, he noticed what he should have seen sooner: the unmarked Crown Vic trailing him. Behind the wheel, that unmistakable oblong head. Arcos.

Saul pulled to the curb a few houses down from Wilson's and on the opposite side of the street. Arcos parked three cars behind Saul. *Obvious.*

Saul considered ignoring him, letting him see how real detectives work. Maybe get inspired. But no, he and Carter would have Saul disciplined for continuing an investigation while on suspension, and, worse than that, they would get in his way.

So, what now? Until he could ditch Arcos, he'd have to back off on Wilson. And where was Carter? It made Saul nervous to see one and not the other, especially since Arcos was the worst of the two. At least Saul's sleepdriving to Mar Vista would give Arcos a nice little diversion to waste his time investigating.

Saul opened the glovebox, removed a bottle of NoDoz, shook out a couple pills and washed them down with the dregs of an old Mountain Dew. He unfolded himself from his plain wrap and took off his coat without looking around, as if he had no particular reason to be on this particular street. He folded his coat, tossed it in the backseat, climbed back in and started the car.

Across from Wilson's house, Streeter, who must have spied Saul from a window, emerged from his front door, impossibly gaunt. Today, in a gray suit.

Saul decided to use Streeter as a diversion for Arcos. He buzzed down the passenger window and waited.

Streeter hobbled across the lawn. As he leaned down to the window, he groaned and held his back. "Gray hasn't left yet."

"Good," Saul said, "but now we've got a problem."

Streeter's eyes widened. "What?"

"Yesterday you asked me about crazy officers, remember?"

Streeter glanced down. "I..." When he looked up, his brows twisted, all the lines on his face tightened. "I didn't mean to."

"It's okay," Saul chuckled. "It's just ironic that yesterday you warned me about the crazies, and now here today I've got one on my tail. Don't look."

Streeter looked. Then exhaled. His face relaxed. "That man is a crazy?"

"That's right. A crazy cop."

Streeter glanced around. He spoke in an almost whisper. "Do you know anyone who can help us?"

Saul shook his head. "No one we can trust. This guy is Internal Affairs. We're on our own here."

"I knew it."

Saul followed Streeter's gaze through the windshield. Wilson walked out of his driveway into the road. His brown hair tousled, his face darkened by two, maybe three, days' worth of stubble. He looked up and down the street.

Before Saul could stop him, Streeter yelled, "Gray!"

Wilson pretended not to hear it and hurried to his Camry.

Saul tapped a finger to his lips. "We can't let Arcos know I'm looking for Wilson."

Streeter glanced at Arcos again. He nodded slowly.

If Carter were here, no doubt Arcos would be out of the car confronting them.

"I have to go," Saul said. "Don't talk to anyone other than me."

Streeter scowled. "I don't talk to crazies."

"Smart. You've still got my card, right?"

Streeter nodded.

Wilson drove downhill in the opposite direction. If Saul made a U-turn, even Arcos might catch on that Saul was following Wilson, so he waved goodbye to Streeter, pulled out, and drove uphill instead.

Arcos followed. Saul made two rights and descended the hill. At the next block, he stopped at the sign. Looked left. Looked right. If Wilson was going to work, he should drive right by here, but there was no sign of him. Had he turned north? Saul would have to find him later, after he ditched Arcos.

Saul turned south, trying again to recall what had happened after he checked into the Roosevelt. He could recall ordering room service—unfortunately. He'd ordered a large sausage and pepperoni pizza, of which he'd eaten half and stashed the rest in the mini-fridge. And then he went back, slice after slice, until only two crusts remained. Which he ate. Then his memory went blank. Had he even undressed before falling asleep?

He wondered if Wayob's victims felt like this. If hypnosis was like sleepwalking. But no way had he been hypnotized. He would know, wouldn't he? Wayob would have to do that in person. What Saul needed was a solid description of Wayob. Saroyan had been useless, Aleman was worse, Rydell was dead and so was Sadie. Now it all came down to Wilson, if Wilson even knew anything about Wayob. Though probably better for him if he didn't.

And why was Saul sore? Yesterday, he'd only walked those few blocks in Hollywood, yet now it felt as though he'd hiked Mount Wilson. He should start exercising more. But exercise made him hungry and he needed to diet. How could he exercise more and eat less?

As he turned onto Sunset, he called Hernandez. He asked her to meet him at Langer's in thirty minutes. Not exactly romantic but if he suggested someplace upscale, she'd want to know why.

"Why?" she asked anyway. "What's going on?"

He could say he needed to ditch Arcos, but she'd know he could accomplish that on his own. The truth, which was so hard to say, was that he just wanted to see her. "Tell you there."

"Okay—"

"And don't park nearby."

Saul turned on Alvarado, and Arcos turned right behind him. *So obvious*. Levy must have said she had Saul's badge or Arcos would have confronted him by now.

He popped on the radio. Dione Warwick was singing *Do You Know the Way to San Jose*. He tapped the steering wheel to the beat, hummed along, and then sang.

Wayob Takes August

At the Skybar at Mondrian, August was checking Ashley's twitter feed for the fourth time when Jacob leaned over and glanced at the screen. "You got home pretty early last night. What's up?"

August had to be careful here. He needed to control the narrative, but what control did he have? At least he'd kept his cool last night when Ashley threw the roses down in her driveway. Although it had seemed like she was completely done with him at the time, she hadn't posted anything yet. And maybe that meant something. With no record of their breakup in social media, it didn't seem real. If he'd broken up with her, he sure as hell would have announced it right away. He was tempted to tweet a peremptory strike or have his entourage start some rumor about Ashley, but he had to hold back. He was broke and spending toward a cliff of insolvency and Ashley was his only hope.

He glanced around at his entourage: Jacob in his usual Dodgers cap. Sydney didn't seem to notice the glob of cheddar the color of his hair that had dripped onto his shirt. He was watching August. They were all watching him. He had taken too long to answer and now he had to say something.

Mark stroked his goatee.

August drained the Bloody Mary that he'd only ordered to maintain appearances, with no intention of actually drinking. Mark followed suit and finished his, as well. Jacob chugged the dregs of his third Bloody Mary and eyed the waitress. Sydney continued demolishing his grilled cheese.

"I broke up with Ashley," August said.

"What for?" Sydney asked the obvious question. His mouth still full.

"She wanted it to be exclusive. And you know me."

They snickered. "Oh yeah." Mark reached across and fist-bumped August.

"Open season, tonight," Jacob said. "Which clubs you want to hit?"

"I don't know about that. I mean, of course we're all going out tonight, but I still might get back with Ashley." August popped an olive in his mouth.

"She know you did her best friend?" Sydney asked.

Although August hadn't wanted to do Raquel—at least not the second time anyway—the look of envy on Sydney's face was worth it.

"And her housekeeper?" Jacob asked.

August motioned for them to lower their voices. "Guys! Not here."

"Chill man. It's cool," Jacob said. But he knew to shut up. After all, it was August's nonexistent money paying his tab.

"Yeah, well, let's not test it," August said. "People tweet everything."

"Hottie alert." Mark tilted his head toward the pair

of bikinis reclining by the pool.

August straightened his shades.

The blond looked away. The brunette smiled lasciviously.

"Yeah," August said, "Ashley might just come around and see things my way. I'm good for her career."

"Oh yeah," Sydney said. "She knows what you're good for." He bulged his cheek with his tongue while pumping his fist toward his mouth.

"Another one?" The waitress's white shorts were practically right in August's face. Her muscular legs were well tanned.

The first Bloody Mary was mixing badly with his hangover from last night. He felt dizzy. "I have to be on *set*," he said.

The waitress bent over the table, further than necessary, to stack the empties on her tray.

"I'll have August's," Sydney said. "Haven't got shit to do today."

Jacob and Mark ordered another round as well.

The waitress propped her tray on her hip. "Three Bloody Marys. Anything else?"

Are the pig tails meant to suggest something about your sex life?

"Just your number," Jacob said.

She giggled, turned, and walked back to the bar slow enough for them to take notice.

"How hot is she?" Jacob said. He bumped fists with Mark.

August stood. "Back in a few."

"Where are you going?" Sydney asked.

"Got to take a deuce," he lied.

He made his way past the bar and the pool which

looked out across Beverly Hills toward downtown, a low haze making it seem further away than it was.

He considered a room and a nap, but how long before one of the guys came looking for him?

In the bathroom, the handicap stall looked reasonably clean. He sat, leaned his head against the wall, and closed his eyes. Just a few minutes of quiet. To recharge.

If he wasn't fucked before Ashley broke it off, then for sure he was fucked now. Stupid to think he could have seduced her into a quick wedding, that he could tap into her fortune before his came crashing down.

He felt light-headed, disconnected from his body. Floating away. No, falling. No, pulled down toward unconsciousness. It was too late to stop it, nor did he want to. He welcomed the numbness.

When he tried to open his eyes, he could not. Something was tugging him down. Down, down, down, into his own subconscious.

—

Wayob awakens and laughs. Laughs at Parker, whose body Wayob could have remained in, but the trap Wayob laid is too good. The foul labyrinth of Parker's memories held pathetically little about the one who holds the Encanto. Parker was useless, his body so heavy it hardly moved. Wayob put it to sleep and found this new vessel, leaving Parker to suffer when he awakens, like Wayob suffered for killing someone when he had no choice—because the priest made Wayob like this. The fucking priest. And then Parker. Parker punished Wayob when Wayob had no choice.

"Saul Parker," Wayob laughs. "How does it feel? Treated like you treated me. All over for you soon. All over. Ha, ha."

"You alright in there?" a man asks from outside the stall where Wayob is sitting on a toilet.

Wayob must behave this time. He must blend in to find the Encanto. Though it is tempting to find Parker first. Watch him fall into Wayob's trap. Wayob longs to laugh in Parker's fat face, his revenge equal to the suffering Parker inflicted upon Wayob, and no more but certainly no less.

Wayob must focus on he who has the Encanto, Gray Wilson, the name Wayob gleaned from the mind of Saul Parker. Wayob must find this Gray and kill him. Perhaps he does not deserve death, but the atrocious priest left Wayob no other option, and Wayob has suffered so much that surely his freedom is worth more than the life of any one man. And Gray's little girl, the one who heard Wayob's whisper from within the Encanto and yet still refused to free him, she must be punished. She shall play a role in the death of her father. For it is her fault that her father must die.

Wayob fumbles with the latch of the stall door until it finally opens. At the sink, a man with dark skin and a red dot between his brows slicks his hair in the mirror.

"Fine sir," Wayob says. "Where are we at the moment?"

The man claps. "I had no idea that you were August Grant. Was that a new character you're rehearsing in there?"

Wayob has no idea what this man is talking about. (Why must awakening in a new vessel always be so confusing?) No matter. Wayob stands before the mirror, his reflection a young man with a round face and strong chin. He turns toward the door.

"Wait," the man says. "Can I get a selfie?"

The man extends his arm, his phone in his hand. A *selfie*? Why not? Why the hell not? Wayob stands beside the man and smiles.

The man's other arm snakes around Wayob's shoulder. Wayob jumps back and shoves the man away. "How dare you touch me."

The man looks scared, as he should. "Sorry, man."

Wayob does not wish to hurt this man, or anyone at all. "This shall not ruin our day."

Wayob exits the bathroom into a large interior space with low cushioned chairs clustered in circles, which turns out to be the lobby of a hotel. A man and two women, all in matching gray suits, idly stand behind a counter. Wayob finds the exit and pushes out.

Blinding sunlight. Wayob emerges onto a balcony. Below, the sun bounces on a pool. Wayob's eyes water as he squints into the glare. Tears ooze down his cheeks. After all the darkness he's endured, the sunlight fills him with ecstasy. "So beautiful."

Wayob descends a curved stairway toward the blue, blue water of the pool, which overlooks a vast city.

"August, where are you going?" asks a male voice.

Wayob turns toward it. Three young men, basically boys, recline in bed-like chairs with white cushions. A girl, her hair in pigtails, lifts aside a red velvet rope to the area where they sit.

Wayob steps in.

"Clogged pipes, eh?" says the big blond man.

From the table, the girl lifts a tray of dishes. Clear bottles of liquor catch the light of the sun.

"The hotties by the pool are checking us out," says the one with the large nose and the hat. "Let's invite them over."

Wayob considers if he can use these boys, who must

88

believe he is the one they see before them, the one called August. Will they help with his hunt? Will they help him kill Gray Wilson?

The girl with the tray latches the rope behind her and walks away toward a bar.

The big blond one jabs Wayob with his finger. "Where did you go, man?"

Wayob grabs the outstretched finger and bends it backward. Something snaps.

The blond oaf screams. "Fucking asshole!"

The oaf should know better than to touch Wayob.

The people in the pool grow quiet and still. At the bar, heads turn toward the oaf and his friends and Wayob. Everyone watching. Music, from speakers all around them, grows louder.

The one with the hat laughs. "Damn, Sydney."

Wayob laughs as well. Then the other one, the one with the goatee and the sideburns tapered to a wiry cruft on his chin, laughs. "Might be a bit harder to get the chicks over now."

The one called Sydney holds his hurt finger to his stomach. "He broke it."

Wayob waves his hands. "I am quite sorry. But this you brought on yourself."

"Like hell."

"Not like hell at all. Trust me."

"Stop whining, Sydney," says the one with the hat. "He didn't mean to."

"Oh, but I did," Wayob says. A test. If the other two stand behind him on this, then perhaps they are useful after all.

"What the fuck?" Sydney says. "I was joking."

"Was I laughing?" Wayob looks to the other two boys. "Do either of you find it funny?"

Their smiles drop. "What's got into you, man?" asks the one with the hat.

"Something urgent," Wayob says. "Who is ready for a quest?"

"A quest?"

"Yes, an adventure. A mission—find Gray Wilson."

"Who the fuck is that?" says the one with the hat.

The man who holds the Encanto.

"A man of no importance. A man in my way. A man who meddled in something he should have left alone."

"Are you saying you want to hurt him?"

"I do not wish to. I do not wish to hurt anyone. But if this Gray Wilson is not stopped then I shall suffer a fate worse than death. A fate I have already endured for much longer than I imagine your young minds are able to comprehend. I assume you would wish to save your fair August from this torture, am I right?"

"He's gone mental," Sydney says. "Take me to the hospital."

"Go if you must. Permission granted." Wayob turns his attention from Sydney to the other two boys. "But we shall not be deterred. Let us depart."

The one with the goatee leans forward and extends a fist. "Okay. I'm in."

Wayob is unsure how to parse the gesture. Perhaps not an act of aggression. The boy holds his hand up as if waiting for Wayob to do something, but what?

Then the one with the goatee bumps his fist against Wayob's half-closed hand. "Khhhhh," he says.

Wayob stifles his urge to recoil at the touch and instead imitates. "Khhhhhhhhhh." He wiggles his fingers. He turns to the one with the hat. "And what about you?"

"This Gray guy really crossed the line, huh?"

"Yes. Crossed the line—good way to put it. He has crossed twice now. And we shall make this his last. We shall find him today."

"I'm with you, I guess. But, dude, quit acting so weird."

"Of course," Wayob says. *Higher dedication is required.*

"So where is he?" asks the one with the hat.

Wayob could, perhaps, have retrieved more from Saul Parker's mind than just Gray's name, but Wayob could not linger, could not risk Parker learning too much, like poor Edward Saroyan. Wayob smiles, thinking again of the trap he laid.

"I just need a quiet place to mediate," Wayob says, "and then I shall find Gray Wilson."

"Since when do you meditate?" asks the one with the hat.

"Come." Wayob steps over the velvet rope. "Let us retrieve our vehicle and begin pursuit."

Wayob waits, not sure where the vehicle is, but he does not wait long. The hat and the goatee both nod at Wayob and begin walking together toward the exit.

"Seriously, guys?" Sydney calls after them.

Only Wayob glances back at the oaf. Wayob smiles. Things are looking up.

As they exit the hotel, Wayob walks between his two loyal boys. "This shall be fun," he says. "I have never had a gang. My own posse."

"What are you talking about?" says the one with the goatee. "We've only done everything together since ninth grade."

"Not like this," Wayob says. "Not. Like. This."

Gray's plan

Gray throws open the door to Ashley's office at the bottom of the turret and is relieved to see his portrait of the large man still on the easel. He finds his paint supplies in the desk, replaces the portrait with a fresh canvas, and channels his frustration into each stroke of the brush.

An image materializes before him like a wave, washing all the ways he's imagined Ashley and Claire in bed together back into a dim recess of his mind. Although it's a landscape and not a portrait of the fortune-teller he'd planned on painting, he's happy just to be painting something other than a black blotch. Last night, he started to worry, so a landscape is fine with him. It strikes him how the view he's blocked in, across Beverly Hills to downtown, differs from what's out the window. It's from a lower elevation than Ashley's perch above the city, and from somewhere more to the east, a perspective he's never quite seen before, yet the haze, the angle of the light on the buildings, matches exactly what he's seeing outside right now. Weird. Still, it feels good to paint.

The problem is what to do next. He never told Claire that this year there would be no bonus, and now, with no way to catch up on the back payments, it was only a matter of time until the bank foreclosed on the house. They should have bought somewhere more affordable than Silver Lake. But the amount of money he needs is nothing to Ashley and her father. Paying off his mortgage and credit cards would be like grains of sand from the beach to Evan and Ashley York. And she'd even offered whatever he wanted. The problem is what she might say about it. Maybe no one would believe that he'd literally held her body hostage, but people might believe that he'd blackmailed her in some way. And a thing like that, even just a rumor, could ruin him as an artist. No one would buy his work.

He sets down his brush and pulls out her phone in its hot-pink case. He scrolls through the nudes he took before she called this morning. According to Dave at work, some guy sold a snapshot of Niran Lima half-disguised in a hat and sunglasses for sixty grand, so these could easily cover his debt and bankroll his new painting career, maybe even Mindy and Tyler's college.

When he gets to the photo of her touching herself, a sour taste rises in the back of his throat. He has to delete them all. He can't sell them any more than he could accept Ashley's money. There would be no way to explain the windfall to Claire, much less to Mindy.

He selects all the photos he took, but before moving them to the trash, he hesitates... Ashley is a wild card. He assumes she won't retaliate just because he needed a few hours to make sure he could paint something other than that horrible black blotch, but, just for the sake of insurance, he logs into his email and sends the nudes to himself before deleting the evidence from her phone. Once he gets back to his own body, once he gets his bar up and running and sorts things out with Claire, he'll delete the email. No one will ever know.

A deep voice booms from the hallway. "Ms. York?"

Gray trots down the hall to the living room. Standing near the door is a man built like a truck bulging beneath a black suit and tie. He has dark skin, a big, rounded head.

"Ready to go?"

"Go where?" Gray asks.

"Your screen test. You didn't get Don's message?"

"I'm not ready."

He looks Gray up and down. There's paint on his T-shirt and jeans.

"Just throw something on. They've got wardrobe and makeup for you." He wears what looks like an expression of practiced patience, like this isn't the first time he's come to get Ashley and found she isn't ready. Must be her driver. Andrea mentioned his name —what is it? Clarence?

"I've got a headache," Gray says. "Let's reschedule."

The man's brows come together, a big show of concern. "Sorry to hear that. I've got stuff in the car. Fix you right up."

"I need to make a phone call," Gray says. The screen test means a lot to Ashley. He has to at least let her know what's happening.

The man's eyes narrow. A look of determination. "You can call from the car."

As Gray starts toward the kitchen, the man starts

after him. "I need to make a private call," Gray says. "If you can't accept that, talk to the hand." Gray has no idea how Ashley talks to her people but being bossy is sort of fun.

In the kitchen, Andrea is chopping a cantaloupe on the island counter. A lock of hair falls over her eye.

"I'm going outside," he says, heading for the door. As he walks, he taps the screen to wake up the phone —and trips over a ridge in the floor. As he reaches out to catch himself, he drops the phone.

"You okay, Ms. Ashley?"

He squints at the circular door in the floor, which he'd vaguely noticed before. Below the two half-circles of glass, framed by sleek steel, wooden stairs lead down into darkness. "What's down there?"

"You're making a joke, right?" Andrea flips a switch on side of the island.

Light floods the stairway. Hundreds of wine bottles line the wall.

"Of course," Gray says. "I have a wine cellar."

Andrea scrunches her brows together.

Gray picks up the phone, hurries outside, and shuts the door behind him. The phone still works but now it won't unlock without Ashley's passcode.

He stares at the screen. Without the passcode, now he can only call 911. It rings in his hand. The name *Don* appears on the caller ID.

Gray answers.

"Ashley, darling. What's the matter?"

"I've got a headache," Gray lies.

"A headache? Ashley. I've got a headache. We've all got headaches. Please, take something and get in the car."

"It's not going to help. I just need a few hours,

okay?"

"You understand this *is* Sean Penn, right? And Charlie Kaufman? Just tell me what you need. I'll have it delivered to set."

"I just need some time… I'm not feeling like myself right now."

"Feeling? Doesn't matter how you feel; you're an actress, Ashley. Pretend. Make *them* feel. And I'm not just talking about the role. You need to sell Ashley York, the whole package, the smart charismatic beautiful woman who everyone wants to be around. They can't get enough of you. Of course, you know all this, right?"

"I guess so, but—"

"But you'll feel great once Shana works her magic. All you have to do is get in the car."

"Great, it's just…" But what can he say? The real Ashley will be pissed. More pissed. Who is Don anyway? Why should *Ashley York* have to do what anyone says? "Let's do it tomorrow."

"Ashley, baby." Don's voice sails up two octaves. "Would that I could. You have no idea what I went through to set this up *for you*. You've got to be there, or they'll go with someone else. You want to be an actress, right? That's why you hired me. That's why I'm working so hard for you. If you bail on this, you know how it is, how word gets around. You won't get another shot. This is Sean Penn, Ashley. Sean fucking Penn! So, what do you say?"

Clearly, canceling this one appointment would make things much worse for Ashley, and she could ruin his chances of making it as an artist. But maybe it doesn't have to be that way. Maybe in Ashley's body, he could pull off the screen test. He's come a long way since his eighth-grade acting fiasco in *12 Angry Men*. Maybe while he's still in her body he can get an audition for himself. Her recommendation might be more valuable than actual talent. If he can get into acting, maybe he *can* support his family, without the headache of running a bar. He could make time to paint between acting gigs.

And he would like to meet Sean Penn.

"Okay," he says.

"Great." Don pants into the phone. "You really had me worried there, Ashley girl. Thank you, thank you."

"Remind me where is it again?"

"Paramount, my queen. Just put your pretty self into that luxurious car of yours and relax. Clayton knows where to go."

After ending the call, Gray returns to the house and follows Clayton out the front door. Sunlight glistens on a pink Bentley Limo. Clayton opens the back passenger door. The seats are, of course, upholstered in pink leather.

"I need to borrow your phone," Gray says.

"In the car," Clayton says.

Gray frowns. He's beginning to dislike Clayton.

Clayton stares back. He blinks. "Sorry I called Don."

Gray shrugs and slides into the backseat.

The Bentley is not a full-length limo but spacious enough to sport a bar below the divider between the back and the front. The booze nestled into the dark polished wood is mostly schnapps and vodka, plus two bottles of gin. No Scotch. Not that he needs a drink. He wants one, but he's still trying to come down from Ashley's vape. After this screen test, he'll imbibe—after he meets Sean Penn. If he drinks before switching back into his own body, will he wake up sober?

Clayton folds himself into the front seat, starts the car, and adjusts the rearview. "Me," he says, "I think you'll get this one."

Should Gray be nervous? The whole situation seems so surreal. "I still need your phone. My battery's dead."

Clayton passes his phone back, an oversized Samsung in a rubber case. Gray inhales. He should have called Ashley back hours ago.

She doesn't answer. Is she still at his house? Instead of leaving a message on his own voicemail, he texts her.

Where are you? They roped me into your project. The show must go on, right? I'll do my best. Call me.

If she looks at the phone, she'll see the text. And if Claire happens to see it, she'll assume it's from one of his coworkers, hopefully.

At the top of Ashley's drive, the gate lifts. Clayton slows as he passes the booth and nods to the Black guard with a shaved head. The guard nods back, that knowing way of nodding, like some unspoken understanding between the two men.

Clayton accelerates smoothly down the winding road, past giant gates and hedges. As they round a curve where the road cuts into a mountain, LA sprawls below in a haze, and it hits him. What is he thinking? *I can't act.* The last time he even tried was eighth grade when he puked his lines out all over the stage.

Ashley and Andrea

Ashley enters the Whole Foods on Crescent and scans the shoppers: a man in flannel is smelling the coffee choices, a woman in yoga pants tows a little girl who insists on hopping from one tile to the next, and no one notices Ashley York, because the person they see is this random man.

The anonymity is sort of nice. No whispers, no pictures, no strangers introducing themselves. It would be hell for Raquel, who loves drawing attention to herself. Ashley had thought it was fun too, when they were younger, but now she's over it.

Andrea shops here on Tuesday mornings, regardless of how little Ashley needs her to buy, and sure enough Ashley had spotted her tango-red Audi in the lot below the store. The question is, will she listen? Will she believe that it's really Ashley in the body of this strange man? At least it's hard to hang up on someone's face.

In the aisle of health-food bars, Andrea's waif-thin figure is unmistakable, even from behind. Andrea removes an almond-chocolate bar from a box near the floor, but instead of the basket hooked over her arm, she slips it into her pocket. She looks around. When she notices Ashley, she smiles and shrugs. Then turns her back and walks away.

Ashley hurries after her. "Andrea," she says softly.

Andrea whirls around, gripping her basket with both hands like it's a shield. "I don't know you."

Down the aisle, a blonde with blue bangs glances up from the box of cereal she's studying.

"It's okay." Ashley offers her palms. Just blurting out that she was Ashley wasn't going to do any good. "Ashley sent me. Can we talk? Let get coffee."

Andrea's brows crinkle up. "How do you know Ashley?"

"That's what I want to talk about." Ashley glances toward the woman with the cereal, as if being overheard was her biggest concern.

"Okay. We can go to the café."

Andrea leads. They weave between the checkout line and a table offering free samples of cashew dip, which Andrea stops to try. Ashley realizes that for the first time in her life, she doesn't have to worry about calories. She marches to the coffee bar, where a barista with a large mole on her chin greets her, and orders a double large caramel macchiato, all for herself, and a café au lait for Andrea.

After the barista completes the coffees, Ashley pops the lid off her macchiato and savors the sweet, foamed milk, the three hundred and fifty calories that don't matter at all.

She finds Andrea at a small table, gazing out the window at the traffic on Wilshire. She pulls up a chair and launches into the speech she'd prepared. "What I'm going to tell you is unbelievable. I wouldn't believe it if it hadn't happened to me. I need you to hear me out."

"I don't even know who you are," Andrea says.

"We'll get to that. I know you've been working for Ashley York for almost a year. You came to LA from Spain on a student visa."

Andrea glances at the exit.

"I'm not a stalker or anything," Ashley says. "I just need you to listen. I know you met Ashley at a silly Samsung commercial while you were a waitress at Providence, working double shifts. But then Ashley hired you in order to give you more time for auditions. I know how she likes her clothes sorted by color and her magazines ordered by date.

And last night, she invited you to live in her guest studio."

"She told you all this?" Andrea says.

Ashley shakes her head. "No, she didn't tell me. This is the part that's hard to believe but I swear to you is absolutely true: I am Ashley."

Andrea's dark eyes widen then narrow. Her brows plummet. Her head swivels slowly from side-to-side.

Ashley continues. "I'm trapped in this man's body, and he's in my body right now. If you saw Ashley York, he wouldn't know any of this information, if you asked."

Andrea studies her. The corner of her mouth twists upward. "If you're Ashley, then I guess you'll know what she—or you, or whoever—has hidden in the bottom drawer of her nightstand?"

Ashley inhales sharply. "You snooped through my stuff?"

Andrea shrugs. "I wasn't sure where to put the socks at first."

Ashley thinks of the stolen almond bar in Andrea's pocket. *You lie.* She takes a quick look around. At the table behind Andrea, a silver-haired man seems engrossed in his sushi and a hardback by Michael Connelly.

Ashley leans forward. "A vibrator. A big black one."

Andrea laughs. Then, a laughter wells up inside Ashley too, and the stress that has been building suddenly becomes too heavy to hold on to. They laugh together. And the laughter lifts Ashley up and away, as if this whole situation, somehow, is happening outside of herself.

Then, Andrea abruptly stops laughing and tilts her head. "What did you want in your smoothie yesterday?"

"Kale and carrots," Ashley says without hesitation.

"What about your magazines?"

"The issues of Vanity Fair on the coffee table in the parlor? I like them fanned out in chronological order with the most recent one on top."

Andrea's eyes widen. "But…how can this be possible?"

"I have no idea."

"I guess some things make more sense now," Andrea says. "This morning, you were—"

"He," Ashley says. "Gray. The man in my body is named Gray."

"Right. *He* was giving me the googly eyes."

"Probably would have made his wet dream if you'd come on to him."

Andrea snorts. "*He* found your weed."

"That's better than finding what's in the bottom drawer." She wants to laugh about the dildo again, but it isn't funny anymore. She tilts the paper cup back and shakes the dregs of her macchiato into her mouth. If not for Andrea watching, she'd lick the foam from the inside of the cup.

She stands. "Come on. I need you to get me past my own security."

Andrea glances out the window. Cars are collecting at the intersection. "What do you think would happen..."

"What?"

Andrea rises. "If this got out in the press?"

"No one would believe it."

She looks sort of disappointed. "Guess not."

Ashley collapses the cup in her hand as she skirts around the register to the exit. The automatic doors swoosh open. The underground garage is lit with harsh fluorescent tubes.

"Did you tell August?" Andrea asks from behind her. The sound of her heels on the concrete echoes off the walls.

Ashley tosses her cup in the trash bin by the carts and turns to face her. "What for? We broke up."

"You did? When?"

Ashley glances at Andrea. "Yesterday."

Andrea tilts her head, almost smiles. "For good?"

"Definitely. I'll follow you back to my place, okay?"

They pass Andrea's car, but she keeps walking. "So, what if...?"

Ashley stops. "What?"

Andrea looks around. She speaks softly. "You're totally done with August, right?"

Ashley nods. "He's a jerk." She squeezes herself sideways between a pair of SUVs. Gray's car is in the opposite row.

Andrea follows. "Did you know he came on to me?"

When Ashley glances back, Andrea's face reddens slightly under her dark complexion.

Now it all makes sense. Last week, when Ashley came home and August was there with that sheepish-stupid grin on his face... And why, after that, he only came over when Andrea wasn't around.

"Did you hook up?"

"No, but..."

"But you want to?"

Andrea nods and turns redder.

Ashley fumbles around for Gray's keys and unlocks the door. "Go ahead if you want. It's your funeral."

Andrea's reflection smiles in the window. Ashley opens the door and climbs into the car.

"You're awesome," Andrea says. "Thanks."

Ashley didn't feel awesome but what could she do? It was a free country. And she didn't want to jeopardize the connection she had made with Andrea. "Let's go. Just make sure Sammy lets me through."

"Okay. What are you going to do?"

"I'm going to get my body back."

Ashley shuts the door. She grabs Gray's phone from the cup holder, glances at the screen. There's a text from an unknown number, but it's obviously from Gray. He's planning to attempt the screen test as if he's her. "The show must go on?" *Bullshit.* A bad impression is worse than no impression at all. People never forget a bad performance. She calls the number...

No answer. She throws the phone down on the seat beside her, reverses out of the parking spot and steers around to Andrea.

"He's at my screen test," she shouts.

Andrea leans down and looks in through the window. "Yeah. He's pretending to be you."

"Not if I get there in time. Call Clayton and tell him there's an emergency. They have to wait for me at the gate. Tell him I'm Ashley's cousin."

"Is that going to work? Even if Clayton believes me, Gray will just say you don't have a cousin."

"He'll play along if he knows what's good for him. I'm heading over there. They've got a ten minute head start, but since I'm already out of the hills, I might be able to beat them. I'll text you Gray's number so you'll know to answer if I call."

Ashley speeds up the ramp toward the daylight, a pure white rectangle growing wider. Where the ramp meets the road, her tires squeal as she turns. Even if she gets her body back, she won't have time to rehearse. But that's fine. She rehearsed the hell out of yesterday.

She tries the number again that Gray texted from. Still no answer. Traffic slows to a standstill. A complete clog. She must wait. Wait an inordinate amount for each driver to slowly accelerate toward the intersection ahead. By the time she finally reaches the light, the maroon minivan in front of her insists on stopping at the yellow. He could have made it through.

She calls her own number. It goes straight to voicemail without even ringing.

A text comes in from Andrea.

Andrea:
Clayton knows you don't have a cousin. I said to put you on the phone with Ashley but he won't do it because "she's already in makeup."

Ashley screams. The minivan moves forward and stops again. Although the light is green, traffic is backed up to the next light which is still red.

She opens apps on Gray's phone at random. His email—a bill from Verizon, American Express, and a recent message from Gray Wilson to Gray Wilson. She opens it and sees the photos attached. Explicit photos. Of her body. All of it. She scrolls through the *Playboy*-style poses. In the last photo, her legs are spread, exposing everything.

Behind her, a car honks. Traffic is moving. She glances again at the photos. Such awful lighting. And the expressions on her face!

She floors the gas, the phone still in her hand. She jabs at the trash icon until the email is deleted and gone. Then she opens the trash, finds the deleted email and deletes it again. After half a block, the minivan, of course, stops at the next yellow. She slams the brakes and swerves into the turn lane. As she passes the van, its driver, a woman with big curly hair, actually has the nerve to honk. Ashley buzzes down the passenger window to make sure the woman sees the middle finger thrust in her direction.

As soon as she gets back to her own body, she'll sic her lawyers on Gray. This is identity theft taken to a whole new level, and she won't stand for it. Even if the photos were just for jerk-off material, it's not okay.

Traffic stands still. She honks. "Fuck, fuck, fuck!"

Her life was great—well, maybe not great yet, but it was going to be. She was going to land this role. But not now. Now Gray is going to fuck it all up.

What does he think he's doing? He can't be serious. He hasn't starved and rehearsed and exercised and endured countless hours of torturous coaching.

Here it is, the day of the most important opportunity of her career—of her life so far—and thanks to some freak anomaly of the universe, all her preparation is wasted. Lost. Sean Penn will believe Gray's shitty attempt at acting is actually her. Even if Gray has some acting experience, this is a complex role, three roles, really. A schizophrenic with multiple personalities: one who loves a man, one who loves a woman, and one who hates them both. And she had worries, even before all this happened, that the role might be beyond her capabilities as an actor. The most positive review she has ever received described her as *melodramatic*. But if there's any way to reach Gray, to switch bodies back in time, she has to try. If she gets arrested for breaking into the studio, then that's on Gray. She has to give it all she's got. Because this movie could be amazing. It might change the way people see themselves in society.

She throws Gray's phone out the window. It clatters on the asphalt, bounces, and skids into the intersection where the tire of a Prius smashes it to pieces. She smiles and drives on with a new sense of freedom. The best she's felt since awakening in Gray's body. The best she's felt in years. Since before boarding this rollercoaster of fame she thought she wanted. Now, whatever happens, it's on Gray Wilson—and Gray is going down.

Denial

Saul arrived at Langer's before Hernandez. He sat in the usual corner booth by the window, his back to the wall. Outside the window, Arcos wandered around the intersection of seventh and Alvarado, as if he thought Saul wouldn't notice him among the pedestrians.

While Saul was waiting, he went ahead and ordered a salad.

She strode into the restaurant. Her raven hair with its streak of white stood in stark contrast to her gray blazer.

"Hi," she said, lingering by his side of the table. Waiting for him to get up because, after breaking the ice last night at the Castle, now they were huggers.

There was no way for Saul to slide out of the booth without thrusting his belly out practically right into her face, but this was a chance to get closer, like he'd always dreamed of, and if he hesitated for one more second, he'd blow it.

Just as he started to slide out, the waitress arrived and blocked his exit. She set his salad on the table.

Hernandez slid into the booth across from him. She ordered the pastrami sandwich, and the way she pronounced *pastrami* made his mouth water. He stirred the dry lettuce around in his bowl.

"You're not ordering lunch?" Hernandez asked, probably aware he had an appetite the size of the ocean and the salad was no more than a sponge.

"I'm not here to eat," he said.

Hernandez nodded. Her lips tightened as if restraining a smile.

"What?" he asked. Was she laughing at him?

"So," she said, "it turns out Wayob in Guatemala was more than a legend. There were actual murders. There was an investigation."

Saul's heart pounded against his chest. "Do tell."

"Not much to tell, unfortunately, because the chief of police, who was investigating the case himself, was shot by the Guatemalan army. They claimed he was attempting to assassinate the president."

Saul was startled by the empty mug plopped down in front of Hernandez. The waitress filled it with coffee. Then, refilled his.

A police chief attempting an assassination? Of the Guatemalan president? It sounded crazy. But...it also sounded like Wayob, his Wayob. Had he hypnotized the police chief into getting himself killed?

"What was the motive?"

"Don't know. I'm still trying to find someone else who was around back then. The chief's family seems to have disappeared."

Saul's stomach roiled. He swigged down the top third of his coffee.

"Should I go down there?" he asked with no desire to actually leave LA with Wayob around. But he couldn't expect Hernandez to go, not with her son in school, and all the slack she'd had to pick up while Saul was on suspension.

"You don't speak Spanish," she said. "Let me work the phones first and get a sense of what's down there. Might be nothing."

"Good idea." He poured cream in his coffee, refilling it back to the brim.

"I drove all the way to the Lunas' at seven this morning, and they weren't home. There was a flyer on their door from some kind of payday lender, so my guess is they were gone all night."

"Same thing Saturday," Saul said. "I slept in the lot outside their apartment."

It was odd, she agreed, but all they could do was keep checking.

"So, what's going on?" she asked, meaning it was time to reveal the big reason he'd insisted on lunch.

I wanted to see you, Saul thought to himself. "Check your eight."

She glanced over her left shoulder, out the window. Across the street, Arcos held his phone to his face. Hard to miss.

She combed back her shock of white. "You should have told me they're on your ass. Now I have to take your badge."

"You think Levy admitted she doesn't have it? Arcos has been on me all morning. Why didn't he take it?"

Hernandez frowned. Saul instinctively reached into the front pocket of his pants. His badge-wallet should be there. But it wasn't. Something had felt off all day. The missing weight against his leg.

Last night, he'd had his wallet when he checked

into the Roosevelt, and then what happened? He ate pizza and fell asleep. Then, somehow, he'd awakened in Mar Vista, with no memory of driving there. The bad feeling in his stomach rose to his throat. Where was his badge?

Hernandez laughed. "You're right. Levy's a chickenshit."

"Does she know you're here?"

Hernandez sighed. "No. She dropped a fresh kill on me, which now I have to investigate sans partner."

"Who's the vic?"

"Jenna Collins, a.k.a. Starla. She was a high-end escort with a website and a handler, but her body was discovered behind the Quality Inn on La Brea."

The remnant of a nightmare flickered out of reach in the back of Saul's mind. Déjà vu. He felt sweaty. His armpits were soaked.

"I could look over the murder book." Although he had no desire to see the body, he had to know what was bugging him. "If you think it would help."

"Levy would kill me. You can't go near the PAB."

Hernandez was right. Now that the case files had been digitized, it wasn't so easy for her to show him. He couldn't access the LAPD network while on suspension, and if he was caught looking at her screen, there would be consequences for both of them.

A glass shattered beside them, dropped by a busboy clearing the table. Clapping erupted from the kitchen and spread throughout the restaurant.

"You okay?" Hernandez asked. "You look like a wreck."

Saul swallowed. "Didn't sleep well."

She nodded. Her brows conveyed understanding; she knew how he felt about Sadie. But she had no idea he'd driven to Mar Vista in his sleep, and how could he tell her without sounding unstable?

She slid her hand across the table a few inches closer to his. "Want to talk about it?"

She was reaching out—maybe not to hold hands, but this was an invitation—and more than anything, he wanted to connect. So he told her again about Sadie. How, after he prevented her from shooting him, she'd smiled as she turned the gun on herself, like she was not dying so much as outsmarting Saul.

His chest tightened. "Her smile wasn't real." *It was like a mask.* "I think she was afraid."

The waitress delivered Hernandez's lunch on an oval plate. A three-inch stack of pastrami sandwiched with buttered toast, cut diagonally, sided with a pickle and curly fries. Saul's stomach rumbled.

"Sounds awful," Hernandez said. "For you and for her."

Saul swallowed. Hard to admit just how much it had affected him. Although he'd seen death before—he'd shot six men, including Brown—Sadie was innocent. The way she'd offed herself right in front of him was awful. The power Wayob had had over her.

The waitress refilled Saul's coffee. He poured in cream. The tan and white swirled so close to the rim he had to lean down to sip it without spilling any.

"Wilson could be the next victim," he said. "When he came out to his car this morning, he looked sort of confused."

"Like he was hypnotized?" Hernandez hefted a sandwich half with both hands. She had to compress it to take a bite.

Saul snagged a coil of fries from her plate. "Hard to say. I couldn't interview him with Arcos on my tail."

He chomped the fries. *Needs ketchup.* He swallowed and told her about Wilson's detour to Beverly Hills yesterday.

It was strange, Hernandez agreed, but not quite suspicious. "What if Wilson is a dead end? Rydell was crazy. No telling if he was following Wilson or not."

But if Rydell had been hypnotized, maybe he wasn't crazy at all. Either way, it didn't imply that Wilson knew anything about Wayob.

"I'm going to stop by Sadie Wu's," Saul said. "Maybe she had a suspicious new friend. Maybe her parents met Wayob and can give us a description."

Hernandez dropped her unfinished sandwich-half. "You're on suspension." She wiped her hands with her napkin. "You can't talk to them."

"I was with their daughter when she died. They might *want* to talk to me."

"Arcos and Carter will find out. Maybe you don't care about your job, but I need my partner back."

Saul's stomach clenched. Arcos and Carter were the least of his worries. "If I don't stop Wayob, who will?"

"I get it," she said. "Let me talk to Levy. I'll tell her Sadie Wu is connected to Rydell—"

"She closed the case on Rydell."

"But we've got a new body now. She can't ignore that."

"Worth a try," he said, but they both knew Levy lacked the balls to interfere now that IA had taken charge of the investigation into Sadie's death.

Saul helped himself to another handful of fries.

"Just promise me you won't go over there," Hernandez said. "Maybe I can stop by after work, undercover, as a civilian. I don't stand out as much as you."

Saul glanced down at his belly. It filled the gap between him and the table. He gulped down the mouthful of fries.

"I mean that in the best possible way," she said. "I really do."

He glanced up at her. She smiled. It looked genuine. Saul had no right to feel hurt. She was right. He *did* stand out. Way, way out. And it was up to him to change that.

But for now, he could only change the subject. "I need to borrow your car."

She blinked. "My Mustang? You're kidding, right?"

"I need to ditch Arcos," he said. "We can use my car as a decoy."

She glanced over her shoulder. Arcos had disappeared for now, but almost certainly he was still lurking around.

"If he stops you," Saul said, "you can say you're returning my plain wrap to the motor pool while I'm on suspension."

Her shoulders slumped. "I just paid it off."

"I'll treat her like a princess," he said. "Don't worry."

She slid the key off her keyring. "If I find a scratch, you'll have a lot bigger problem than Wayob on your hands."

He waved his palms in the air in mock defense. "If you want to come with me and drive, I could use the help."

"I wish I could." She leaned forward. Her brows tensed. "But I've got this other case."

Saul nodded. All victims deserved justice. Hard to put any one above any other.

Outside the window, sunlight glared off Arcos's oily

head as he strode past. He peered in at them, so obvious he might as well press his face to the glass.

Hernandez waved at him. Saul grinned.

Arcos quickly glanced the other way, as if something across the street had just caught his attention.

"So, where's Tweedle Dumb?" Hernandez asked.

"I'm wondering the same thing. Seeing Arcos alone makes me nervous."

"Maybe he's acting as a decoy for Carter."

"You think they're that smart?"

She shook her head and laughed. The skin crinkled around her eyes. "Hell no. Where does IA find these guys?"

"I might admire their conviction—if they weren't after my badge."

"When a stupid man is doing something he is ashamed of, he always declares that it is his duty."

Saul chuckled. "Who said that?"

"George Bernard Shaw." She leaned forward. "I hear they live at Carter's. Arcos's apartment is just for appearances."

"Not surprised." Whether or not their relationship extended beyond work hardly seemed worth discussing. "I should go before he comes back." Saul pushed himself out of the booth. Felt around in his empty pocket. He checked his other pocket. It contained the keycard to his room at the Roosevelt. Nothing else. An arrow of panic shot through his gut. Where the heck was his wallet?

"Mind spotting me?"

"So, I do you a favor, and my reward is to buy you lunch? Something seems backward here."

"I'm buying; don't worry. I just forgot my wallet."

"Smart. Now no one can take your badge."

But he didn't feel smart. He felt off. "I owe you."

"That you do," she said with a slight smile. "And I intend to collect."

He made his way to the back of the restaurant, steered around the yellow "wet floor" cone by the restroom, and pushed out through the back exit and into the alley. To avoid Arcos, he detoured on Westlake to Wilshire, where Hernandez had parked her red Mustang.

He folded himself into the car. On the passenger seat beside him was a hardback translation of the *Tao Te Ching*. Hernandez had a lust for philosophy, a desire to expand her horizons. One of her many attributes he admired.

To make sure no one could track him, he powered down his phone. He rubbed his eyes. The coffee at Langer's had lacked a sorely needed jolt. He popped another NoDoz.

As he drove up to the light, he kept one eye on the rearview. No one behind him.

He merged onto the 101 north. Free and clear. For now.

—

Saul exited the 101 and tacked west on Hollywood Boulevard. Stopping by the Roosevelt was maybe not the smartest idea, but where else could he have left his badge? It was more valuable than his Glock. The badge was like a key to the city. When people saw it, they tended to open up.

Since his legs were still sore and he was in a hurry, he drove past the surprising amount of street parking and turned into the alley behind the Roosevelt, which contained the vehicle entrance. Ahead, the alley was cordoned off with yellow crime scene tape, behind which five or six uniforms were standing around.

Saul rolled up to the valet stand and heaved himself out from the Mustang. "What happened?"

The valet was a squat man with a block-shaped head. He glanced toward the alley and shrugged.

Saul had a bad feeling in the pit of his stomach.

He entered the back lobby and boarded the elevator along with a young couple and their stroller. The guy had a sparse, unkempt beard, like maybe he'd trimmed it once or twice in his life. He held his key card to the scanner and pressed three. Same floor as Saul.

The elevator ascended. The doors opened. Not wanting an audience for his wide load walking the narrow hall, he motioned for the couple to ahead of him.

The guy motioned to the stroller. "After you." He waited. So did his wife.

Stalemate. Saul hurried to his room.

At the door, he held his keycard to the electronic lock. No beep. The little light above the knob flashed red. He tried again.

"Excuse us," said the guy with the beard.

Saul turned and pressed against the door. The couple wheeled their stroller past. The baby inside was swaddled in a blue blanket, sound asleep. Saul examined the keycard. No room number, but he had a clear memory of the clerk printing "312" on the cardboard sleeve, which Saul must have left on the nightstand.

He blew on the card. Held it against the lock. The red light flashed.

Four doors down, the woman narrowed her eyes at

Saul while her husband keyed open their door.

"Must have demagnetized," Saul said. Without his badge, the best he could offer to alleviate their suspicion was a sheepish smile.

She hurried the baby into their room.

Saul rode the elevator back down to the lobby. Maybe they had disabled the card after he missed checkout at ten? He marched to reception. "Did someone check me out?" He handed his card to a clerk, who had dark hair gelled to his scalp.

"I apologize for the inconvenience, sir." The clerk tapped Saul's card to a scanner and frowned. He typed into his computer. Frowned some more. Glanced furtively at Saul and scrolled and typed. He shook his head.

"Anything?" Saul asked. If housekeeping had turned over Saul's room, hopefully they had found his badge and handed it in.

"One moment." The clerk disappeared through a door embedded into the wood paneling behind the counter.

Saul turned and leaned his back against the counter. A half-flight of wide stairs descended to the marble floor of the lobby, which echoed every footfall of the people passing through, every whisper. Anyone could be Wayob or someone he'd hypnotized.

On one of the padded benches that flanked the lobby, a woman gazed up from her phone, looking directly at Saul. She wore a thin T-shirt over a black bra or bikini top and had wet hair. Did she recognize him? Or was it just his unusually large size?

Before Saul could react, she stood and marched to the front entrance. Pushed through the glass doors and out into the Hollywood sun.

117

"Officer Parker."

Saul turned. "It's detective."

The man standing by the clerk had a tense face. Same black pants and white shirt as the clerk, but no coat. He stood erect with an air of importance. "I'm Gary, the director of guest services. Please join me in my office." He motioned toward the door behind the counter.

Although the office was spacious, it looked out on a brick wall that blocked most of the light. Saul sank into the cushioned chair facing the oversized oak desk and the brick wall. A bad feeling twisted in his stomach.

Gary closed the door and hurried to the desk. He set down his phone and picked up a brown sandwich bag, which was folded closed. With his thumb and forefinger, Gary lifted it and held it away from his body. He carried it to Saul, dropped it in his lap, and returned quickly to the desk. He sat behind his computer and used his shirt sleeve to buff the spot where the bag had been.

Saul unfolded the bag and peered inside. It contained his badge-wallet. Nothing else.

"That's everything," Gary said. "Now we would greatly appreciate it if you left the premises quietly. You're no longer welcome here."

A feeling of panic expanded in Saul's chest. "What happened?"

Gary shook his head. "Nothing happened, okay?"

"Look. I didn't eat enough yesterday. My blood sugar was low. I think I might have been sleepwalking last night." Saul opened his wallet. "I'll gladly pay for any damages."

Gary looked down at his phone. "You didn't do

anything."

Saul straightened. Maybe Gary had just noticed something on the screen, but to look down at that moment—it looked like he was lying.

If Saul had caused some kind of damage, they would just give him a bill. This was something worse. "So what's the problem?"

"No problem, detective. Bad things don't happen at the Roosevelt."

"I've been coming here for years." Saul heaved himself up from the chair. "You owe me an explanation. Please."

"Nothing happened. You were never here." Gary came around the desk. He kept his distance from Saul as he marched to the door where he performed a curt bow. "I've got another matter to attend to."

"Wait," Saul said.

But Gary, and the dark secret he refused to speak of, had disappeared through the door.

If Saul had done something, why hadn't he woken up? He couldn't have been hypnotized. He wasn't susceptible to hypnotic suggestion. He had failed the tests performed by stage hypnotists at the Castle. And Saul would remember if Wayob had tried to hypnotize him, wouldn't he? Could Wayob have blacked out Saul's memory? Was that even possible?

In his wake a pair of guards entered and stood against the back wall and waited for Saul to leave.

He got to his feet and faced them.

The younger guard glanced at his pal. The older, maybe thirty-five, narrowed his eyes. He wanted to fight. If he knew Saul was LAPD, he couldn't care less. Saul was tempted to indulge him, but there was nothing to learn here. The message was clear: there would be no cooperation, no questions answered.

At least he had his badge back. He whistled the Warwick tune as he strolled by the guards. They trailed close behind him all the way to the back exit.

While waiting for the valet to bring up the Mustang, Saul stepped into the alley and called Hernandez. He asked her to check the incident report for what had occurred in the alley.

"No need," she said. "That alley leads to La Brea, right? That's my scene: Jenna Collins. What are you doing there?"

Saul hesitated. He wanted to tell her but what could he say?

"I was on my way home to get my wallet. Just happened to drive by. What happened with Arcos?"

She snickered. "He pulled me over. Can you believe that? He actually pulled me over like he was making a traffic stop and asked for my paperwork. The balls on that guy."

"Yeah, brave but stupid. He still on you?"

"No, I'm back at the PAB."

As the valet pulled up from the garage, he rumbled the engine of Hernandez's Mustang. Saul covered his phone and turned away.

"Where are you now?" she asked.

"Stoplight. What about Carter?"

"I haven't seen him. When I asked Arcos, he changed the subject. It seemed to upset him."

"Strange."

Across the alley, a half-open dumpster reeked in the heat of the sun. Saul grimaced. If Carter was lurking around here somewhere, Saul would be easy to find. "I'd better go—"

"Wait, how's my baby?" Hernandez asked.

"I'll have her back by the end of the day, don't worry. She drives great."

"I'm not worried. I know you value your life."

Saul laughed.

"Just call me after you talk to Wilson, okay?"

Saul promised he would and ended the call. He tipped the valet a five. Folded himself into the Mustang and gunned it out of the alley. Away from the crime scene. Watching the rearview. No sign of Carter.

—

Before driving to Intrepid Solutions, Saul called to verify that Wilson was there. His voicemail picked up. Saul redialed and asked the receptionist for Wilson's supervisor.

The supervisor introduced himself as Brad Davies, and when Saul asked about Wilson, he laughed sarcastically. "Gray? He quit."

Saul felt a surge in his gut. "When did he give notice?"

"Give notice? You'd think, right? Common courtesy. But no, he just quit with a text message last night. His new job better be rock solid because he burned his bridge here."

This is not a coincidence. No way. "Do you have the number for his next of kin? He's not picking up on his cell."

"Hold on." Davies punched his keyboard.

Ahead of Saul, the light turned green, but the intersection was backed up from one light to the next. He was blocked.

"I've got his wife's number," Davies said, "but I can't give that it out, I'm afraid. Company policy." He sounded, perhaps, slightly remorseful.

"It's an emergency contact, right? This is an

emergency."

"Not my employee. Not my responsibility."

Saul clenched the wheel. "This is a murder investigation."

"Is he involved?" Davies sounded hopeful.

"I don't know yet. It's LAPD policy not to release details of an ongoing investigation. But I'll tell you this anyway, because I'm worried. Wilson might be in danger. And he's not the only one."

"Sorry," Davies said. "Wish I could help you."

"I can get a warrant," Saul lied. "You're just slowing me down here. Don't be that guy."

"Hey, I'm just doing my job. I don't appreciate your tone of voice." Davies ended the call.

Saul punched the wheel. Wilson's resignation was starting to seem justified. Perhaps it had more to do with Davies than Wayob or anything else.

Gray

In the backseat of Ashley's pink Bentley, Gray tries to sketch the back of Clayton's head.

Instead of Clayton, the person he ends up drawing is Andrea. He starts with the profile of her oval face, then sketches a window around her head and shoulders. She's driving a car. If he'd planned on drawing her, he'd have visualized capturing her waifish beauty, the way she stood in the kitchen with the cantaloupe, the lock of hair across her eye. This time, the problem is not his hand working against him but his mind's eye. When he looks at the paper, he can only picture Andrea from the point of view of a car passing in the opposite direction, on the narrow part of Beverly Park Drive below Ashley's house. He draws the four interlocking rings of the Audi symbol. Déjà vu. He's never seen Andrea's car—he's sure—and yet he's positive it's an Audi. A red one. *Weird*.

"Here we are," Clayton says.

Gray looks up as they turn off Melrose and roll through the double arched gate of Paramount Studios.

His pulse quickens. The screen test suddenly seems more real than it had before. They glide past the security booth. Beyond it, on the opposite side of a roundabout, a guard hurries to move the orange cones that block a side street leading further into the studio lot.

As they turn on the street, another guard, too scrawny for his security shirt, runs ahead, past a row of brownstones built to look like a street in New York City. Behind them, the familiar world wanes away beyond the gate.

The road narrows between large windowless buildings the color of sand, each labeled with a stage number. The guard motions for Clayton to park behind a black Lexus.

As Gray heaves the car door open, he catches a perplexed expression on Clayton's face reflected in the mirror.

Once he's out Clayton presses a button on the center console and the door shuts on its own. Now he remembers that the door had closed automatically after he got in the car. There must be some button to open it from the backseat as well.

He looks around. Bold capitals stenciled on the building declare it "STAGE 12."

"So, what am I supposed to do?"

Clayton shrugs. "Don't worry, you'll do fine."

The scrawny guard reappears in an electric golf cart. "I'll take you to wardrobe, Ms. York." His boyish cheeks blush bright red as he fails to make eye contact.

Clayton nods goodbye, leans against the driver's side door, and takes out his phone.

Gray climbs into the white cushioned seat behind the guard. The guard drives through the stage entrance, which is big enough for a four-ton truck to pass through. They pass lumber stacks and sheetrock, a living room set surrounded by cameras mounted on tracks and cranes, and people with clipboards and screenplays milling about.

Gray's heart beats hard. He has to pull this off for Ashley so she doesn't hold it against him that he's in her body. If he doesn't ruin her career, then maybe she won't ruin his.

They pull over near a queue of people waiting beside a table draped with white cloth and decked with baskets of muffins, bagels, fruit, juice bottles, and an urn of coffee.

Before Gray can disembark, a girl in a pink skirt with fake lashes hurries up the cart and beckons for him to follow her. "Shana's ready for you."

She leads Gray past long racks of clothes to a bright dressing room. Shana turns out to be a six-foot Black woman in a tube top with wavy blonde hair. She greets Gray with air kisses, one for each cheek, then ushers him into the swivel chair, where she wraps him in a blue barber cape.

"I need to practice my lines," Gray says.

"First, you need your hair done," Shana says, with a smile. When Gray doesn't smile back in the mirror, Shana adds, "You're going to blow them away, sweetie. Trust me."

As Shana brushes, spritzes and combs, she talks fast, her voice high with excitement. But Gray is too dehydrated to concentrate. He needs to drink something, preferably with caffeine, before the lightness in his dried-out brain becomes a full-on headache.

Shana whispers to her assistant, who snickers then

attempts to cover it with a cough. Shana riffles through a pile of magazines on the counter below the mirror. Both seem to be watching Gray for a reaction.

Shana stops smiling. "You feeling okay?" she asks.

For the first time, Gray notices her Adam's apple. Not that it matters that she's transgender, and he feels pang of guilt that the revelation surprised him. He glances down.

"Ashley York. Such a privilege." A man with an Australian accent parades into the dressing room, his hair moussed up into spikes. Trailing behind him are a pair of waifs, one blonde and the other brunette.

"I'm Paul Davies, and I'll be your costume director today."

Shana moves aside as Paul squeezes Gray's shoulders, painfully, while issuing a fountain of compliments. He spins Gray's chair around to face the dressing room.

A lanky brunette emerges from the wardrobe holding up a clothes hanger with a ribbon of white fabric.

"I present to you your dress for today, Ms. York," Paul says with a slight bow, as if expecting a standing ovation.

"It's so beautiful." Shana clasps her hands to her neck.

Gray feels like he has drifted out into deep water. His stomach knots and rumbles, just like it did in eighth grade when he auditioned for a play—only to get close to Laura. When he came out on stage to say his line, what came out instead was half-digested macaroni, like little white worms stewed in stomach acid, all down the front of his shirt, his shoes, the floor. The audience had laughed at him as did the entire cast, especially Laura.

"Are you alright?" Shana asks.

"Guess I'm just a little nervous about the audition." More than a little. Much more.

"Ashley York is beyond an audition," Paul says. "This is a screen test."

Gray feels flushed. Sweat oozes from his armpits. His whole plan seems ridiculous now, to ace Ashley's screen test and put in a good word for himself. What was he thinking?

"Kimmy wore your dress for the lighting test." Paul reaches up to indicate the blonde waif standing behind his right shoulder, who is nearly a head taller than him. Seeming to realize he looks awkward, he withdraws his hand. "I promise you, it's a knockout."

But dress or no dress and despite Gray's disguise in the cute package of Ashley York, it's still going to be him standing up there, having no idea what he's doing —in front of Sean Penn.

But maybe if he's sick he can reschedule? And he has a feeling that if he's going to ask, he'd better ask the boss. "Where is Sean Penn?"

"Mr. Penn is on set with Zac," Paul says. "They'll be ready for you in twenty minutes, just enough time for Shana to finish your hair."

Shana nods.

"Who's Zac?" Gray asks and immediately regrets it from the way Paul's eyes widen and he exchanges a look with Shana.

"Zac Efron, sweetie," Shana says.

Paul raises both hands. "Your agent didn't tell you? That's ridiculous. You need better communication. I happen to have a friend who's an amazing agent—"

"No," Gray says. This is getting out of control. "I

mean, he told me, but…before I get up there, I need to discuss character motivation." He'd heard the term "character motivation" in a movie once; it sounded important.

"You'll do fine." Paul moves behind Gray and begins kneading his shoulders again. "Look at you. I'll have my agent friend call you afterward. His name is Buckley. It doesn't hurt to talk, right? You two are going to hit it off. I just know it…"

Gray hardly hears what Paul is saying. He longs for the solitude of his garage, where he can paint without anyone watching him, where he can layer over his mistakes until his painting looks exactly like he intends. But at the screen test everyone will see all his mistakes, and how many takes will they give him? Two? Three? How can he pretend to know how to act when just the thought of public speaking makes him nauseous? Even the shitty software job he quit beats getting up on stage. Once Brad, his supervisor, decreed that they "reduce undocumented discussions," Gray hardly had to speak at all.

Shana shepherds Gray over to a folding screen, where Kimmy helps him change behind it. Because the dress leaves so much exposed, he has to strip out of his underwear and bra and squeeze into a bodysuit. In the front it forms a deep *V* of chest, exposing the sides of Ashley's breasts, and there's not much more fabric on the sides of the dress, just thin strips of fabric connecting the front to the back, exposing his hips and upper thighs. The bodysuit doesn't leave much to the imagination.

When he emerges from behind the divider, his cheeks are red in the mirror. *Ashley wouldn't blush*, he thinks. Goosebumps break out on his arms and legs.

There's a chill in the air. Even the Kimmy's tank top has more fabric than his dress.

"You look a-mazing!" Shana says.

"I think we've got a winner." Paul throws an arm around Kimmy, the other around the brunette waif.

Gray crosses his arms, feeling uncomfortable.

Someone knocks lightly on the dressing-room door, a timid knock that seems distinctive given how everyone else just barges in. Shana exchanges another look with Paul and goes to check.

The scrawny guard who drove the golf cart edges in through the doorway and flattens himself against the wall as Clayton almost shoves him aside to enter.

"Some kook is claiming to be your cousin," Clayton says. "I told him to get lost, but he convinced me he's been to your house before. You look dope, by the way."

"What's his name?" Gray asks.

"Gray Wilson," the guard says. "He says it's an emergency. Sorry to bother you, but no one picked up." He points to the black office phone beside the magazines with a blinking red light. "My boss wanted to make sure he isn't legit before kicking him out or whatever."

Thank goodness, Gray thinks. Ashley got his message. Even if they can't switch back to their own bodies right away, she can at least tell him how to get off this train speeding toward a cliff.

Gray steps toward the guard. "Where is he?"

Shana grabs his arm and pulls him back. "We don't have time."

"You really have a cousin?" Clayton says, his beefy frame blocking the door.

Yep, Gray thinks, *I definitely don't like Clayton*. "He's a distant cousin. If you don't let me go talk to him this will just take a lot longer than it has to."

Clayton reluctantly moves aside.

The scrawny guard follows Gray out of the dressing room. Gray hops in the front of the golf cart, surprised to find he has more control than he thought. Clayton climbs in the back, glaring at him. The cart sinks under his weight.

As they accelerate through the soundstage, the guard casts near-constant sidelong glances at Gray's breasts. Gray pulls up on the straps, but there simply isn't enough fabric to actually cover them.

"Look out." Gray points at a stack of plywood. The guard swerves, narrowly missing it.

What would Ashley do? Gray smiles and arches his back.

Ahead, sunlight pours in through the stage door. They drive out into it and turn onto the narrow road between stages. They pass mock storefronts and a bank.

Gray twists around in his seat to face Clayton, who sits like a boulder in the back of the cart. "When we get there," Gray says, "I need to talk to him alone, okay?"

At the roundabout near the studio entrance, a tour group has gathered around a pair of young guides in studio T-shirts.

"Hold up," Clayton says. "Too many people."

The guard slows down.

"Doesn't matter," Gray says. "Just get me there."

They carry on toward security, steering a wide arc around the tour group at Clayton's insistence. The tour guides finish their spiel and lead the group in the same direction.

Parked by the security shack is Gray's car, and the person who hops out of it looks like his doppelgänger. She marches toward them, her gait less precise than his, toes twisted inwards, her face determined and desperate. There is something different about the way she pulls the corners of her mouth, too far down toward her chin. Not the way Gray would frown, but close.

A sunburned guard with a crew cut runs after her from the security shack, his shirt coming untucked. "Hey! Stop!"

The guard driving the cart slams the brakes a few yards away from Ashley.

"It's okay," Gray hears himself saying in Ashley's voice, as if from a distance or a dream. As he exits the cart, the people in the tour group train their cameras and cell phones on him, and Clayton is saying something, which Gray ignores. He's mesmerized by his own visage, inverted from what he sees in the mirror. *This is how others see me.*

"Is that what you're wearing?" Ashley says. "Seriously?"

Gray glances down at the dress as she pulls him aside.

"Ashley," Clayton shouts from close behind them.

Ashley in his body is taller than Gray in hers. She leans down and growls into his ear, "Found your photos."

He steps back, feeling exposed, as if it were his own body that had been stripped and posed in those photos, which he had no plans to use, but obviously there's no chance she's going to believe that now.

With one hand, she grabs a fistful of fabric below his right breast and pulls him closer. "You want to act? Act like this hurts a lot worse than it does. You're not going to do the screen test."

She draws back her hand, which is his hand—which looks naked without his wedding band, which he left by the bathroom sink, last night—and swings.

Her hand smacks his cheek. He feels the sting but is too stunned to move. His eyes water.

The crowd gasps and murmurs.

"Asshole!" She balls both hands into fists.

Gray steps back, gingerly rubbing his cheek where she slapped him. "I'm sorry."

Clayton grabs her arm and twists it behind her back. When she screams, it's Gray's voice, but higher pitched than he'd have screamed. "Sorry? You're sorry?"

Clayton twists her other arm back, forcing her to bend over.

"Let me go," she says, "or you will be sorry!"

The scrawny guard had jumped from the cart and is ripping the Taser from his belt, not noticing or pretending not to notice that the attacker is already subdued. He fires. "Take that, you bastard."

Her body jerks and goes limp.

Clayton lowers her to the ground. "You didn't have to do that, man."

Clayton nods toward the cameras and the phones. The guard seems to shrink two sizes smaller than he already is.

At the sight of his own body lying there on the slate pavers, Gray's throat tightens. He kneels beside Ashley and tries to hold up her head. She groans. The sunburned guard squats down with a pair of handcuffs and tries to roll her sideways to cuff her arms behind her back.

Gray shoves him away. She has every right to be angry. This is his fault.

Tears stream down Ashley's cheeks, so easily it seems. He always found it hard to cry.

Clayton comes around behind Gray and grips his shoulders firmly. "I'm sorry, Ashley girl. So who is this guy, really?"

The crowd circles in. A teenager dressed in black squeezes through a pair of fat guys in tan shorts, both with T-shirts tucked tight over their guts. All with phones, of course, pointed at him. What will Claire think?

Gray allows Clayton to lift him to his feet. How can he and Ashley switch back? He plants his legs wide to prevent Clayton from pulling him away. "I still need to talk to him," Gray says. "Is there like an office or something where we can take him?"

"No way," Clayton says. "I'm responsible for your safety."

The sunburned guard clicks the handcuffs on Ashley.

"Let's get you out of here, girl," Clayton says to Gray. "You're not thinking clearly." Then he raises his voice. "You could sue this studio into the ground." He tows Gray away by the arm, bulldozing a path through the crowd, who keeps filming despite the additional guards who have arrived and are shouting for everyone to move along.

Gray's head feels too heavy for his neck. He needs to sit. He needs to process seeing his own body outside of himself. But he can't abandon Ashley. He digs in his heels. "Get those handcuffs off him. We have to get him out of here. He's family."

Clayton puts one arm around him and uses his

other hand to block Gray's face from the cameras. "I'll take care of it. But first I have to get you to a safe place." He nudges Gray forward with his massive arm that feels like an oak branch in a tailored suit.

Gray reluctantly starts walking. It will be good to get out of this crowd. With all the attention surrounding him, maybe it's better to stay away from Ashley for now. He'll call her and tell her how to use the charm. Hopefully it will set things back to normal.

"That guard overreacted," Gray says to Clayton. "I want him released before things get worse. Let me deal with him on my own."

"After we get you squared away." Clayton holds up his hand to a guard and whistles. "Bring the cart," he shouts. He motions Gray toward the double doors of the building nearby.

"No way I can do the screen test today," Gray says. "Not after all that."

Clayton chuckles low inside his chest. "I'll take care of it. Don't worry about a thing."

The doors lead to a circular lobby for a screening room. Gray sinks into a cushioned bench, his mouth too dry to swallow. Posters for various Paramount classics adorn the walls: *There Will Be Blood*, *The Virgin Suicides*, *Rear Window*.

Clayton keeps watch by the doors. "You'll feel better in the car. We'll get some ice on your cheek. It's going to be fine, by the way. Hardly red at all."

Gray pictures the bar in the back of Ashley's pink Bentley where soon he can get a drink—a real drink—and just the thought quenches the dryness in his mouth. His head feels lighter.

Wayob Gives Chase

Wayob's frustration grows into anger. They've been driving for hours, and his posse keeps jabbering. He cannot concentrate. The one called Mark, who insisted on sitting back here and crowding Wayob's personal space, points out one showy blonde after another. The one called Jacob, who drives the vehicle, stops again.

"Must you stop at every light?" Wayob asks.

"I do when she's next to us." Jacob honks and waves to the woman in the vehicle beside them: another blonde. A pale fleshy thing, insignificant compared to the beauty once held by Wayob's bride. Behind the glass of her vehicle, she smiles back, specifically at Wayob in August's body. She rubs her tongue over her lips. Disgusting, but not nearly so vile as Wayob's bride turned out to be.

Distracted again now, Wayob must concentrate. "Quiet!"

He closes his eyes, trying to ignore all the external sounds. Until, in his mind, he can make out the sound of he who has the Encanto, a feat which took Wayob hundreds of years to learn. Listening to Gray Wilson's mind in the darkness, he homes in on the direction.

"Dude." Mark interrupts Wayob's meditation again. "Are we getting close?"

Wayob slaps the empty seat in front of him. "How many times must I ask you for silence?"

"I was just asking, was all."

"You were just asking. You are of no use to anyone. Thanks to your incessant remarks about hotties in convertibles, we have traveled too far. We must go west now."

Mark looks out the window.

"Do you have an address?" Jacob asks. "I mean, your new meditation thing is really cool and all, but if I knew where we were going—"

"Go westward. Gray Wilson may also be traveling. I might know, if you could give me one moment of peace."

"What do you have against this Gray guy? You don't really mean to hurt him, right?"

"I have nothing against him," Wayob says. *But if I do not end his life, I shall suffer a fate worse than death.* "Now, please, I must concentrate."

"What are you talking about?" Jacob asks.

Wayob wants to scream. He wants to exit the vehicle, despite all the problems he encountered when he tried to hunt alone. At least alone, he has silence. Wayob inhales. Patience. He cannot tell these fools about the Encanto. They would want it for themselves.

"Just get me to him," Wayob says. "I will do what needs to be done." He squeezes his eyes shut. "Now be quiet. I am asking you as kindly as I can."

"We've got your back," Jacob says. "Just tell us what's going on."

"Do you understand the language of English?"

Jacob says nothing. Mark says nothing. They both seem to find something to focus on beyond the windows of the vehicle. Do they think he is joking? Wayob *must* kill Gray. Wayob does not joke. Except, as a part of his revenge, Wayob did sort of perform a joke on Saul Parker. Wayob laughs, which makes him lose his concentration. The trap he laid for Parker. "Parker," Wayob growls.

"Who's Parker?" Mark asks.

"I was merely thinking to myself. Now stay quiet."

The fucking priest died too soon for revenge, and the priest shall be the last to wrong Wayob and go unpunished. And who can blame Wayob for this? No one. Wayob only takes revenge in equal measure to the wrongs inflicted upon him.

Wayob watches the angle of sunlight change on the palm trees that pass outside the window. Jacob has yet again chosen a road that loops in the wrong direction. Now Wayob must begin his meditation all over again. He closes his eyes. Breathes in. Breathes out. Tunes out the sound of the engine. Retreats down inside himself. He tries to focus, tries to find the sound of Gray's mind. If he could find whoever is now in Gray's body, then he would have the Encanto, for Gray would have left the Encanto along with his true body. But Wayob can only hear the mind-sounds of he who holds the Encanto. It creates a marker on the holder's mind. Not that he understands at all how. Fucking priest explained nothing before banishing him to this existence.

If Wayob were to end the life of this vessel, if he were to endure the pain of dying once again, could he get closer to Gray? At least he could free himself from these vapid jabbering fools. However, this he can do without suffering through death, if he sees someone sleeping.

Wayob recalls the exhilaration when he first discovered his ability to transmigrate without dying. Back in Guatemala City, when the Policía imprisoned Wayob in a cell, Wayob left his vessel at the time and found his way through the iron bars they believed could contain Wayob and into an officer asleep at his desk outside the cell. If only Wayob could transmigrate from further away.

"Dude!" Mark says. "This who you're looking for?"

Wayob opens his eyes, ready to strangle the fool, as Mark shoves a phone device in Wayob's face. On the screen is an image of a man—the very man Wayob pursued in the vessel of Rydell—and he is attacking a young woman.

Wayob snatches the phone from Mark and pushes him back. "Personal space," Wayob says. "How many times must I tell you?"

"Damn," Mark says. "Don't take it out on me."

"What is it?" Jacob slows the vehicle and turns his head, straining to see.

"This dude just slapped the hell out of Ashley York." Mark smiles as he looks toward Jacob's reflection in the rearview mirror. When he glances back at Wayob, he seems to struggle to look serious. "It's the guy you're looking for, right? Gray Wilson? Guess your subconscious was telling you something after all. We were practically at Ashley's before you said we had to go east all of a sudden. Maybe he was with her."

"Perhaps," Wayob says. Though he was not merely *with* her; Gray must be in this Ashley woman's body, and she must be in his body. Wayob is sure of it. He practically heard it in the sound of Gray's mind. Wayob understands why she attacked him—oh, he knows—for he too has felt anger like hers but a thousand-fold stronger for the fucking priest who separated him from his body and imprisoned him inside the Encanto.

Wayob points at the screen. "Where is this?"

"Looks like the Paramount lot. Remember? When we considered that sidekick role for you in *Transformers*?"

"It is to the west of here, no? How far?"

"We'd be a lot closer," Jacob says, "if you had just said go to Paramount instead of '*go east, go west.*'"

"Go there now," Wayob says. "Go fast."

"Makes sense why you're after him now," Jacob says. "You think they've got something going on?"

"I'm not after him. Not anymore. We must find her." Wayob tilts the phone device toward Mark.

"Going to let Ashley have it, huh?" Mark says. "Guess you don't want to get with her again."

Wayob laughs. "This will be the last time we see each other." So, this vessel, August, has had relations —perhaps has even mated with—the girl whose body Gray now possesses. Perfection.

This morning, when Wayob discovered the distance between his new vessel and Gray Wilson, he fell into a state of furious despair. But now he shall have the upper hand, because in this vessel, Wayob can get close to Gray Wilson and the girl, Ashley, without suspicion. Very close indeed.

If Wayob had probed the mind of August, he could have discovered this sooner, would not have wasted so much time driving around with these vapid fools who seem in constant need of affirmation, always talking of nothing. But it is overwhelming to peer into the mind of a vessel—all the disgusting memories. Wayob had nearly lost himself under the avalanche of information in Saul Parker's mind, and nearly lost control. And by peering into a vessel's mind, Wayob exposes himself, for as he peers into the vessel, the vessel can see into Wayob. August must not learn of the Encanto, like Edward did. Foolish Edward Saroyan, who desired a body for himself with functional legs, and who wanted revenge on poor Wayob. Wayob knows all about revenge. Fucking priest. *No.* If August discovers what the Encanto can do, he will try to take it from Wayob, and then Wayob shall have to kill August, too.

"Is there no shortcut?" Wayob growls as Jacob stops at yet another intersection.

"This is a shortcut."

In the vehicle beside them, a fat girl waves. She shoves her saggy white arm out the window with her phone. Wayob jeers for the photo.

When the light turns green, Mark says, "We need to think about this. Ashley's got a shit-ton of fans. You don't want to be like the dude who slapped her."

"She's got no talent," Jacob says. "You've had girls twice as hot, and there are plenty more. Hell, they'll fuck us just for a chance at you."

"Ashley's got money, though," Mark says.

"August doesn't need money, numb-nuts. And it's Daddy's money, anyway. Not like she ever did anything. We earn ours. We'll be loaded after *Quantum-Man*."

Money. Wayob knows, from all the effort he spent whispering to Gray's subconscious, tickling Gray's desires to persuade him to use the Encanto, that Gray wants money. What he desires most of all is time for himself—time he believes can be purchased with money. And Ashley has lots of money. But Wayob knows better. Wayob knows. Eventually Gray will reflect upon his own pathetic life and succumb to a whim of nostalgia. He will dial back the Encanto. And trap Wayob once again inside the dark, dark nothing, alone.

"I don't care about her fucking fans," Wayob says. "But I do need to see her alone."

"That's what I'm sayin'," Mark says. "Let's go to her house."

"What if she does not go home? We can waste no time."

"Text her. She's your girlfriend, right?"

Wayob tosses Mark's phone back to him. "You do it. I have no patience for such communication."

"Better do it from your phone."

"Fine." Wayob finds the phone belonging to August in his pocket and tosses that one to Mark as well.

Mark fumbles it, dropping it on the floor between his feet. "Careful," he says as he retrieves it.

Jacob makes a U-turn and heads north into a neighborhood where each house is surrounded by expansive plots of green land. As they ascend a hill, each house seems larger than the one that came before it.

"She's not responding," Mark says. "But someone tweeted her pink limo leaving the studio. We can beat her home."

"Very good. Take me to the house that is Ashley's."

Once they near Ashley's, Wayob will proceed on foot. He must leave these fools. They cannot be allowed near the Encanto. If any one of them happened to hold it in such a way as to come to own it, it will transport Wayob back inside and trap him there.

As they drive up the same street where earlier they had turned eastward, silence—merciful silence—finally descends on the vehicle. They reach a gate. It opens. They follow the steep windy road up through a canyon, up a hillside of brown weeds, past rows of tended vines with autumn leaves of red. At the top of the mountain are vast palaces surrounded by fences and fields of green.

Near the summit, a row of trees with bark peeling from their trunks lines the road.

"This is it." Jacob slows as they approach a palace with its own road and a gate.

Wayob points toward trees to the right. "Let me out here. I shall go in on foot."

"We can't leave you stranded," Jacob says. "If you want privacy, we'll just hang by the pool with her hottie maid."

"The one in the Audi?" Mark says. "I could get with that."

"Yeah, Andrea."

"No!" Wayob hates contact, but he must. He must make his point. He leans forward, reaches across, slaps the back of Jacob's head. "I must go in alone, understand?"

"Whatever, dude." He adjusts his stupid hat and laughs, as if Wayob has made some joke.

Clearly, Wayob must try harder. These fools must obey. They cannot be allowed near Ashley's palace, or near Gray Wilson, or near the Encanto. Wayob has suffered too long alone in the dark nothingness to risk going back. Wayob balls his fist and, with all his might, strikes Mark in the ear. Mark's head impacts the window with a satisfying thud.

"Jesus," Jacob says.

Mark raises his arms defensively. Makes no effort to strike back. "What the fuck?"

Wayob wipes his hands on his shirt. Wayob is still the alpha. "My orders are to be obeyed. I shall go in alone."

"Whatever," Mark says. "You're the boss."

Jacob stops the vehicle by the thicket near Ashley's gate. As Wayob gets out, Mark informs him, as if Wayob cares, that they'll go pick up Sydney from the hospital. "Then we'll have some ladies over. So don't expect us to come get you."

"I wouldn't dream of it." Wayob swings the door closed.

As the fools drive off, Wayob enters the thicket. He climbs up a fence. On the other side, a vast field of green grass surrounds the palace that is Ashley's, and beyond her palace, the city of Los Angeles lies sprawled out in the sun, full of promises. Wayob deserves it all.

Who Knew Sadie Wu?

In front of Sadie's home, Saul parked the Mustang and stared at the rust-colored stain on the asphalt. A Prius drove over it. Saul scowled at the driver as she descended the hill and turned left.

By being here, Saul was breaking his promise to Hernandez, but Wilson was AWOL, and idling the investigation would be worse than breaking his promise, worse than facing the Wu family. Wayob was out there somewhere, and Saul had to find him.

The front door was lacquered black, closed tight against the bright afternoon. As he approached, he watched where he put his feet on the uneven slate walkway.

The door unlocked and opened, and Saul looked up. The man standing there was unmistakably Sadie's father. Same square chin. Same high prominent cheeks. Same wiry way of holding himself like a tree in the wind. The resemblance brought Saul back to Sadie's death, and he relived it all over again, her mask of laughter as she ate the gun.

Wu stood there, his mouth turned down, squinting against the sun and the tragedy and the waste. He was a short man, maybe shorter than Sadie, and thin. Which gave Saul an idea of what to search for, perhaps a connection to her death.

Saul clasped his hands. "Mr. Wu, I am very sorry for your loss." He introduced himself and reached to shake Wu's hand, to maybe pat him on the back or hug him, but Wu didn't lean in.

Instead, he shook his head. Inhaled a deep ragged breath. "It was you… I saw your picture." He stepped out of the house and tried to push Saul back from the doorway.

Saul dropped his arms and stood his ground.

Wu balled his hands and pounded Saul in the chest with the side of his fists. First one hand and then the other. Again and again, as he moaned one long mournful note.

Saul accepted it. Because he'd failed to save Sadie's life. Because she'd had her whole life ahead of her. He should have let her shoot him, let her live instead of him.

As Wu's rage dissolved into exhaustion, Mrs. Wu appeared in the doorway, a head taller than Mr. Wu, pale and blonde with dark bags below her eyes. Saul felt like collapsing, or like retreating to the car and driving away.

She put an arm around her husband. "Let him in, Hiromi."

He turned toward her, leaned his head into her chest, and sobbed. Saul's throat tightened. He wanted to cry too. But he had to stay calm. He had to get answers.

She ushered Mr. Wu inside and gestured for Saul to

follow. She led him to the living room, where Mr. Wu withdrew and collapsed on the couch. Mrs. Wu whirled around to face Saul. Fixed him with a cold stare.

Saul inhaled. "I don't know what the other detectives may have told you—"

"They didn't tell us shit," Mrs. Wu said, her face cold. "But they sure had a lot of good questions about you. Like why would you be meeting our daughter in the middle of the night?"

"Last night was the first time I ever saw her. I thought it was a chance encounter at first."

"Is that so?" She tried to sound sarcastic, but as her pitch raised, her voice cracked. "Then why would they seem to think you had something against her?"

"I'm under investigation by Internal Affairs," Saul said. "It's a matter of protocol when there is a shooting. They have to cover all the bases. But I was there. Your daughter... Sadie, she turned the gun on herself. I was trying to stop her."

"No. She would never do anything like that. Whatever you think you saw, you're mistaken. Sadie did not kill herself. If you're here to ask more questions, like if she was unhappy at school or at home, then get out now."

"Do you mind if we sit down?" Saul tried to sound soothing.

Mrs. Wu stared at him.

"I'm here to get to the bottom of this," Saul said. "It won't bring your daughter back, I know. But she wasn't acting on her own." Saul seated himself on the recliner and waited.

On the couch across from him, Mr. Wu seemed to collect himself, nodding slowly as if coming to some kind of acceptance.

Mrs. Wu remained standing. "What does that mean? You make it sound like she committed a crime."

"Nothing like that," Saul said. "Sadie was the victim."

"You've got that right."

"I'm trying to find out what really happened. Why was she in the middle of the road with a gun?"

Mr. Wu swallowed. "Sadie was a straight-A student. She would never do anything like this. She was my little girl."

"I understand," Saul said.

Mrs. Wu stepped toward Saul and clenched her fists. "You understand? What do you understand? You don't know anything about our daughter."

Saul kept his voice calm. "Tell me about her."

"They always say the parents must be out of touch," Mr. Wu said. "But that's not us. We knew our daughter."

Each man is an island onto itself, Saul thought. Hernandez would know whoever said that. Saul shifted forward in the recliner. An eerie silence drifted in the dim light filtered through the curtains, which covered the two windows in the room, one behind Mr. Wu and the other beside him. "I believe...someone manipulated her. She may have been hypnotized."

"Who would do that?" Mrs. Wu asked.

"Did she have any new or unusual friends?"

"No," Mr. Wu said. "She spends all her time with Bethany and Isabella. They've been inseparable since middle school."

Mrs. Wu went to the window beside her husband and peeked through the curtain. An oblique bar of light divided the room.

"No boys?" Saul asked. "Or men?"

Mr. Wu shook his head. He glanced up toward his wife. She closed the curtain. "Not outside of school."

"Anything unusual happen recently? Anything out of the ordinary at all?"

"No," Mrs. Wu said without turning around. "Nothing."

Above Mr. Wu hung a thirty-inch framed photo of a steep hillside above the ocean. From the hillside, an oak tree arched toward the sky.

When he noticed Saul looking, Mr. Wu turned toward it. "That's one of Sadie's photos from Big Sur," he said. "She was going to be a photographer."

Saul rubbed his hands over his face. Sadie was an innocent teenager who'd had so much to live for. "Where did she get the gun?"

Mrs. Wu turned from the window and fixed her husband with a stare. "We don't know."

Mr. Wu pressed his lips together.

Saul said nothing. He'd hoped that the gun Sadie used would trace back to Wayob, but now it was clear the gun belonged to Hiromi Wu.

"You want to see her room?" Wu stood, brows knotted, almost pleading. "Some of her best work is up there."

"Love to," Saul said. He needed to search her bedroom anyway.

As he heaved himself up from the chair, Mrs. Wu marched past. "I have to clean the kitchen." She wiped her eyes and disappeared down a hallway.

Mr. Wu led Saul to the stairway by the front door. He lunged up the steps. Saul followed, the stair planks creaking under his weight. By the time he hit the third step, Wu was already at the top. Saul's legs were incapable of moving any faster. *Exercise. Need to exercise.*

"Did the Internal Affairs detectives check upstairs?"

"Carter did."

"Carter?" Saul stopped midway up the stairs to catch his breath. It surprised him that Carter had searched beyond the forensics at the murder scene, or that he'd done anything at all without Arcos following at his heels.

"He's the one with the mustache, right?" Wu asked. "While I was out this morning, he came back to see her bedroom. Laura let him in."

In Sadie's bedroom, light poured through a window above her desk. Outside the window was the twisted limb of an oak. Below it was a flat roof where the first floor extended out beyond the second. Photos lined the walls, fog and ferns and Big Sur redwoods. Mr. and Mrs. Wu on a rocky beach. A portrait series of two girls about Sadie's age, one Anglo, the other Latina, posing on lifeguard towers. A candid shot of the same two girls and Sadie, their arms intertwined and feet buried in the sand.

"That's Bethany and Isabella," Mr. Wu said.

"Cute girls."

The bedroom got to Saul. All her photos and the corkboard of selfies with her two friends, the three of them always laughing. The pile of stuffed animals arranged in the cubby under her window. Saul knew why Wu had wanted him to see her room, this cocoon of a teenager excited about life, and about her future— as if seeing her eat the gun was not enough for Saul to put everything he had into stopping the bastard who somehow invaded her head.

He approached the bifold doors opposite the bed.

"Mind if I look?"

"I guess not."

As Saul opened the closet, Wu peered in behind him. The dresses and shirts were small enough to be children's clothing, except the style was too chic. Saul found only one flannel, a baby-blue and white plaid. He pulled it out.

"Are you looking for something in particular?" Wu asked.

"Did you notice what she was wearing when you identified the body?"

Wu rubbed his face and looked down. "No."

"That's normal," Saul said. When identifying a deceased loved one, the shock could be overwhelming. A parent should never have to see their child's body. Saul returned the shirt to its hanger. "She had on a men's flannel shirt. It came down to her knees. A large tall, or maybe an extra large."

"That doesn't make sense," Wu said.

Saul nodded. "Do you or your wife have anything like that?"

"No." Wu looked down at himself. "I'm a small."

"You might want to wait downstairs," Saul said. "I need to search her room. Is everything how you found it?"

Wu planted himself in the chair at the desk. "I made her bed. That's about it."

The bed was a double, two pillows, white sheets, and a thick pink comforter. Saul went over and pulled back the covers. The sheets looked clean. He kneeled down and examined them. Three long, dark hairs clung to the pillow. Sadie's hair. And also, a gray hair —two and a half, maybe three inches long. Saul clutched it carefully between his thumb and forefinger.

Held it up to the light. Wu's hair was solid black. And this gray hair seemed too thin to be Asian. Probably not Latino, either. It was the wrong color and length to be Mrs. Wu's or Bethany's or Isabella's. And certainly, it wasn't Sadie's.

"What is it?" Wu's voice climbed an octave.

"Just a hair," Saul said. "Probably nothing."

Wu inhaled through his nose. "Maybe I *should* wait downstairs," he said but remained slumped in the chair.

Saul pulled a plastic evidence bag from his coat pocket and dropped in the hair. *Could be everything.*

Ashley's Pony

Ashley awakens on the ground with a pair of studio guards standing over her and surrounded by a crowd of tourists taking photos of her agony with their phones, probably video as well. A glance at her hands reveals she's still in Gray's body.

The shrimpy guard, who looks too young to work here, helps her to her feet, while the meathead who Tasered her grumbles an apology. "Look, I know you're Ashley York's cousin and all, but this isn't the place to air your dirty laundry. We've got policies and procedures we have to follow to keep everyone safe."

At least Gray had the brains not to press charges.

She drives to a strip mall on Sunset and enters a store called *Phones* with strobes in the window and bad house music. Using Gray's card, she buys a disposable smartphone and checks her twitter feed.

The photos of the confrontation are no surprise, but the comments like, '*Ashley York gets what's coming #RichBitch*,' are disheartening. As badly as she wants her body back, sometimes she's sick of being Ashley

York.

She crosses the parking lot to escape the noise of *Phones* and calls Gray.

He answers hesitantly. "Hello?"

"Is the screen test rescheduled?"

"Um," Gray swallows. "Clayton said he'd handle it."

Clayton will call Don, who will be anxious for her to get right back in the saddle. But Ashley knows the best way to delay Don is to avoid him. He'll make up an excuse for her rather than admit he's out of touch. And if anyone can persuade Sean Penn to give her another shot, it's Don.

"When Don calls, don't answer. No matter what."

"No problem," Gray says. "And for what it's worth, I wasn't planning to do anything with those pictures."

"Then why take them?"

He sighs. "I didn't think it was a big deal. Look at what's already on the web."

Ashley wants to scream. She wishes she'd *punched* him in the face, even if it was her face. She calms herself before responding. He's not worth it. "You don't know anything about me," she says. "Why did you even go to the screen test? I told you how important it was."

"Don and Clayton practically forced me into it," he says. "I thought it might help you if I went."

"You wanted to help me? Then why switch bodies in the first place?"

"Look. I'm sorry." His apology rings hollow, as if he knows it's not okay.

"I don't want your apology. I want my life back."

"I'm with you there," Gray says. "At least, I want to be me again. The charm is in the garage on my workbench, I think."

The sidewalk is almost as noisy as *Phones*. Traffic barrels up through the intersection toward the Sunset Strip. She turns back toward the lot, toward Gray's car. "Where did it come from?"

"A fortune-teller," he says. "At the Day of the Dead festival, downtown."

Holding the phone to her ear, Ashley unlocks Gray's car and sinks into the driver's seat. "So how does it work?"

"I'm not sure, exactly. She doesn't speak English, and when I accepted it, I never expected I'd wake up the next day as you."

"But you knew the second time, right?"

"No. I sort of had someone else in mind. I wasn't sure anything would happen at all."

"So why me?" Ashley says. "This whole damn thing is like a nightmare."

"Look for a round stone with a snake," Gray says. "You have to turn the snake. If nothing happens, try sleeping, and I'll go to sleep too. Oh, and don't hold the stone in your hand when you turn the snake. It stabbed the hell out of my hand."

Ashley closes her eyes. "Assuming this actually gets us back to normal, what's next?"

"I don't know..." Gray says. "I'm making some changes in my life. I need to figure some things out—"

"Uh, no. I'm talking about the charm. No offense, but I don't want to be you again."

Gray laughs. It sounds forced. "It's that bad?"

"Bad timing," she says. In truth, if not for the screen test, it might have been interesting to experience life in his body.

"I guess I'll destroy it," he says.

"Promise me."

"Promise."

She ends the call and checks Instagram. It's just as bad as twitter. Her anger mounts as she scrolls through her feed. It was bad luck that the tour group happened to be there to photograph the whole incident, the slap and Taser—but still, it was Gray's fault. He was the one who had used the charm twice. Even if she could forgive him the first time, the second time was deliberate. He doesn't get it. This is *her* life he's fucking with.

He deserves a little gift, she decides, to commemorate their time together: his own image that can never be erased. Beside *Phones* is the Sunset Tattoo Studio.

Inside, the walls of the narrow space are lipstick-red and lined with framed posters of tattoos. There's a black leather couch and a black lacquered counter, and behind the counter, a stocky woman in a wife-beater shirt, no bra, her arms tattooed from wrists to shoulders in busy black ink.

Ashley approaches. "I want a tattoo on my butt."

The woman's expression remains blank. "You have a design?"

"I think so." Ashley glances at the photos behind the woman. Most people she knows wouldn't be caught dead with a Harry Potter tattoo, but that's not embarrassing enough for Gray. "You have other examples, right?"

The woman opens an iPad and hands it to Ashley. Pictures of tattoos are organized into albums. Ashley scrolls past tribal, Japanese, realism, and dives into the kitsch album where she swipes past Bambi, cartoon cats, and a baby mermaid riding a seahorse. She pauses on a doe-eyed My Little Pony surrounded by butterflies and hearts and stars. The pony is pink with baby-blue wings and a long flowing mane of blue hair.

"This is the one," Ashley says.

The woman tilts the iPad, and the image rotates one-eighty, such that it's upside down for Ashley and right side up to the woman. She studies the image. "How big you want it?"

"How big can you make it in an hour?"

She zooms out. "I could do a three-inch version without the stuff around it in an hour and a half. But we don't have to do it all in one session, if you want bigger."

"Three inches should be big enough."

"Take some time and think about it. This is a permanent piece of body art, and you need to be sure. I'll be here when you're ready."

"I've thought about it." Ashley says more forcefully than she intended. "I know I don't look like the kind of guy who would want this tat, but I've got my reasons, trust me."

"Hey, I don't judge. I just want you to be happy is all."

She leads Ashley to a back room and begins gathering her tools from the candy-red metal cabinet. Ashley undresses and lays face down on a cot lined with white paper.

The tattoo artist spreads her tools and inks on the nearby table and pulls up a stool.

Ashley laughs. Gray deserves worse. What if Don can't delay the screen test? What if Sean Penn already has someone else he wants to cast, some other actress with more experience. She tries to force herself to feel angry instead of relieved at the thought of a missed opportunity.

As the tattoo artist begins, Ashley feels the scratching sensation on her butt cheek, which seems to spread to the back of her mind—is she taking things too far by getting this tattoo? Honestly, how much does she care about the screen test? It's not just that the role is out of her league; it's the months and months of commitment. Is a movie really worth so much time? What else could she do with her life?

Kids. She knows for sure now, from her time spent as Gray. A boy and a girl, just like Tyler and Mindy, would be amazing. It would be hard to provide a stable home environment as an actress, with all the traveling and long days and late nights. Sure, she could hire all kinds of help—that's what her dad did—but Ashley wants to raise her kids herself. And preferably not alone.

It must be hard to stay together for so long. She wonders if Claire still cares about Gray in some tangled, twisted way, because clearly she's checked out. Maybe all relationships become like that over time —like hating the person you love. Ashley has never stuck around long enough to find out. Is it even possible for two people to stay in love long enough to raise a child?

Her butt cheek starts to burn. Like the time she fell off her scooter, trying to ride it down the stairs, and scraped her knee. That was right before her mother died, when Ashley was five, when the adults in her life seemed to answer every question with the word '*cancer*,' as if cancer actually said something about who her mother was.

The memory of the hospital—its long quiet hallways and serious nurses, everyone whispering high over her head— makes Ashley shiver. She remembers how Michelle, her first nanny, shoved her into a room with the harsh smell of antiseptic and a frail, shriveled woman propped up on a bed.

"Ashley, it's so good to see you," the woman had said, trying to smile. She sounded like Ashley's mother, but her mother had hair, thick blonde hair.

Ashley had tried to squeeze back out through the door, but Michelle picked her up and carried her in. "Say hello to your mother."

She plopped Ashley on the bed by the woman, who Ashley refused to believe was her mother. The woman wrapped Ashley in her twig-like arms that snaked with all kinds of wires and tubes. They both cried. Eventually, after Ashley managed to squirm off the bed, Michelle took her home. She should have stayed at the hospital. If she ever got a do-over, she'd go back to that moment and hug her mother back.

After the funeral, after all the strangers patted her on the head and said '*cancer*' and '*sorry*' and not much else, and then her dad drove them back to their home to Bel Air. That night, Michelle moved into his room.

In the weeks following, her dad took a break from work, and they stayed out at the house in Malibu. Those few weeks were the happiest of her childhood. They *were* her childhood: playing on the beach with her dad and Michelle. On her sixth birthday, her dad gave her a golden puppy, who she named Rexi.

But a few days later, her dad returned to work and Ashley was sent off to a summer camp in Idyllwild where Rexi wasn't allowed, and where Ashley cried herself to sleep every night.

When she finally returned from camp, Michelle was gone, and Shayla was the new nanny and she made

Rexi stay outside in a pen that had been built around Ashley's playhouse. It dawns on Ashley now, as the tattoo artist attacks her butt cheek, how much Raquel, with her D-cups and Brazilian blow-out, looks like Shayla, who must have been in her early twenties when she was hired. The same age as Raquel is now.

It feels like a cat dragging its claws over and over on the same patch of skin. Ashley wants it to stop, but she grits her teeth and bears it, like she did when Shayla levered herself between Ashley and her dad.

It started one of times when Dad slept at work because of some big deadline, but Shayla told Ashley it was because Ashley bothered him. So, when he came home, Ashley kept to herself. Meanwhile, Shayla threw decadent adults-only parties where she acted all bubbly and fake while she sat with him at the head of the table, touching his arm and laughing at everything he said while Ashley had to eat in the kitchen.

The fire was the breaking point. Shayla used it to force Ashley out of the house. It had been cold outside, and Ashley had only meant to warm her playhouse with just a small fire, but the little curtains caught fire, and they made so much smoke that she couldn't see the flames well enough to stop them. The smoke burned in her lungs and her eyes. She and Rexi almost choked to death before they escaped. The fire department came with hoses and put out the fire, which by then had turned her playhouse and the nearby hedge into ashes.

That night, Ashley listened at her dad's door while Shayla—who had moved into his room by that point—went on and on in her shrill voice about how Ashley was too much to handle, a delinquent who deserved to be committed for her own safety, and for theirs.

Ashley wanted to apologize to her dad for the fire, but Shayla was always hovering around, always talking over Ashley when she tried to say something.

The next week, Ashley got packed off to the Oakhurst Academy for troubled girls in Santa Barbara. She went without a fight because she thought it would be the end of Shayla, who was hired to be Ashley's nanny. Instead, somehow, Shayla persuaded her dad to get married again.

They let her out of school for the wedding, which was held on a private island in the Caribbean, but by then it was too late. There was no way to stop him from walking down the aisle.

The marriage ended after a few months, followed by an intense year of legal battles during which her dad became more distant than ever. He let her move home, at least, but Shayla had gotten rid of Rexi by then and the house was empty without him.

After the divorce was finalized, her dad gradually came out of the fog. He became more attentive to her. And she forgave him for the neglect, because although he dated occasionally, the women never moved in, and he'd never even brought one home. If Ashley's plans for the two of them ever collided with a date, he'd quietly cancel on whatever woman he was seeing. As he often said, Ashley was the most important girl in his life. Even when he'd thrown himself deep into his work, if Ashley called him, he always made time for her.

He still does. Whenever she goes a few days without calling him, he calls her. So, it's strange that he still hasn't returned her call after the message she left this morning.

The artist puts down her tools and hands Ashley a

mirror. "I finished the outline. Check it out." She angles another mirror toward Ashley's butt so Ashley can see the pony prancing on Gray's left cheek surrounded by pink, irritated skin. It looks like a drawing by a pre-teen girl. No need to fill it in. It's more than Gray deserves already.

"I'll come back and get the rest later," Ashley says.

"You don't like it?"

"No, it's good," Ashley says, but she doesn't feel good.

As the artist bandages her butt, Ashley notices her hands are trembling.

So Close

Outside Sadie's, Saul folded himself into Hernandez's Mustang. To get the hair sample analyzed, he'd have to ask her for another favor. He pulled out his phone, powered it on, and saw she'd already texted, asking him to call her.

He dialed and started the car. In front of him, a Mercedes SUV had parked too close for him to maneuver around it. Hernandez answered and filled him in on her news as Saul eased the car backward. She described how Wilson had attacked Ashley York and was Tasered by studio security, and how Ashley then, surprisingly, fawned over him.

A rim grated against the curb. Saul slammed on the brakes.

She stopped talking. "What was that?"

"Nothing," he said.

He had to go forward. No other option now. He turned the wheel, clenched his teeth, and pressed the gas...ever so gently.

The rim grated against the concrete, even louder

than before. The vibration reverberated through the car, from the wheel to his shoulder, which held the phone pressed against one ear.

He spoke over it. "Do me a favor and look up Ashley York's address. Dollars to donuts she lives in Beverly Hills, in a gated neighborhood north of Sunset."

As he rolled away from the curb and past the Mercedes, the clacks of Hernandez typing came through the phone.

"Beverly Park," she said. "How did you know?"

"That's where I followed Wilson yesterday. He watched her gate for an hour."

"Weird," she said. "You think they had some kind of fling?"

"I don't see it. Wilson's not plugged into Hollywood. It must be something else. Can't be a coincidence that Rydell was following Wilson and now this. Maybe Wilson is Wayob, although I don't think so. He might be the next victim, though. Or maybe Ashley."

"You really think their confrontation has something to do with Wayob?"

"That's what I intend to find out," Saul said. "Can you find a number for Wilson's next of kin? He's not picking up on his cell."

"I'm slammed with the Collins case right now. It might be faster if you stop by his house."

"I'll try again, but I'm going to hit Ashley's first."

"Seriously? You think she'll see you?"

"If she cares about her safety."

"Ooh. Get me her autograph while you're there."

"Ha."

"Call me afterward?"

Saul agreed and tapped off. Ashley York and Wilson took priority over the hair. He'd give it to Hernandez later.

—

As Saul approached Beverly Hills, the sunlight grew softer, filtered through haze. He turned north on San Ysidro and drove past where Wilson had parked yesterday and up to the gate. He badged to the guard, and the guard nodded and opened the gate.

Saul rolled through. After the guardhouse and garden area, the road narrowed and rose. It banked up a dry hill and turned, and after a couple of miles seemed more like remote desert wilderness than the middle of LA. Then the road parted around a manicured median and leveled out, revealing a sparse row of mansions with manicured lawns.

Ashley York had her own guard stationed in a four-foot-wide booth in the middle of her driveway with an arched gate on either side, one for coming, one for going. The iron bars of the gates were bent and twisted into geometric shapes and freshly painted with black paint—probably painted once a year. The gates were mounted on stone pillars connected to a wooden fence. As Saul rolled up to the booth, he could see through the gate. The driveway cut a lazy arc through a vast expanse of tended lawn bathed in warm light, punctuated by long shadows of palms. Below the lawn, the house featured a stone turret on the eastern side.

The guard slid open the window to the booth. He was a muscular Black man, his head shaved bald.

Saul flashed his badge. "Ashley home?"

"I'm afraid I can't answer that, Officer Parker."

Beside the guard, a black dog leaped up and

clamped its big paws on the windowsill. It tilted its head, cocked its ears, and sniffed the air.

The guard pulled her back by the collar. "Down, Shera."

"It's Detective." Saul smiled.

The guard's arm jerked as Shera squirmed against it. He winked. "Lot of detectives drive a Mustang, do they?"

"Some do," Saul said, though Hernandez was the only one he was aware of who drove a personal ride on the job. "Mind opening the gate?"

"You got a warrant?"

"Not exactly."

"Then I can't exactly let you in."

"What's your name?"

The guard scratched Shera's head. "Sammy."

"Sammy who?"

He hesitated. "Johnson. I'm just doing my job here. You understand, right?"

"Of course." Saul nodded. "So, call your boss and let's get this settled."

"I'm afraid I can't do that."

"I believe you will."

Johnson crossed his arms. "And why is that?"

"Your job is to protect Ashley York, am I right?"

Johnson nodded.

"Well, she's in danger. And if anything happens, I'll tell the world that I came here today to warn Ashley, and Sammy Johnson refused to even call her."

Johnson frowns, shuts the window, and picks up a phone.

To Be Mindy's Hero

Gray rolls over in Ashley's guest bed, which feels less obtrusive than sleeping among the personal things in her bedroom. He's almost certain he must sleep for Ashley to return to her own body, but sleep will not come. He's too drained to really sleep, thanks to the Scotch he sucked down in her limo, in a useless attempt to forget that most of his time here had been wasted. He wasn't about to make any demands on Ashley when there might be consequences later on, but if she was still feeling generous after they switched back to their own bodies he might just have to accept.

He imagines the portrait he started of Charlie silhouetted in the doorway, the way he wanted to paint the sunlight streaming in from around him. And even more than Charlie, the person who Gray truly wants to paint is the fortune-teller, the way she looked in the candlelight, pain etched into every line on her face, shadows almost as dark as that horrible black blotch.

His eyelids pop open, and sunlight pours in

through the expansive windows of Ashley's guest room. He's still in her body. Exhausted and, at the same time, wide awake. Is this what it's like for Claire?

He sits up in bed, grabs a notebook from the bedside table, and starts doodling. The lines converge into a city skyline, LA, with buildings sprawling from downtown to the Santa Monica Bay. A bank of low clouds roils over the Pacific. In the foreground, he sketches grass and the lawn below Ashley's house. Although Gray hasn't seen it from this point of view, he's quite sure this is exactly how it looks. *Weird.*

On the bedside table, Ashley's phone riffs a pop tune he doesn't recognize. '*Front Gate,*' according to caller ID. He answers.

"There's a Detective Parker here to see you," says Sammy. "He thinks you're in danger, but I told him everything's cool while I'm around."

"In danger from who?"

Sammy chuckles. "The dude who attacked you today, or someone he knows. Some shit."

Gray smiles. "Oh. I don't think we need to worry about him."

"That's for sure," Sammy says. "He won't get near you again. Not while I'm around. No way. Hold on..." Sammy muffles the phone.

Gray lies back on the bed. Will the police go to his house? Have they already? Doesn't seem like they can do anything since he, as Ashley, isn't pressing charges. The detective is probably just here to try and change Gray's mind. As if that will happen. Maybe he doesn't have to worry about the police, but Claire will be freaking out. She must have heard all about the slap by now.

Sammy continues. "He's saying other people are in

danger too. He wants to talk to you in person."

But Gray is more worried about causing more trouble if the detective asks a question that he can't answer in the same way Ashley would. "I'm kind of busy right now. Tell him Gray Wilson is completely harmless. I'm not at all worried about him, and he shouldn't be either."

Sammy agrees and ends the call.

Gray sets the phone aside and lies back on the bed. He closes his eyes. The sooner he goes to sleep, the sooner things can return to normal.

Thud.

The sound came from downstairs. Like a sack of potatoes dropped on the floor.

"Andrea?" Gray calls out.

Silence.

If he goes to check it out, he can forget about falling asleep. A familiar headache from the Scotch leaving his system is building behind his temple.

He reaches for Ashley's phone, but he's still locked out of the device, of course, and there's no point in calling her. By now, she must have turned the obsidian snake, hopefully.

The windows cast rectangles of orange on the wall, which shiver as a cloud passes over the sun. Gray wraps himself in the comforter. Ashley is right about the pictures he took, about him holding her body hostage. Deliberate or not, he has no right to be here.

Was it only yesterday that Mindy drew him riding a tiger? It seems like so long ago. He longs to be her hero again, to hold Tyler in his arms. He even almost looks forward to the inevitable questions Claire will ask once he's back in his own body. He has to tell her he's quit his job. It's time to face life head-on.

Saul Takes a Hike

At the booth, Johnson hung up and shook his head. Saul considered charging the gate. A formidable work of iron, for sure, but only as strong as its weakest link. The hinges would yield to the two tons of Crown Vic at his disposal. But if he smashed through the gate, Johnson would call 911. That was a given. And then he could forget about Ashley's cooperation, the whole point in coming here.

Saul glanced around and nodded, as though he appreciated what he saw. "I can see you keep it tight around here, but what about before your shift? Not everyone is as diligent as you."

Johnson tapped an iPad. "We keep a log of everyone who comes and goes. Including you, although you're only going."

"Who else is down there, besides Ashley?"

"Just the maid and gardener," Johnson said, "and my orders are to keep it that way."

Saul pulled a card from his wallet and passed it out the window to Johnson. "Call me if Wilson shows up."

"Sure thing." Johnson chuckled. "After I kick his ass."

Saul backed up the drive and into the road. He drove up the hill until he was beyond Johnson's line of sight from the guard booth and pulled over. Took out his phone and zoomed in to his location on the map. Wayob wouldn't give up, Saul knew, and so nor would he.

He drove up to Mulholland and turned right. Wound his way through the curves. Past the million-dollar views of the San Fernando Valley and the mountains behind it, burned by recent fires and now sunshine as the day downshifted from afternoon into evening. At the light where Mulholland crossed Coldwater, Saul turned onto a narrow road which led down into Franklin Canyon. A couple of miles below the gate, he parked at a dirt turnout and glared up at the daunting climb to Ashley's property. Yes, he was going to hike. He was that desperate.

He shoved Hernandez's small binoculars in his pocket, unfolded himself from the Mustang, and pulled off the new coat and tie. He tossed them back inside. What did Ashley know? Did she even know anything?

He started up a narrow trail, which snaked its way up the canyon, and was almost instantly out of breath. The trail steepened to the point where he had to scramble on hands and knees, half-sliding and wading through loose dirt and gravel, half of which seemed to lodge in his shoes. He had to remind himself of the urgency, that it was only a matter of time before Wayob claimed his next victim.

He passed rocks the color of dark mustard, radiating heat from the sun like an oven. He removed his button-up, tied it around his waist, and stretched up his T-shirt to mop the sweat and the dust from his face. At least tomorrow when he woke up sore, he'd know why. He pressed on.

The trail seemed to end near a rock outcropping. Saul swatted his way through a thicket of sage and walked out onto the rock. It was like emerging into a different world. A moist wind blew cool and constant. Mansions peppered the opposite rim of Franklin Canyon, beyond which the LA basin stretched from downtown to the Pacific. Miles and miles of pavement and cars. Slow streams of red and white light moved through the long shadows cast by the buildings, most of them stucco but some made of glass, which mirrored the sky. Beyond downtown, the San Gabriels rose up like sentinels in the haze.

He eased himself down. Dangled his legs from the side. Too exhausted to care that the sandstone might crumble under his weight. He wiped his face again and noticed his right pant cuff was shredded. The cost of new pants plus the Roosevelt would consume most of his paycheck for the week. Not that money mattered, not compared to stopping Wayob.

Saul removed his shoes and emptied the dust and gravel into the wind. Shook out his socks and laid them on a rock to dry. Maybe that oversized flannel shirt Sadie wore belonged to a secret boyfriend. Could be a lot of reasons for her having it. But if she kept it from her parents, then no telling how far her secret life went.

"Parker-Parker-Parker-Parker," she'd sung. Sadie with Wayob's musical, mocking cadence. She had laughed as she raised the gun, like it was a toy.

From out over the ocean, a shifting cloak of clouds

spread toward the city. Saul shivered. He put his shoes on, heaved himself to his feet, and took out the binoculars. He scanned down the hillside to Ashley's immense lawn, which seemed almost alien against the dry scrub that surrounded it. Her house was built from large stones. The main part of the house had three balconies, a deck, and an immense wall of windows. The roof was tiled with terra cotta and sloped steeply upward. Above the peak was the turret. It was the house of a princess, an LA princess. But smaller than he'd expected, maybe three thousand square feet, certainly less than four. And it seemed all alone up there surrounded by so much land. Alone and masked by the glare of the sunset on the windows.

Scattered about her lawn, a dozen brown rabbits nibbled peacefully on the grass. The lawn rolled down to a dull fence of sun-faded wood that made an arc along the cliff. Two rows of crossbeams connected by posts at uneven intervals, with the top row no more than three feet above the lawn. Easy to climb over *if* he could get up there.

He pocketed the binoculars and started back across the boulder. The outcropping seemed to shrink in the growing shadow of the cliff. The wall of the canyon rose up at a near vertical, all loose rocks and dust. He was going to have to scramble on hands and knees if he had any hope of reaching her property at all. Near his foot, a white rabbit leaped into the sage. If there was any such thing as real magic, he could count on the rabbit to help him up the cliff.

Watch Him Sleep

It is late in the afternoon when Wayob sits in the sun in the cut grass field that is the garden of Ashley York and overlooks the city and the ocean. Wayob, in the vessel of August Grant, folds his lower legs toward his body, interlocks his fingers in his lap, closes his eyes, and focuses all his energy on the desperate sound of the mind of Gray Wilson. Wayob inhales. He breathes out...

Deep within, inside the blackness, Wayob finds Gray's mind. Coming closer. *Come to me, Gray.* Wayob shall have his freedom soon. Soon indeed.

Wayob hears an engine approach the opposite side of the palace from where he sits. He waits. A door closes. The engine drives away. He keeps his eyes closed and his mind focused on the sound of Gray's mind. And from the resonance of the low hum, Wayob knows Gray is close. He is in the house.

Wayob stands.

Below Ashley's palace, clouds of gray have enveloped the ocean and the west side of the city.

Wayob enters Ashley's palace through a garden doorway, which turns out to lead into a kitchen. Inside is the skinny woman who, many hours ago when they passed her vehicle, Jacob had called "the hottie maid." Her hair is tied back and her skin is the color of copper, several shades lighter than Wayob's once was, back before the odious priest imprisoned him inside the Encanto.

She is putting dishes into a cabinet, and for a brief moment, Wayob considers backing out the door and trying some other entrance to the palace, but it is too late. She turns toward him. An annoying grin spreads across her face.

Inconvenient, Wayob thinks.

"You'll never believe what happened to Ashley." She approaches Wayob. This woman has no respect for Wayob's personal space.

Wayob steps back. "I know far more than you. Where *is* Ashley?"

"That's what I'm trying to tell you. The guy that slapped her. He might be in Ashley's body. It sounds crazy, I know, but—"

"Yes, yes." Wayob tries to sound calm. "So you know of the Encanto?" If she knows, then she will want to take it for herself. Wayob shall have to stop her.

The woman steps closer. "So, wait, you believe me? She told you too?"

"Yes, that is what happened," Wayob says. "She told me." His skin crawls. She is so close, he can feel heat coming off her. Wayob wants to create more space between them, but now he cannot afford the luxury. Not yet.

"What's the En-cant-o?" She puckers her plump lips

and presses herself into Wayob.

Wayob laughs. Of course. Why would Gray tell anyone about the Encanto? He wants it for himself. "It is nothing. Forget it." Wayob is grateful that he does not have to kill this woman, but still, she needs to get out of his way. The sickening sweet smell of her soap oozes off her face. Wayob backs away. He bumps into the refrigerator.

"What's wrong?" she says. "Ashley doesn't care if we hook up."

Wayob tries to resist his urge to push her back. Wayob must be smart. Use the influence that August holds over her to his advantage. But now she presses her lips into his—in the same manner that his young bride once did—and shoves her tongue into his mouth. It feels slimy, like a fat worm that tastes of mint and overripe fruit.

It is all Wayob can do not to retch. He shoves her back. "Not here," Wayob says, his voice strained almost to a whisper. "Go to your house and I will meet you there."

"My apartment? Think you can wait that long?" She flutters her dark lashes. She turns and saunters to the counter, swaying every curve she can. She hops up and sits on the counter facing Wayob. She slides the strip of cloth she wears as an undergarment down her thighs, over her knees.

"Stop it," Wayob says. "Get down from there."

"Why don't you come get me...down?"

Her voice sounds just like his bride's did, somehow, even though the language is different. Fear and anger transfix Wayob where he stands.

She raises her feet, points them at Wayob, then kicks off her panties toward him. She opens her legs and reaches down to grip the counter between them. A lascivious smile. She slides forward, spreads her legs, her crotch pressed against the back of her wrists. She laughs, and now she looks like his bride as she jumps from the counter and comes toward him.

No, Wayob thinks. *Not here. Not now.* His young bride died centuries ago. This palace that Wayob is in is where Ashley York lives. This woman, yanking at his belt, she is not his bride.

Wayob's voice fails him. He can only manage to hiss, "Stop it."

His hands clamp her neck. She moans, her voice high and thick with pleasure. She tears apart his belt, zips down his pants, reaches in, and gropes around. Then, understanding seems to dawn in her eyes. She claws at his arms. But he cannot stop now. He saw her with the fucking priest. She gave him no choice.

With all his strength, Wayob squeezes. He squeezes and throttles until her body goes limp. Until she is no longer his young bride but just some flaccid doll of a skinny woman who would have screamed if Wayob had let her have even a sip of air. And her scream would have alerted Gray. He would have dialed back the Encanto, and then Wayob would have been trapped alone in the deep terrible darkness, disembodied.

Was she lying about the Encanto? Probably. Almost definitely.

He releases her body. It collapses at his feet, and her head knocks like a drum on the hatch embedded in the floor. Wayob regrets having to kill her. If only she could have understood all that Wayob has been through. If she had suffered even a fraction of the centuries that Wayob spent alone in the Encanto, she would have done the same as Wayob. No one would blame Wayob for killing her, not if they knew.

He listens. The house is silent. He drags her body aside and opens the hatch in the floor. Wooden stairs descend below ground. Wayob lifts the woman and carries her sideways down the stairs. Her feet rake the many bottles of wine in racks along the wall.

He drops her at the bottom and returns to the kitchen.

Wayob grimaces at the disgusting panties on the floor. They had nearly hit him in the face. Beside the sink is a rag. Though the cloth is dirty, it is still a million times more agreeable than the foul panties. Careful not to touch them, Wayob rolls them into the rag. He holds it away from himself as he stands, and throws the rag with the panties into the dark open door of the cellar.

In the living room, Wayob's every footfall on the wooden floor seems to echo. He moves slowly past the two-story windows, quiet as he can. Will Gray fear August? He should be wary of anyone sneaking into the house.

Beyond the living room is a large parlor which contains a grand piano and a white sofa. Never before has Wayob seen a house so vast and uncluttered, so immaculately clean—you miss such marvels, spending your life in utter darkness. Does anyone live here besides Ashley? This is wonderful, just walking alone in the quiet.

After finding no one on the first level, Wayob creeps up the stairs. In the bedroom to the right, he finds the young Ashley York, who must still be Gray, otherwise Wayob would have returned to the Encanto and been trapped inside.

Gray is stretched out under plush white covers, dozing like royalty in Ashley's body. It would be so easy to strangle him before he wakes, but Wayob is smarter than that. Wayob killed the last holder of the Encanto, who was in the body of Luis Luna at the time, and what good did it do? Before Wayob could destroy the Encanto, Abuela had given it to Gray.

Wayob has spent far too much time tortured and alone in darkness to take such a risk again. The next holder of the Encanto might never set Wayob free.

Wayob searches as fast as he can without making any noise, afraid that Gray will awaken at merely the stirring of the air. There is a phone on the nightstand, but the drawers are all empty. Wayob kneels on the floor and looks under the bed. Nothing.

But Wayob has an idea. Can he make Gray his next vessel? Is it possible with Gray in Ashley's body? Barbaric priest. Should have told Wayob how this works.

But since Gray is sleeping, Wayob could try to transmigrate into Ashley's body. If it works, he should be able to probe Gray's mind to find out where he hid the Encanto. Then, Wayob shall destroy it and kill Ashley in Gray's body. And then he will be free to live Ashley's luxurious life. Wayob deserves this much. After all he has suffered, he deserves more.

As Wayob sinks into the cushioned chair beside the bed, he must swallow his laugh. Gray does not stir. Wayob leans back and closes his eyes. He concentrates on the darkness. Finds the sound of Gray's mind, closer now than ever before—definitely still in Ashley's body.

Wayob imagines himself lifting up into the ether. His mind, descending down upon Gray. Dominating him under the weight of all that is Wayob. Wayob imagines how peaceful life will be in Ashley's palace above the city, alone. He drifts off…

Rosa and Abuela

Rosa knew something was truly wrong when Abuela refused to have her hair brushed that morning. Abuela had been breathing raggedly for weeks, maybe months, yet she refused to see a doctor. She stirred the quinoa around in her bowl, as if spreading it against the sides made it look like she'd eaten some, and insisted that Rosa go to school. Rosa shouldn't have, but she went anyway, for there was no denying the will of Abuela.

It was great that Abuela cared so much about education, but what was the point? What was she going to do with a degree and no documentation? And USC was too expensive. They couldn't afford it, even before her father's murder, and now without his income there was no way she could possibly pay. Yet Abuela insisted it would work out and tuition would be covered somehow, like the sum was just going to fall from the sky. Maybe Rosa could cover tuition for somewhere less expensive, if she had a green card, or a visa. Then she wouldn't have to wash dishes in a Thai restaurant that only paid in tips shared from waitresses, many of whom were skimming. And what could Rosa do about it? Nothing. She might even be fired tonight for missing her shift. But there was no way she could have gone to work after she spoke to Abuela, after class, and she sounded so far away that Rosa had rushed back home to their small apartment.

Abuela lay on her back in bed, gasping. It sounded more like drowning than breathing, as if her lungs were filled with fluid, and Rosa didn't want to think about that.

She climbed in beside Abuela. There was hardly room in the narrow twin bed. She held her tight, just like Abuela had been holding Rosa her whole life. She nuzzled her white tresses and inhaled, but instead of the gardenia perfume that Abuela always wore, there was only the smell of stale skin and lotion. She smelled almost like a stranger.

The bedroom seemed smaller now than it ever had. On the wall near the door was a carving of the Virgen de Guadalupe, her red dress faded from all the years of Abuela's hands running over it every time she left the room. When Abuela lost her eyesight, she didn't go blind. She saw with her hands.

Abuela's lips quivered. She restrained a cough. Outside the one narrow window, the sun was sinking.

"Deja que una pobre vieja muera en paz," Abuela said.

Rosa sat up. *Let her die?* She was only sick. Abuela could not die. Not yet. Rosa would not let that happen. "No te estás muriendo. Los médicos te ayudarán."

Abuela coughed spasmodically. She tried to cover her mouth with the handkerchief balled up in her hand, and it unfurled. The fabric was stiff and specked with brown. Dried blood.

Rosa's tears came on suddenly. All the time she'd wasted denying Abuela's decline, she should have been doing something. She could not lose Abuela too. She just couldn't. Her shoulders shook convulsively.

No, she needed to be strong, like Abuela. Rosa wiped her face on her sleeve and reached for her phone. Abuela's hand came down on Rosa's arm, the thin bones of her fingers loosely covered with skin.

Abuela could practically read minds, just from the slightest action or the tone of a person's voice. That's why, at Rosa's insistence, she'd started telling fortunes as a way to make extra money.

"Es la hora," Abuela said. She insisted Rosa let her go, let her die at home in peace, here with Rosa. All these years, it was Abuela who had made all the decisions, but not this time.

Rosa wasn't ready to be alone. Not even a week had passed since she had lost her father. She would give anything just to have one more day with Abuela. *Just one more day.* She dialed 911 and requested an ambulance.

"No," Abuela said. "Estoy lista para unirme a Miguelito."

Rosa was a kid the last time she'd heard Abuela refer to her late husband by his nickname. The Guatemalan army had shot him, but Abuela had been vague about the circumstances, which Rosa suspected were the reason that they had fled Guatemala when she was two. After crossing into Mexico, they were robbed—Rosa knew that much—and something had happened to her mother, something so horrible that Abuela and her father didn't want to tell her. *When you're older*, they'd promised. But now her father was dead, and Abuela was so sick she could hardly speak.

Rosa remembered the endless walking, how cold it was after they crossed the US border, her father commanding her to lie still as spotlights swept over them, as trucks plowed through the sand inches from their hiding place, as militiamen with their guns and their loudspeakers boomed their hatred across the desert in the night.

She was glad they came, though. Despite the many hardships, Rosa loved it here in LA.

Abuela coughed into the handkerchief for what seemed like hours. She wiped her mouth. Fresh blood smeared on her chin. Rosa should have called 911 sooner. She should have listened when Abuela started beginning sentences with *When I'm gone…*

But she hadn't been this bad until after the funeral. Now Rosa doubted if Abuela could even get out of bed on her own.

"Todavía está con nosotros," Abuela said. "Tu padre. Mi Luis."

Rosa understood the feeling. Her father had been such a huge part of her life that it was hard to let go. And she never saw the body, because Abuela had had it cremated, so there was no sense of closure.

In the weeks before his death, he'd become sullen and hardly spoke. Rosa had assumed it was his job, that he might be losing it. But now she realized he must have known about Abuela, how sick she was. He must have been desperate to help her. Of course he was.

What had he done?

"¿Qué hizo?" Rosa asked. "Dime, Abuela. ¡Por favor!"

"Todavía está con nosotros," Abuela sputtered out

between ragged breaths.

Why did she keep saying that? And how could he still be with us? Did she think he was trapped in some kind of limbo?

Between fits of coughing, Abuela ordered Rosa to forgive him. He was only trying to help. It was Abuela who had sinned, she said, for she was the one who had kept the Encanto all these years and she didn't tell them what it was. She kept the secret to protect them, but in so doing, she'd doomed her only son. For if he'd known about Wayob, the evil spirit trapped inside the Encanto, he would never have freed him.

And then giving away the Encanto was the only way to stop the spirit, Abuela insisted. The only way to trap him back inside. Her eyes squeezed shut. "Debería haberlo destruido cuando tuve la oportunidad." Tears streamed through the crevices on her cheeks. Her mouth twisted into a grimace.

Rosa frowned. She wasn't sure what Abuela was talking about but it was frightening to see so much strain on her face, which typically radiated so much kindness. Rosa smoothed her hair against her head. "No tenías otra opción."

Abuela's eyelids flicked open. But she seemed utterly lost behind the clouds in her eyes. "Antes de que. Debería haberlo destruido en Guatemala. Pero tenía miedo. Como el mono. No podía dejarlo ir. Yo no…" Her lids fluttered closed. Her breathing slowed. She seemed to have fallen asleep.

It made no sense. No sense at all. Why would she smuggle a thing she knew to be evil on the arduous journey from Guatemala and then keep it here where she lived with her son and Rosa? But she must have had a reason. Rosa trusted her completely.

Where the hell is the ambulance? She dialed 911 again, but they were on the way. Nothing more could be done.

She went to the bathroom and got a towel, which she used to wipe the smeared blood from Abuela's chin. The tension in the lines around her mouth seemed to ease. Rosa got back in bed and held her, her grandmother, who had loved her like a mother as well.

The sun dropped away to the west. It bounced off cars on the freeway and through a slim path between the warehouses, through the window, a bright slit of pulsing light on the wall. For a moment, the whole room glowed. Dust sparkled in the arm of light as it moved toward the worn Virgen de Guadalupe. Then it was gone. Leaving the room cold and dull, echoing with wind from the freeway and the dry sound of tires.

Nightfall

As dusk descended, wind whipped through Franklin Canyon and chilled the sweat on Saul's skin. He was thirty feet from Ashley York's fence, but the terrain was almost vertical, the soil loose and dry. With each step up, he slid back down.

The sound of someone whistling carried on the wind. The *Mission Impossible* theme song.

At the top of the cliff, Sammy Johnson leaned over the fence. "I'd give up if I were you."

Saul grimaced. "Don't think I can make it?"

"I've seen idiots half your size fail. But go ahead, try. If you get close, I'll come back and Tase you."

"I'm trying to protect her."

"You're welcome to apply for the job," Johnson said. "But for now, she's hired me." He turned and disappeared beyond the rim of the cliff. Resumed whistling. The melody fading into the twilight.

"Damn it," Saul said aloud to no one. *Must be hidden cameras in the fence.* How long had Johnson watched his struggle? He was right though. There was no way

Saul could climb any higher.

Saul reluctantly turned and began to retreat. He had to crab-walk downslope. His butt dragged in the dirt. He was thirsty and had nothing to drink, and he was so hungry he felt light-headed.

He lumbered back out onto the boulder outcrop, his chest heaving for air. Clouds had carpeted the city. All but the tallest buildings. Their spires pierced the roiling mass. Beacons of light above a glowing sea. Then they too were swallowed by the clouds. Wayob was down there, somewhere beneath it all. Saul had to find him. But how? The lives Wayob had taken seemed to have nothing in common. No parallel thread.

By the time Saul caught his breath, the fog had slid into the canyon. Vapor rolled over the boulder and submerged him too in the whiteout.

Beneath the boulder, he found the trail. By a very faint glow in the mist, he navigated his way down the switchbacks. The fog seemed to muffle his footsteps. The blur drifted around him. A face came to Saul, a dream-fragment conjured from the gloom. A woman. Her smile, coy. And as she sauntered toward him, Saul realized they were in the hallway at the Roosevelt. But that was all he could remember before the memory faded into the mist.

He stopped. Closed his eyes and focused. In the blackness, instead of the woman, he imagined the face of Saroyan—cowering. Eyes wide. What could it mean?

He snapped his eyes open and shivered. Saroyan had admitted to killing Luna. He'd said that his body had acted against his will, and now Saul believed him —Wayob was responsible. He should question Saroyan again.

He reached the road and trudged toward the vague outline of the Mustang. His legs heavy as stumps. Behind the Mustang, a shadow loomed. A truck. As he neared, the driver's door creaked open and a light popped on inside the cab. A dark figure hopped down. The light circled on the pavement. Toward Saul.

Saul crouched low, drew his gun, and scrambled toward the Mustang. The figure with the flashlight came around the car and leaned over the windshield, his light on an envelope. As he slid the envelope under the wiper, light bounced off the glass and illuminated a uniform. A park ranger. He had a dark brown beard, a solid two inches thick.

Saul holstered his gun. "Wait."

The beam swung into Saul's face. Saul pulled his badge and waved the light away. "Do you mind?"

The ranger lowered the flashlight. "You're out of your jurisdiction."

Saul motioned around him. "This is the middle of LA!" he said, though he knew this was a national park. "I've got a right to pursue a felon."

"I didn't get a call about that."

"I didn't have time for the courtesy," Saul said. "I've got lives at stake here. How about a break on that ticket?"

The ranger shook his head. Tapped the little printer clipped to his belt. "You're in the system now. It's out of my hands. Easiest just to pay before the late fees."

"I'll file a report," Saul said. "This will come back on you."

"Good luck with that." The ranger climbed back into his service truck and reversed.

As the headlights swept over Saul, he snatched the envelope from Hernandez's wiper. $256 for parking after dark. He crumpled the ticket and shoved it into his pocket.

The truck rolled unhurried down the hill. High above the canyon, the beam of a helicopter swept the fog.

Saul folded himself into the Mustang. Retrieved the NoDoz from his coat. Shook the bottle. Nothing. He tapped it against his palm, but it was empty. He needed something. He was tired and famished, the night was slipping away, and he was getting nowhere.

He fired up the Mustang and rolled down through the canyon toward the city. Saroyan was recovering downtown in the Good Samaritan ICU, and Silver Lake was on the way there. Maybe Wilson had come home.

—

Gray snaps into semi-consciousness. His head throbs. This always happens after he drinks. He blacks out and then wakes up an hour later unable to fall back to sleep.

Before opening his eyes, he knows from the tone of the silence that this is not his house, and he is not alone. He struggles to focus and rolls over. He's still in Ashley's guest bed, but he should be back in his body by now, shouldn't he?

A faint light filters in through the windows. The white chair by the bed sort of glows, and draped over the chair, dark as a shadow, the figure of a man leans to one side.

Gray's heart pounds in his throat. The man's chest rises and falls. As Gray sits up slowly, he can just make out the round face and gelled hair. It's August Grant, and he is sleeping.

Why is he here?

Last time Gray was in Ashley's body, when August just showed up at her house uninvited, it seemed weird, but watching her sleep is a whole new dimension of creepiness.

Gray shuffles to the opposite side of the bed, gets to his feet, and sneaks barefoot out of the bedroom and down the hall. He glances over his shoulder. Darkness folds in from the hallway and blankets the bedroom door. Had he dreamed August there?

He descends the stairs. A wall of fog presses hard against the windows. In the living room, the blurred outlines of furniture lurk below the light streaming out from the kitchen. He moves toward the kitchen door. He bangs his shin into a shadow that turned out to be the coffee table. It groans against the floor. Gray stands there frozen for a long moment.

He forces himself to turn, to look back up the stairs. They darken and disappear. For a moment, it seems that August is up there, a shadow within a shadow peering down upon Gray. But there is only silence. Gray sees only his own fear projected up into the darkness.

He exhales and hurries to the kitchen. Beside the fridge, the trap door to the cellar stands open at a right angle. He peers down the unfinished stairs, along rows and rows of wine into the darkness. He's afraid to look away from the darkness. Afraid to approach.

"Andrea? You down there?"

Perhaps the light has burned out. But then why doesn't she answer?

Almost right behind him, August practically sings, "Andrea has departed early."

Gray tenses. He turns. August is standing almost right on top of him. Gray stumbles backward. Though he's a head taller than August, he's dwarfed by August's intensity. August stands rigid, every muscle tensed, his face tight and unfriendly. Irises like dark swirls of ink. And he doesn't seem to realize that his nose is running.

"What are you doing here?" Gray asks.

"I could ask you the same thing, couldn't I, Gray?" His tone makes Gray's skin crawl. It's pure malevolence.

He knows. But how? Unless…Ashley told him.

"Look," Gray says. "I apologized to Ashley. We're trying to switch back."

August's brows furrow, and his voice trembles as he speaks. "Unfortunately, I cannot allow that to happen."

"What?" He struggles to imagine what August could mean.

"Don't play coy with me, Gray." Spit sprays from August's mouth. His breath reeks of onions. "You thought you could fool poor Wayob, but now I know why *she* was angry with you. You had me following Ashley, with her in your body, because I knew you held the Encanto. I should have expected it, but you're the first one who after switching into the body of another went back and retrieved the wretched device. Clever, very clever."

"Who's Wayob?"

"I am Wayob."

Gray wishes he had let the detective in. He glances around for a phone but there isn't one. "You need to leave." If he runs, will August follow? He sounds crazy, calling himself Wayob. He turns toward the door. If he makes it outside, maybe he can outrun August and make it around the house, up the driveway to the guard booth.

August edges sideways, putting himself between Gray and the door. Gray steps back along the opening to the cellar. He'll go around August's other side. If he tries anything, Gray will shove him down the stairs.

"I hate doing this," August snarls.

Gray charges past, zeroing in on the door. The fog presses in against the window.

August dives into him and knocks him forward.

Gray's knees slam into the tile. He catches himself with his hands. "Help! Andrea!" Gray crawls toward the door.

August jams his elbow between Gray's shoulder blades. "You're making this worse for yourself." He grabs him by the hair and yanks him back. All Gray can focus on is the pain.

"Give me the Encanto and you may live."

August knees him in the spine, and his legs collapse under the weight. He needs to turn around and fight head on, but August has him pinned flat on his belly. He can't reach him. Can't push him off. August's hands slide around his neck, cold and bony. Gray squirms and accomplishes nothing. The hands tighten like a vise.

"If you will not give me the Encanto, then you must die," August says. "This is not my fault, you understand; I'll be tortured if I don't kill you. In the reverse situation, you would not hesitate to kill me."

"Wait." Gray chokes. Unsure if he's said anything at all.

August loosens his hands. "What?"

Gray gasps for air. "You're talking about the charm, right? The stone thing with the obsidian snake."

"Yes, the Encanto. If you only understood how

much I have suffered, you would surrender it gladly."

"I will," Gray says. "It's caused me nothing but trouble."

August releases Gray's neck. "I knew you had it here. Where is it?"

Still pinned to the floor, Gray wrenches his head to the side, but he can only see white tile and the stairs leading down into darkness. If he could get something to use as a weapon… "I left it in the car," he says, glad that August can't see his face. "Let me up and I'll show you."

August eases off his back but grips Gray's elbow as he gets to his feet. He stands back with his arm extended, as if he'd rather not be near Gray at all.

Gray glances over August's shoulder at the door that leads out to the garage. "It's in the garage."

August releases his arm and moves aside. "If you're lying, I will kill you."

"How do I know you won't kill me after I give it to you?"

"You will have to take that risk."

Gray walks toward the garage. Not inclined to try anything with August so close behind him. He pulls the door open.

"It's right there in the white Mercedes. On the passenger seat." He steps aside, motioning for August to go see for himself.

August, his face eager and mouth slightly open, edges past him and approaches the Mercedes in the dark garage.

Gray whirls, shoves the door closed, and opens drawers at random in search of a knife but the best he can find is a drawer full of flatware. He hears August wrench the door back open behind him. He grabs a fork and leaps around the island. Avoiding the opening to the cellar, he turns and spreads his feet, ready to defend himself. August is already nearly upon him. Gray swipes the fork at August.

August steps back and laughs, his laughter like a mask that Gray has no desire to see behind. His eyes seem to reflect Gray's fear back at him. The pinpoints of August's pupils are not just on him, but *in* him.

The thought of harming another human being almost freezes Gray, but August seems to have no qualms about killing, and Gray cannot let him near his house. *Must protect my family.*

August grabs for the fork. Gray withdraws. Then rams his head into August's stomach. August falls backward, hitting his head on the base of the island as he comes down hard on the tile. Gray loses his balance and drops the fork in order to catch himself on August's chest.

He grabs August's feet and twists him around. His hands scramble for purchase. Gray kicks him backward, headfirst into the cellar. He screams as he falls into the blackness. His body thumps into the stairs.

Gray hops around the opening and pushes the door. It doesn't budge.

Just a few feet below, August snarls in a strange language as he struggles to get upright. Gray drops to his knees and examines the hinge. It's latched into a groove to prevent it from moving. He yanks the hinge from the groove and the door starts to close, but the hinge is hydraulic, designed to slow the door's movement. He shoves all his weight against it, and slowly, ever so slowly…the door closes.

But there's probably a way to open it from below.

Gray leaps up. With adrenaline surging through his body, he shoulders the steel refrigerator, rocking it back on its wheels. Ignoring the strain in his back, he rolls it across the floor. The plug jerks from the wall. Just as August starts to push the door open, Gray manages to roll the fridge on top. August bangs and shoves from below, and the fridge rocks a little but remains in place.

"You think this will stop me?" he screams.

Gray slumps against the kitchen island. All the energy drains out of him. Maybe the little man screaming in the cellar isn't really August. Gray is sitting here in Ashley's body, so it's no more crazy to believe that someone else could be in August's body. Someone insane. With each passing moment, Gray becomes more convinced that it might not be August down there. He called himself Wayob because that's who he is.

Wayob stops fighting against the trap door. "I only have to kill one of you," he says. "You can live out your life as Ashley. Her beautiful body shall be yours."

"That's not going to happen," Gray says.

"You think I want to hurt her?" Wayob says. "I do not wish to harm anyone. I wish only to be left alone, but I have no choice, you see? If I do not kill her, then when you return to your own body, I will be trapped inside the Encanto, trapped in darkness a million-fold worse than this cellar. This is no fault of yours, Gray; Abuela gave you the Encanto, so it will be her killing Ashley. It's Abuela's fault. Her and the fucking priest who cursed me into this miserable existence. You and me, Gray. We are innocent."

Does he expect Gray to believe all this? After nearly strangling him? Even if he's telling the truth, Gray will not trade Ashley's life for his.

"You're not killing anyone," Gray says.

The refrigerator resumes rocking. Glass bottles clatter inside.

"You cannot keep me trapped in here," Wayob says. "I will find you, Gray Wilson. I will find you. No matter where you go. I can be anyone. You hear me? I am offering you a better life. Give me the Encanto, and I shall give you your dreams."

Gray closes his eyes, rubs his hands over his face that is Ashley's. Dreams? How can he think about dreams? All he wants is to get back to normal.

Claire's New Husband

Claire struggles to see through the fog of insomnia. Her life is so far away, unreal. How can Gray just stroll into the living room, all nonchalant, like everything's normal? Like just another normal night with plain old Gray?

She clicks off her phone and stares at him. "Nice time at work?"

He looks around the room as if taking it in for the first time. "I guess so."

You guess so? Like she's clueless. Does he think she might have missed the video of him that's blowing up on Instagram? He knows she follows Ashley York. She tries her best to quell the accusation from her voice. "Why didn't you call me back?"

"I didn't get the message."

Yeah, right. "I only called you like a thousand times."

Mindy bursts from her bedroom, dashes toward Gray, and hugs him around the legs. Gray leans down and hugs her back, ignoring Claire as if she doesn't exist at all.

Claire unlocks her phone, and there he is: her husband slapping Ashley York in the face. And with a surprising number of likes.

Claire launches off the couch and holds out her phone. "Mind explaining this?"

His brows flicker only for an instant. "Later." He plops down on the floor, crosses his legs, and turns his attention to the coloring book Mindy hands him.

Claire kneels down and shoves her phone in his face. As she plays the video, his lips tighten. Of course he's not surprised, because, after all, he was there.

"Why the fuck would you do that?" Claire says. "Explain."

Gray's eyes widen. Mindy looks down at her drawings, but yeah, she heard. So what if she heard her mom cuss? Does he really think she's going to go her whole life and never hear a bad word?

"You wouldn't understand," he says.

"Damn right. How would you even know where to find Ashley York?"

Gray pretends not to hear her and focuses on the drawing Mindy has shoved into his lap. "Who's the elephant?"

"His name is Paul," Mindy says. She points to the scribbly man riding him. "And this is you."

Claire throws up her hands. "You can't just ignore me."

Gray stares back at her. "I don't want to talk about it now."

Claire stands, feeling like she's the only adult in the room. "Well, too bad. Man up."

"We'll talk tomorrow, okay?"

Claire is speechless. Mindy holds a new drawing in

Gray's face, imitating how Claire held her phone, mocking her anger and insistence.

Gray takes the drawing and thanks Mindy. He hugs her, squeezing his eyes closed.

Claire feels like she's watching a movie where she missed the beginning as he carries Mindy's drawing into the garage.

Fine. If Gray wants to make a fool of himself, then why should she care? The consequences are his responsibility. Claire sits on the couch and scrolls through Instagram, though she's unable to focus on the images.

She gives Mindy the thirty-minutes-to-bedtime warning and goes to check on Tyler. He's fast asleep in his crib.

From the hallway, she hears their bedroom door close. Is Gray seriously going to bed right now? Doesn't he know she needs help?

She throws open the door and finds him lying on the bed. His eyes are closed. On his chest is the stone thingy with the black snake he got at the Day of the Dead.

She snatches it off his chest. "What is the deal with this thing?"

He jolts upright. "Don't touch it!" He reaches for her hand but she steps back.

"Fine." She throws it down and stomps on the hideous black snake with the ball of her slipper. It makes a satisfying snap.

Gray gasps. He falls to his knees and snatches the stone from the carpet. It's basically fine, except that the snake has broken off. He tries to shove it back on the stone, tries to hold it in place, but it won't stay. "No, no, no." He runs his hands through the carpet searching for more pieces. "Do you have any idea what you've done?"

This is insane, Claire thinks. "Do you?"

Gray gets up and pulls a phone from his pocket, but it's not his phone.

"Where is your phone?" Claire asks. Did he drop it again? Maybe he really had missed her calls.

He dials and holds the phone to his ear, turning his back on her. Who is he calling? There is something truly different about the way he's been lately. And he's built a wall around the change, a big, gray stone wall. And Claire is on the opposite side.

She wants to feel angry. If she could get angry, then they could fight. And if they could fight, they could get through this—whatever this is. But she can't feel anything other than tired, because last night she woke up at three a.m. again and couldn't go back to sleep.

A truly insane thought dawns on Claire: what if Gray slapped Ashley because of her? Could he be *that* jealous of how much time she spends scrolling Ashley gossip? It's just a way to amuse herself. It's not like she's obsessed with it, not the way he's obsessed with his painting.

Gray paces back and forth, making one call after another and getting no answer, acting like she doesn't exist at all. Her pulse races. For some reason, she's drawn to his obstinance. She can see now that even if she'd slept, this change in Gray makes no sense. No sense at all.

—

Ashley keeps calling Gray but can't get through, and now Claire is standing very close, staring with those her electric blue eyes of hers. She takes the phone from Ashley's hand.

"I don't care about Ashley," Claire says. "I just wanted to know what's going on."

Ashley has to look away from the intensity in Claire's eyes, because a part of her wants the release, to give in, to let go like she did the first time when Gray's body was more like a dream. But how can she now when she might be trapped here forever?

What Ashley needs is to get back to her own body, her own house. But now Claire has broken the charm and Gray is— Why won't he answer? How could a stone cause them to change bodies anyway? *Can't think.* If the house wasn't such a disaster, maybe she could think.

Ashley shoves past Claire, lifts a pile of clothes from the stained carpet, drops them on the bed and begins folding.

"What are you doing?" Claire says. "Some of those are mine."

"Then help me."

"Chill out. I'll clean up some, okay?"

Realizing there's no chance she can calm herself with Claire in her face, Ashley leaves the bedroom. She needs to do something.

In the kitchen, she attacks the dirty dishes in the sink. There are so many she has to move them onto the counter to make enough room to wash them. She feels Claire's eyes boring into her back.

Ashley turns just as Mindy parades past Claire with a cute look of intent. "Can I help?"

Something surges deep in Ashley's heart. "How about I wash and you dry?"

Mindy nods with enthusiasm. Claire, with a lot of head shaking and sighing, helps Mindy find a towel and a little stool to stand on.

After the dishes are washed and dried, she begins putting them away. She doesn't feel like asking Claire where things go, so she opens random cabinets, looking for a place to stack the plates. She finds a cupboard containing four shelves of spices in such disarray that it makes her skin crawl. She begins moving them from the cabinet to the counter. Three bottles of thyme, two half-empty. Two full bottles of cayenne pepper. Oregano, bay leaves, turmeric. A box of ground black pepper, which looks like it hasn't been used in years.

"What are you doing?" Claire asks.

"Sorting." Ashley glances at her. "Height or alphabetical?"

Claire stares at her in amazement. "Why do you care all of a sudden? It's been like this for five years."

"Alphabetical is better." Ashley places the basil on the left and wasabi on the right, leaving a lot of space between them.

Tyler whines through the baby monitor by the stove. Ashley and Claire lock eyes. His sobs ramp up to a wail.

"Way to go," Claire says. "You woke up Tyler." She storms out.

Mindy drags over her little stool, and, at her request, Ashley dishes out little samples of some of the milder spices for her to taste. Beneath all the canisters and the dust, Ashley discovers the shelves are lined with floral contact paper that has faded to brown. She cleans it and begins replacing the spices in neat rows. Having order, even just in this small part of this small kitchen, calms her.

Switching bodies, she thinks, can't be as simple as twisting the charm Claire broke. That would be...

magic. What if Gray has no idea what he's talking about?

When Mindy leaves to get changed into her PJs, Ashley goes into the hallway bathroom to check out her tattoo. It doesn't hurt so bad now, thanks to the Advil she took. She peels off the bandages, cleans the three-inch outline of the prancing pony with a damp towel, and smears on the greasy ointment she bought at the tattoo shop. She buckles her jeans and splashes cold water on her face.

Is Gray's life really so bad? It sure seems more fulfilling than hers, her never-ending quest for a meaningful role. If she had a little girl like Mindy, then maybe her wealth would be worth something. She could stay home with her. Every day, they would play in the pool. Ashley would give her a puppy. And Tyler: he's so cute. But these aren't her children. None of this is hers. Crazy to even think like it could be.

—

Claire stands outside the bathroom, listening to the sound of water running in the sink. Something's not right. What's Gray doing in there? Without knocking, she opens the door. And he's just standing there in front of the mirror. Mesmerized by his own reflection.

"Why are you looking at yourself so much lately?"

"I'm not," he says.

"Ha-ha." Claire laughs with the highest level of sarcasm she can muster, because he's been in here the whole time she was putting Tyler to sleep. And this morning, he shut himself in the bathroom for hours. Maybe not yesterday, but the day before, he was certainly checking himself out every chance he could. Hard to believe this is the same man who often just wets his hair before heading to work so it looks like he took a shower.

So what's changed?

This is the insomnia. That's why everything feels strange and nothing makes sense. If she could just close her eyes, just for a minute… Claire leaves Gray alone without saying another word and drags herself to the living room couch. Before she can lie down, she notices something move outside on the deck. Outside the window, where there should be only darkness, there is a hand pressed against the glass. Someone standing out there, peering in.

Claire screams. Then, realizing who it is, she screams again. "*No. Way.*"

Ashley York steps back from the window into the darkness, too late not to be noticed. Claire runs across the room, flips on the outside lights, and shoves open the door. It really and truly is Ashley York, standing on their deck, and she's holding a giant stuffed bear.

Ashley waves sheepishly.

Claire, incredulous, turns toward Gray, who has come up behind her, and somehow he appears not to be surprised at all. She blinks and swivels back to Ashley, who lets herself in and shuts the door behind her. She's wearing white tank top and jeans, which are, of course, form-fitting. The stuffed bear might weigh more than Ashley does.

Claire never imagined what she'd do if she actually met Ashley. It always seemed like she lived in some other separate LA, a world apart from Claire. It seemed impossible that she could be standing here in Claire's living room. *But here she is.* It occurs to Claire to take a selfie, but all she can manage to say is, "No way. You are not here."

"What's with the bear…Ashley?" Gray has his arms

crossed when he should be groveling for Ashley's forgiveness after what he did.

Ashley holds the bear in one arm and moves toward him. She doesn't seem mad at all. "It's for Mindy," she says.

Claire grips her phone. Something is not right. "How do you know our daughter?"

Ashley fixes Gray with an intense look. A look that says a lot.

He turns to Claire with an almost imperceptible shake of his head. "I wanted to surprise you. I have a friend at work whose niece works for Ashley."

Claire stares at him. *That* is the best he can come up with? "You don't have friends at work."

Mindy appears in her PJs. Obviously, she has been listening. She glances from Claire to Gray. "For me?" She reaches hesitantly for the bear.

"Absolutely." Ashley kneels and gives it to Mindy. The bear has curly brown fur, a white muzzle, and black beady eyes spaced too far apart. Mindy hugs it and it engulfs her. Ashley picks up Mindy and the bear, its head craning over her shoulder. She lifts her above her head and spins her, almost exactly the way Gray does when he wants to make her laugh, and that's exactly what happens. By the time Ashley sets her down, Mindy is giggling uncontrollably.

She falls on the bear. "Do it again!"

"I need to talk to your father. Alone." Ashley glances from Gray to Claire and then turns toward the kitchen.

"What's going on here?" Claire says.

"I want to see his paintings," Ashley says. "They're in the garage, right?"

Gray shrugs slightly and follows her.

Claire lunges after them. "Paintings? Seriously?"

The doorbell rings. Ashley's head swivels toward the front door. "Don't answer it."

Like Claire would bother with whoever's at the front door while Ashley York is standing right here at the entrance to her kitchen. She puts her hands on her hips. "How do you know he paints?"

The doorbell rings again, followed by hard rapping.

"Gray, get that, please," Claire says. Maybe Ashley will make more sense without Gray here to lie for her. *Office-friend's-niece? Pl-ease.* Just because she's exhausted doesn't make her an idiot. She wonders how much time they've spent together, and why Ashley would have anything to do with Gray?

"Don't." Ashley holds out a hand. "Turn out the lights."

The knocking grows louder, but Gray just stands there.

Ashley approaches the row of switches on the wall, but she's living in a dream world if she thinks turning out the lights will stop whoever is knocking so insistently.

"We have a sleeping ten-month-old," Claire whispers.

"Don't answer it," Ashley says. "It might not be safe."

Claire has to stop herself from laughing. Ashley must think that anyone who lives outside her Richie Rich neighborhood is besieged by crime. "Don't worry. I'll get rid of them. If they're looking for you, you're not here."

As Claire starts toward the door, Ashley whispers frantically to Gray.

Claire cracks the door and peers out. And sees

nothing. Only darkness and fog.

She flips on the porch light, undoes the latch, and opens it up all the way. Fog rests over the neighborhood like a blanket. The air is still, heavy, silent. Nothing stirs. Nothing at all.

The chaos is inside, behind her, where Ashley's whispering has moved to the kitchen. It's not really even whispering; it's more of a squeaking, like a chipmunk chattering.

Claire closes the door and locks it. As she turns, Gray hurries out of the kitchen and down the hallway. "Where are you going?" she asks.

He ignores her. *Fine.* Now maybe she can get some answers out of Ashley.

In the kitchen, she watches in amazement as Ashley squats down and hugs Mindy with a weird familiarity, as if she and Mindy go way back.

"Okay," Claire says. "What's the deal?"

"She was thanking me." Ashley gets to her feet. "Isn't that right, sweetie?"

Mindy nods. "I ready for my story now."

Claire reaches down and gives Mindy a gentle pat on the back. "Go find your father. I think he's in our bedroom." Claire stares at Ashley, who looks sort of wistful as Mindy hurries out.

"What I'm asking," Claire continues, "is why you're really at my house? The way my husband attacked you, I was expecting to hear from the cops or your lawyers, not you in person—here, on our back deck."

Ashley glances away. She fiddles with the alphabet magnets on the fridge. When she finally speaks, the words come out slowly. "Gray was upset that I showed his painting to an art-dealer friend of mine, because it's a work in progress. But Gray is a brilliant artist." She grabs the doorknob to the garage, like she owns the place, and glances back at Claire. "He told me to go ahead and look at his stuff."

"Wait." Claire moves to follow her. Gray never shows his unfinished work, not even to her, and now he gave a stranger permission to dig through it?

"Alone," Ashley says. "I look at art alone."

Mindy's footsteps return to the kitchen, but Claire keeps her eyes on Ashley. *Alone?* With anyone other than Ashley, Claire would call bullshit. But what else could explain Ashley's presence? Claire is too tired to think.

Mindy pulls on Claire's shirt. "Daddy said you wanted to read to me, Mommy."

Wow. This must be serious if Gray turned down a chance to read Mindy's bedtime story. "Fine," she says to Ashley. "But he doesn't finish anything. You'll see."

If this wasn't Ashley York, no way Claire would let her dig around in the garage alone. She lifts Mindy, and her new giant bear, and carries them to her little bed. Sure, Gray has talent, but why would Ashley care? No way they're having an affair. Not even a friendship makes sense, but what does? She liked Ashley better back when she'd existed in a glitzy version of LA that was completely apart from Claire's world. Once she gets Mindy to bed, the three of them are going to have a long and no doubt unpleasant talk. And, probably, she'll stop following Ashley on social media.

As she tucks Mindy in, hurried footsteps brush the carpet in the hallway. "Gray?"

She gets up and peers out in time to hear the door to the garage open and close.

Claire says good night to Mindy and turns out the

light.

"What about my story?"

"If you're still awake when your father comes to check on you, he'll read to you."

She shuts the door. Mindy knows better than to protest. That might work on Gray, but not her.

She considers changing clothes, like she would for any visitor, but now it would be too obvious. Instead, she grabs the hoodie she left on the couch, which will at least cover her faded T-shirt.

As she pulls the hoodie over her head, she feels a creepy stare and glances out toward the deck. There's a man standing there, almost exactly where Ashley stood, peering in the window. A big man in a suit with disheveled gray hair and a look of determination. He looks oddly familiar.

Claire fixes him with a fierce look. "I'm calling the police."

He presses a police badge against the window.

Charlie Lost It

Charlie peeks through the curtains at the crazy on his front doorstep. It's the crazy with the bald pate smooth as putty that was almost arrogantly oiled, the one Detective Parker warned him about. The crazy knocks again. But anyone with even a lick of sense knows better than to open up for a crazy.

Across the street, outside the Wilsons' window where the crazy woman with the giant stuffed animal was spying in on them, a giant bird of paradise casts strange shadows through the fog. No sign of her now. If Charlie had their number, he could warn them. His daughter, whose house he's living in for three months while she's out of the country, didn't even have a phone book. Good thing he stayed inside. If he'd gone to warn the Wilsons in person, he'd have run into the bald crazy who is now on his doorstep. Crazies are everywhere, and now there is no chance of sleep tonight. Not without the Oxycontin, which he stopped taking.

The crazy holds up a badge, not toward the door

but toward the window. The crazy looks right at Charlie. *Can he see me?*

Charlie snaps the curtain shut and steps back. He nearly trips into the wingback chair. He turns out the lights and creeps to the door.

He looks through the peephole. And there's the badge again, as if a badge makes the crazy officer any less crazy. After all, it was an officer who clubbed the bum, and who scared him into the street. Charlie should have told Detective Parker all about it, the way the crazy officer's eyes were out of focus, the mucus running into his mustache. Charlie shouldn't have driven away, but what else could he have done? He wanted to confess, but then Detective Parker didn't give him a chance. What if all these crazy officers are in cahoots?

"I know you're in there," the crazy says. "I need to ask you about Saul Parker. He's under investigation. I'm with Internal Affairs."

"Detective Parker thought you would say that."

The crazy knocks again. "Come on. Open up. Have you seen him since this morning? I saw you talking to him."

The crazy looms forward. His bloodshot eye fills the lens of the peephole.

Charlie falls back against the wall. "I'm calling Detective Parker right now," he shouts. "I'll be sure to tell him you're here."

"You do that. Tell him I need to see him."

In the kitchen, Charlie spreads his stack of papers across the table. Anyone who knows anything about anything knows to keep things organized so they're easy to find. But Parker's card isn't here where it should be, and with the crazy shouting outside,

Charlie can't concentrate.

Yesterday, he scrapped a bunch of junk mail. Parker's card must have gotten mixed into the junk mail somehow by mistake. Charlie turns over the trash can and empties the contents onto the kitchen floor. He kneels and smears his hands through the papers, which are torn and shredded and wet with god knows what. Coffee grounds, eggshells, brown banana peels, expired cheese. Smeared across the floor is everything he's thrown out since last week. Except, of course, for Detective Parker's card. It's not here.

He remembers, distinctly, how Detective Parker had plucked it right out of thin air. At the time, Charlie thought there would never be any need to call him. After all, Parker was only interested in Gray Wilson, who's just a dolt. Charlie knows crazies and Gray is not a crazy; he's just a slouchy dolt who refused to listen when Charlie warned him about the crazies. He was too preoccupied with whatever drove him outside in his underwear. Some problem with his wife, Charlie assumed at the time, but what if that wasn't it? What if Gray *is* crazy?

Anyone with even a lick of sense knows that when you lose something, you have to think back to the last time you saw it and go from there. Charlie recalls how after making the card appear out of thin air, Parker placed it on the side table next to his Oxycontin. Only a half-dose so far today, but now his back is killing him worse than ever—he needs a double.

He struggles to his feet, wipes his hands on his pants, and grabs his phone. When he pushes through the kitchen door to the living room, a blast of cold cuts through his thin shirt. Lights are on. The front door is open. The crazy is standing there in his cheap suit.

Holding Detective Parker's card like a carrot.

"Looking for this?"

The crazy's jacket hangs open. Inside is a shoulder holster. If Charlie wants to live, he'd better placate this crazy or he'll meet the same fate as the bum that other crazy officer shoved practically right out in front of Charlie's car.

"I have to take my pill," Charlie says. He begins crossing the room, slowly. No sudden movements.

The crazy's eyes spark. He rips the card in half, and half again, until it's shredded to confetti, which he showers on the floor.

"From now on," he says. "You talk to me."

Charlie sets the phone on the side table and eases into the wingback. If the crazy intends to end his life, then Charlie should first at least ease his own suffering. He'll just take a half, better to keep his wits about him. But a half isn't much better than none at all, not with his tolerance. To ease the pain even a little, he needs a whole, minimum. He opens the bottle of round blue pills that he's been dreaming about all day and shakes one out in his palm. He salivates. His hand trembles. He lifts it to his lips. The pill has two flavors: first the vague sweetness when it touches his tongue, and then the distinct acidic taste as he crunches it with his right molars.

He swallows. When he focuses again. The crazy is standing right over him.

"You want to call Parker?" the crazy says. "Fine." He takes Charlie's phone and dials the number by heart. He straightens his shoulders and looks up with his mouth slightly open. For a moment, the crazy looks almost hopeful. Then, desperate.

"Straight to voicemail." He drops the phone in

Charlie's lap. Drops his shoulders. His face sours.

Charlie looks down at the plastic phone. A tinny voice suggests he leave a message. Maybe Detective Parker won't get it in time, but anyone with half a lick of sense knows you have to take every chance. "This is Charlie Streeter. The crazy you warned me about just broke into my house and—"

The crazy snatches the phone. "I didn't break in. I was concerned for the old guy's wellbeing…when he couldn't open the door. But, it turns out, you spooked him. You better explain yourself. You hear me, Parker? I know you had something to do with Carter." He hangs up but does not return Charlie's phone.

Instead, he pulls out his own phone and shows Charlie a photo of a cop on a beach. His uniform is pressed and creased, and the hat has gold trim. His mustache looks just like Tom Selleck's. "Have you seen this guy?"

"Never," Charlie tries to say, but his dry mouth bumbles the word.

"That's Carter," the crazy says. "He's dead now. And your pal, Parker, had something to do with it."

Charlie reaches for the pills, but the crazy snatches the bottle. He sits on the loveseat. In one hand he has both phones, and in the other, he studies the Oxycontin. "Jonesing, huh?"

"It's a prescription," Charlie says. "For my back."

"Tell me what's going on, and you can have all you want." He shakes the pills.

Charlie's mouth waters. No point in fighting an armed man half his age. Anyone who knows anything knows that it's better to live to fight another day. The crazies are all in cahoots, all of them. They must have seen Charlie watching. They must suspect Charlie knows, and if Charlie admits it, this crazy will tear him apart like he scrapped Parker's card.

So, Charlie says nothing. He sits there and pretends to listen while the crazy goes on and on about what a good man Carter was. How he was too young to die. If there is one thing Charlie can do, it's sit. He'll sit all night if he has to. He leans back, wishing he could sleep, but the air practically buzzes with the current coming off the crazy.

"What do you think about that, old man? Huh? Don't fall asleep. Help me nail Parker."

Charlie feels emboldened. Maybe because of the pill he already took or maybe it's his need for more, but he's not afraid of dying, he realizes. This crazy, what can he do? "I think you're crazy, is what I think," Charlie says. "You blame Detective Parker for your crazy partner's death? But what did he do? I bet he had it coming."

"Fuck you," the crazy says. He empties the Oxycontin onto the floor: Charlie's last eleven pills. With his black leather boot, he grinds the pills into the carpet until they're nothing but chalky-blue dust.

Charlie stands up. It's not the medicine; it's the gesture. It feels like Charlie's life crushed by the crazy's boot.

The crazy rises from the loveseat. "Sit down."

But if Charlie doesn't stand up for himself, then who will? "You're going to pay for that."

"What did Parker tell you?"

Charlie curls his fingers into a fist. "You're crazy, is what he said. And I should have listened harder."

"Come on. Parker didn't drive all the way here just to warn you about me. He knew I was following him. Tell me something else. Something I don't know."

Charlie snorts. Fishing is what the crazy is doing, trying to scare Charlie into admitting something. This crazy standing over him, nostrils flaring, has no idea about the car in the garage with the dented fender and the shot-out rear window. And Charlie is not about to tell him. He's not going to say anything about Wilson either. Whatever reason Detective Parker had for asking about him, he wanted to keep it a secret. And if Charlie knows how to do anything, it's how to keep a secret.

He'll find someone to replace the glass, someone discreet. No one will ever know. The crazy officer who shoved the bum is probably so far gone he doesn't even remember.

Charlie stares at the blue smear in the carpet. The Oxycontin will still work fine, if he can figure out how to get it up from the carpet. It's just a little dirty, that's all. A little dirt never hurt anyone. Then he sees how out of control he has become. He must fight the urge to get down and lick the blue powder like a dog. He can almost feel the carpet on his tongue—he can taste it. He needs to stop. This is it. Cold turkey. No more.

"You still want it, huh? I bet you'd lick it up from the floor."

Charlie glances up at the crazy's big arrogant face and imagines it with a black eye. He swings.

But the crazy's arm lashes out fast as a snake. He grabs Charlie's fist, nearly crushing it with his meaty hand. He spins Charlie around and twists his arm behind him.

"My back," Charlie screams.

"Your back, huh?" The crazy wrenches Charlie's arm up until he's forced to bend over. "How about now? Does that hurt?"

The pain is excruciating. Charlie hasn't bent over this far in years, maybe a decade. He might never stand up straight again. "Fucking crazy…" He can hardly breathe as the crazy twists him around and pushes him toward the loveseat.

"On your knees."

Charlie tries to carefully lower himself. The crazy shoves him down. Forces his face into the carpet and the blue powder.

"Go ahead, old man. Take your medicine."

Charlie tries not to breathe, tries to hold his mouth closed. But his jaw opens all on its own. Pretty soon, carpet covers his tongue. Fibers lodge between his teeth. His throat goes numb. Disgust replaces the pain in his back. How can he fight a crazy? He can't even fight his own addiction.

Touch

While waiting in the garage for Ashley to fetch the charm, Gray removes the canvas with the awful black swirl from the easel and leans it against the workbench. He shoves aside the boxes that hide his collection of unfinished paintings and digs out the portrait of Charlie he'd started before all this happened. He places it on the easel. It's hardly more than a sketch, and Charlie looks cruel, not at all the way Gray remembers him in the doorway Saturday morning with the sunlight streaming in around him. But everyone looks sinister in silhouette. If he cheats the angle of the sun, the light will capture Charlie's kindness in contrast with the deep grooves that line his face.

Ashley still hasn't returned, so he squeezes a dab of black paint on his palette and selects a small brush. As his brush connects with the canvas, his feels a pull in his hand. Then he sees it in his mind. Another terrible black blur is what he's going to paint. Not Charlie.

He tosses the brush on the workbench.

But there was more than just blackness this time. There was light there too. Light streaming in. A dark angular object. A dim hint of stairs. As if he were looking at Ashley's cellar from Wayob's point of view, assuming he was still there in August's body, looking up through the glass door blocked by the refrigerator.

Something rattles, and Gray starts.

It's the knob on the kitchen door as Ashley swings it open and steps out. "It's totally broken." She holds up two objects: the obsidian snake and the white stone. The door closes behind her. The sight of her in his body still dizzies him.

"So what are we going to do now?" she asks.

He struggles to focus. "Maybe we can fix it?"

"Yeah, I tried that." She shows him how Claire broke the snake off from the stone.

"Well, we have to do something. Our lives are in danger. August tried to kill me."

"Whoa. Okay, what?"

"It wasn't August, exactly. Someone else was in his body. He said his name was Wayob and that he can become anyone."

"Seriously? And you believed him?"

"Not at first, but— If you could have seen his face. Why would he make that up?" He explains how desperately Wayob wanted the charm, or *the Encanto* as he called it, and how he locked him in her cellar.

"So, we're safe for now?"

"I don't know. If Wayob can just become anyone, I don't know how long this will stop him."

"Well, you got us into this, so I hope you have another idea."

He swallowed. They could try finding the fortune-teller. But Olvera would be empty this late on a

Tuesday.

"Wow." She proceeds to the workbench, sets down the two pieces of the Encanto, and studies his sketch. "Starting a new one?"

"Sort of." He picks up the porous white stone and the snake and tries to force them back together.

Ashley kneels and reaches toward his stack of canvases, below the workbench.

"Those are rejects," he says.

She doesn't seem to hear him. She pulls out the landscape of Malibu Lagoon with the burning bush, which he'd discarded before starting the portrait of Charlie.

His heart pounds. He feels naked, more exposed than just skin—here all his hopes, his dreams are spread bare before her in this harsh fluorescent light.

"This is amazing," she says. "The flames are so emotional."

Something surges in his chest. Maybe the painting is better than he thought? She reaches for another one. He should put the landscape away before she gets a better look, before Claire comes out here and makes another negative comment. He can paint better than that now; he knows he can.

But first he inspects the narrow hole in the stone where a spindle anchored the snake like a dial. It must have connected to some internal mechanism that drove the quill to stab his hand.

"We're missing the shaft," he says, squatting beside her and pointing at the hole.

"I ran my fingers through every inch of carpet," she says. "Here, let me see." She reaches for the stone and obsidian snake. As he passes it to her, her fingertips graze his palm—her skin feels like sparks.

Time slows down.

What he could only describe as energy—though it's so much more—consumes him, overcomes his whole body, overrides his vision. First there is pure white energy, then nothing. It's like floating. And though he can't see Ashley, he knows they're together. In this warm, dark place.

They transcend into what seems like some other dimension. They leave their corporeal forms—his body, like a weight, drops away—leaving all of Earth like a memory fogged by time, half-forgotten. It doesn't matter; there is so much newness to explore. He and Ashley could know every atom in the universe and beyond. A childlike excitement bubbles up within him.

Someone screams. Someone here with Gray and Ashley in this non-place. The scream sounds like August.

No, not August. Wayob.

Wayob is here with them. Screaming. As though dying a thousand deaths. The scream goes on and on at an impossible volume that grows from everywhere. The scream swallows Ashley, and then she becomes the scream, and then Gray's own mind drowns in the sound and the scream is all there is.

He's Not Here

Most people would have been wary of an officer at their back door, but not the woman with the curtain of mocha hair that fell across her face as she shoved open the slider.

"What do you want?" She sounded curt, approaching annoyed. And something about her was familiar.

Her skin was pale, almost translucent, the veins in her cheeks visible by the light on the deck. It was her eyes, the color of steel, that were unmistakable. Now Saul recalled their brief encounter on Olvera Street when he was searching for Aleman, who must have been under Wayob's influence at the time. If Wilson was there too, it removed what little doubt remained. It went beyond the realm of coincidence—this was a convergence.

Saul returned his badge to his pocket. "Mrs. Wilson?"

She tucked her hair back behind her ear. "Good work. You solved the mystery of the millennium."

"Do you remember me? From Saturday?"

She squinted at him and shrugged as if Saturday might have been more like three years ago instead of three days.

"At the Day of the Dead, I helped you get your stroller through the crowd." Saul remembered how her little girl, in a pink dress, had smiled up at him.

Mrs. Wilson gripped the handle on the slider. "So, you're stalking us now?"

"No. But I'm afraid someone is."

"Seriously?" She glanced doubtfully behind her. "Who?"

Saul pulled out his phone, which was still off. As he pressed the button to boot it up, his stomach roiled again with an uneasiness. It was more than just worry that Arcos might use it to track him. The home screen came up. He flipped on airplane mode. As he opened the photo roll a sense of dread overwhelmed him, and his eyes squeezed shut. He scrolled with his thumb. Forced his eyes open. It was the mugshot of Rydell. He swiped to the picture he'd saved of Aleman from the MDC's staff directory.

"Have you seen this man?"

She glanced at the phone and shook her head. "No. Why would he be stalking us?"

"That's what I'm trying to find out." He swiped forward to Rydell. "What about him?"

Mrs. Wilson studied the mugshot. "I've never seen him in real life, but his photo was all over the place."

"Mind if I come in? I need to talk to your husband."

She glanced over her shoulder. "Now's not a good time."

Behind her, the room was empty and in the same disarray he'd seen yesterday, except for the additional laundry basket of spilled towels by the couch. The flat-screen was on but muted and showed a news anchor in front of an alley cordoned off with crime scene tape. Then an exterior shot of a Quality Inn—Hernandez's new case.

"It will only take a minute."

"He's not here." She grabbed the door handle. "Thanks for stopping by."

As she tried to close the door, he blocked it with his foot and tried to look casual. As though his shoe just happened to be there in the way.

"His Camry is on the street."

She centered herself doorway, her feet apart. "He took a Lyft."

Saul frowned. If he forced his way into the Wilsons' house, he could forget about their cooperation. However, he'd learned from experience that people who were scared usually opened up. "As you may know, this man was involved in a carjacking and fatal shooting. What hasn't been released yet is that immediately afterward he was seen following your husband through Hollywood."

"But Gray was at work on Sunday," she said. "He was nowhere near Hollywood."

"You know that for a fact?"

She folded her arms across her stomach. A hardness crept into her face. "Is he a suspect?"

"Not at all," Saul said. "But it is suspicious."

"He doesn't know shit, trust me. *If* he was there, then it was just a coincidence."

"I don't believe in coincidences," Saul said. "There's a connection between this man and the man I was tailing when I ran into you at the Day of the Dead."

"What kind of connection?"

What could he say? The fact that they had both acted like someone else on separate occasions would do little to convince her. "All I can tell you is that the man behind all of this is looking for your husband."

"Whatever." She gripped the door. "I'm tired of secrets. Please step back."

Somehow, he had to convince her to help him. So he took a deep breath. "Listen…a young woman is dead, and I believe she was coerced, possibly hypnotized, into taking her own life. Talking to your husband may help me find the man responsible. I have to stop him before anyone else dies."

"I hope you do," she said. "But you're wasting your time here."

"Have you noticed anything unusual about your husband?"

Cold light glinted in her eyes. "Unusual is a crime now?"

"Not typically."

"Ashley York's not pressing charges, so don't worry about it."

"That's the least of my worries," Saul said, although he assumed it was related. "Think about it. What if this killer who can coerce people got to your husband as well?" He shifted forward, his whole body in the doorway.

But Mrs. Wilson held her ground. Apparently, she did not care to keep the usual distance from Saul's girth. She straightened up and faced him.

"I need to come in," he said. "Let's do this the easy way."

She exhaled hot air into his face. "You got a warrant?"

"Don't need one. It doesn't work like TV."

"If you don't leave, I'll call 911 and find out how it works." She held up her phone.

She had called his bluff. All he really had was some odd behavior and a hunch. Not probable cause to enter the premises, even if he weren't on suspension. Using force wouldn't work either. If he plowed his way in, Gray Wilson would clam up for sure. Saul had to lure him out somehow. Make him want to talk.

"We got off on the wrong foot. I apologize. It's no excuse, but I had a rough night last night. Let's talk when you're ready." He stepped back, snapped his fingers, and produced a card.

"Cute." She took the card. Somewhere back in the house, a baby cried. Mrs. Wilson sighed, rolled the slider closed, and locked it. Then she drew the curtains.

Saul descended the steps from the deck to the side yard, where he was plunged into darkness. She had turned out the lights.

He used his phone as a flashlight to find the latch on their gate and let himself out.

Ashley Felt It, Too

Ashley fell back from the warm, dark place—fell down into her body. Into cool dry air, on the floor of the garage. The bleak fluorescent light shone above her.

She had been kneeling when she reached for the Encanto, when her fingers grazed Gray's hand. He had felt electrified. Like a circuit connected between them that snapped them into a darkness. They had floated, weightless, like a plane dropping through an air pocket. An entirely different existence. She'd felt herself drifting through Gray's consciousness while, at the same time, he was inside her. The two of them were just thoughts, intertwined, and floating. She had felt who Gray was, completely, and all at once.

Then, that horrible screaming was everywhere.

Now she was lying on the floor with no idea how much time had passed—an hour or a second or a day —and her head on Gray's chest. *His* chest.

She bolted upright. Felt her face, her breasts, her hips. *Mine. My body.* "Do you have a mirror?"

Gray opened his eyes and blinked at her. He stood

groggily and offered his hand. She reached for it—remembered the electricity—and shrank back. "I think I'll, uh…"

"Yeah." He nodded and looked around, as if he couldn't believe where he was.

She grabbed onto the workbench and pulled herself up.

"You don't need a mirror," he said. "You're Ashley York. What about me?" He gazed at her with intensity.

No one else could understand the impossible experience they had shared. "You're you," she said.

She looked at her slender hand and felt like laughing. She touched her chin, soft and hairless, and inhaled deeply. Even her insides felt younger somehow—more like *her*. Then she did laugh. Giggled like she was six again.

"How did you do that?" he asked.

Did he think *she* had pulled them through each other's consciousness and back into their own bodies? "I thought it was you."

"Did you hear Wayob's scream?" He studied her.

Hear it? She had felt it, deep inside herself, even when she'd had no self at all. "Wayob is the guy in August's body?"

"Yes. I'm pretty sure it was him." He picked up the stone from the floor, where it had fallen. Then, with thumb and forefinger, he gingerly picked up the shiny black snake.

"So, what do we do now?" she asked.

"Get back to our lives, I guess." He slapped the button by the kitchen door. The garage door growled into action.

Ashley felt uncertain. Her life—what was it? Outside the door was fog and the dim, orange ambience of LA. Gray was right, she realized. What else could they do?

"I'm getting rid of this." He held up the stone and snake. "Claire was right to throw it away." He marched out into the moist air.

She followed him. Between the house and a big leafy bush was an overfilled garbage bin, its lid propped half-open. Gray shoved the stone between a pair of slimy white bags. He forced the lid down. But when he let go, it popped back open.

He turned to face her. "I'm so sorry. If I had known…"

Ashley was sorry too, though she couldn't quite say what for. She felt hardened by the experience. The life she'd been so desperate to get back to didn't seem to matter so much anymore. She might even miss seeing his jade eyes in the mirror, the way the bristles on his chin felt in her hand.

Gray squinted up the hill into the fog, as if considering what to say. Traffic hissed in the distance. He shoved a hand in his back pocket and scratched the tattoo he had no idea he had on his butt.

By the side of the house, a man appeared. He wore the same cheap trench coat from the portrait that she'd found in her office—which she now recognized as Gray's from the bold strokes that captured the man so exactly—the same giant shoulders and thinning hair, the same penetrating eyes staring back at her. He paused for a moment behind the trash bin and then hurried past it and around the bush toward the driveway.

"Run," Ashley screamed.

Gray glanced around. "What?"

The man cleared the bush and huffed toward them.

His pant cuffs were ripped and basically solid dirt up to the knees. At least his shirt was tucked in. His hair was matted down and moist, gray at the temples.

"Gray Wilson," he said between breaths, "you're a hard man to find."

"Hold it right there, Parker," another man yelled from across the street in the fog.

Parker tensed his big shoulders and turned slowly.

The second man crossed the street. He held a gun aimed at Parker, she hoped, and not them. Streetlight glared on his sweaty shaved scalp.

Ashley and Gray exchanged glances.

"Dammit, Arcos," Parker said, "put your gun away."

Arcos's face twisted with raw anger. But when he glanced at her, his expression changed. "Oh my god. You're Ashley York!"

She shrugged.

"This man's harassing you, isn't he?"

"I'm not sure what he was about to do."

Parker reached toward his coat. "I'm a detective—"

"Not anymore." Arcos waved his gun. "Step aside."

Parker stepped back, his shoes scuffing the pavement. Arcos kept his gun trained on Parker and showed them a badge.

"We were only taking out the trash," Gray said.

Arcos seemed puzzled. "Spill it, Parker. Why are you here?"

Parker half shrugged. "I wanted an autograph."

"Not going to happen." Arcos motioned Parker toward the street, then fixed his gaze on Ashley and Gray. "You want to file a report?"

Ashley glanced at Gray. Whatever he knew about Parker, he wasn't saying anything in front of Arcos, which made sense because where would they start? *August is locked in my cellar.* Talk about publicity.

"What's to report?" she asked Arcos.

"Don't worry. Parker won't bother you again." He handed her his card. "Need anything else, you call me. Got it?"

Arcos waved his gun and ushered Parker across the street.

"I'll walk you to your car," Gray said to Ashley.

As they walked up the hill, she glanced back. Parker was standing in the road, his hands held up in surrender. He was arguing with Arcos but seemed to be watching her.

"So, who is he?" she asked.

"I have no idea."

"But you drew him."

"I thought I made him up, like a character. I didn't know what to believe when he showed up in real life."

"I thought he was Wayob."

"Yeah, that's what I was afraid of," Gray said, "but I don't think he is. At least he wasn't acting like it. Wayob was out of control."

"Weird." Ashley glanced back at the two men. Arcos was shouting at Parker, but if he was under arrest then where were the handcuffs?

Her white Mercedes stood out from the line of dark cars along the curb. She discovered her key fob in the front pocket of her jeans, where she would never have put it.

"I should come help you with August," Gray said.

A part of her wanted Gray to come, but what could he really do? Assuming Wayob was gone, then it would just be August locked in her cellar. She was so done with August and his creepy flowers and fake smile.

"I'll let Sammy take care of it," she said.

She wondered if Gray had felt it too—the way they had drifted together on another plane of existence, inside each other's consciousness.

She followed his gaze down the hill. Beyond the two angry cops, fog blurred the road into white nothing.

"I should probably go." She wanted to hug Gray, but she was afraid of the sparks, all that electricity that charged into her when they touched. "Your kids are amazing, you know."

"I know." Gray stood in the road, his hands in his pockets as she unlocked the car and got in.

She rolled down the window and waved.

He nodded, his lips pressed tight together. Was he hoping they would meet again?

Ashley pulled out and drove away without looking back. She imagined him waving goodbye as he faded into the fog behind her. That was how she wanted to remember him.

Saul Versus Arcos

Saul was sick of obstacles, and as far as obstacles went, Arcos was insubstantial.

Arcos seemed to have no idea why Saul was here outside the Wilsons', didn't ask who Wilson was, and didn't even seem curious about Ashley York, here at night in a neighborhood so far below the stature of her net worth. All his anger seemed focused on Saul.

And it was better this way. Better to confront him as far as possible from anyone else, because Arcos was coming unhinged. So, while Wilson and Ashley disappeared up the hill and into the fog, Saul let Arcos march him down the street at gunpoint.

Arcos's plain wrap was parked under a massive eucalyptus whose roots had wrecked the curb. He ordered Saul to get in, but getting in would be a full surrender. From the backseat, it would be almost impossible to gain the upper hand. So Saul turned to face him. "How did you find me?"

The gun shook in Arcos's hand. He stepped into Saul's face, his breath stale. "What happened to

Carter?"

Saul had wondered the same thing. Ordinarily, Arcos and Carter were joined at the hip. "Shouldn't you know?"

Arcos frowned, and his already sagging shoulders slumped. All his usual smugness drained away, leaving him looking defeated and ten years older. "Look, Parker, level with me."

"About what?"

Arcos looked at his shoes and back up at Saul. "About whatever you're up to."

"You think I'm up to something?" What he needed to do was to create a distraction so he could disarm him.

"I talked to the old guy." Arcos pointed his thumb toward Streeter's house.

"And?" Saul shoved his hands into his pockets and felt around.

"Hands where I can see them."

Saul slowly withdrew his hands, and in the process palmed a deck of cards and a receipt into his left sleeve. In his right hand, he grabbed a crumpled piece of paper, probably another receipt, and a tin of Altoids. He held them up. "Mint?"

Arcos shook his head. "You're not going to open that."

"They're just mints." Saul shook the tin as if that proved it. Then with a flick of his wrist he made them disappear into his right sleeve, along with the crumpled paper. "I guess you knew I was tailing you this morning," Arcos said.

"You were? Why would you do that?"

"The old man doesn't know shit. He was a decoy, right?"

"A decoy for what?" he asked.

"You tell me." Arcos's voice, which was already high, shot up in pitch. "Why would Carter go nuts?"

Saul paused. Up the hill, the fog had thinned a bit. Wilson and Ashley were standing by a white Mercedes. "What did he do?"

Arcos stared at Saul. "Don't pretend you haven't heard."

If Carter had done something, Hernandez would have been dying to tell Saul, but he'd turned his phone off because he was afraid of being tracked. "My phone died."

Arcos glanced down at the road. His voice cracked. "You threatened us."

"The man I'm investigating is extremely dangerous. I told you to back off, for your own protection."

"You have no investigation, Parker. You're on suspension."

"You want to spout IA bullshit? I've got lives at stake here—maybe even Carter's life."

"Carter's dead."

Saul inhaled sharply. He waited for Arcos to continue, but he said nothing further. His eyes went watery in the streetlight.

Arcos without Carter; it seemed impossible. For a moment, Saul tried to let go of the animosity between him and Arcos. He asked as gently as he could, "How?"

"He was shot. A witness claimed Carter was stealing a car, but he'd never do that. Straight up no way." Arcos looked away. "If I had just given him a ride."

Saul could think of one reason for Carter to steal a car—Wayob made him—but he wasn't about to share this with Arcos, who was still aiming his gun vaguely in Saul's direction. Saul would be hard to miss.

"Carter said he saw inside you." As Arcos turned back to Saul, shadows from the eucalyptus in the streetlight swam across his face. "What the fuck does that mean?"

Hair prickled on Saul's neck. The fog was closing in. "Tell me exactly what he said."

"He pulled a gun on me," Arcos said, "and the thing is, to even think that he'd do that is ridiculous. There's just no way."

Saul said nothing.

Arcos swallowed. He squared Saul in the eye. "You and Carter. Were you… Were you getting together, after hours?"

The hesitation, the naked concern on his face. So, the rumors were true. Arcos and Carter had something going.

"No." Saul almost felt sorry for him. "Of course not."

"Then why would he say that?"

"When did he say it?"

"Last night. Outside that shithole you visited in Mar Vista. He said you were trapped. And he laughed, like you two had some inside joke going."

Saul blinked. A figment of a dream came back to him. And in this dream, he was inside an apartment— it was Saroyan's apartment—in the darkened bedroom. Standing in the shadows by the bed where Saroyan slept under a blanket.

It was just a dream—*had* to be a dream. He hoped. And yet his heart hammered against his ribs. A vise tightened on his gut.

He needed to know. "I have to go."

Arcos waved the gun. "I don't think so. You have to help me clear Carter's name."

Saul glanced down the hill to where he'd parked the Mustang two houses from the Wilsons'. It was hard to feel like helping a man who made his demands from behind the barrel of a gun.

With a wave of his hand, he made the crumpled paper appear, as if out of thin air, between his fingers. He flattened it out. "This might clear him." He held the receipt up sideways so that Arcos couldn't read it.

As he slowly turned it, Arcos drew closer to see, the gun only inches from Saul's chest.

Saul flicked the receipt and made it disappear while simultaneously popping the other one out in his outstretched left hand. "Oops. Here it is."

Arcos turned his head to look. Saul grabbed the gun, wrenched it sideways, and tore it from his grip.

As Arcos reached for it, Saul stepped back and turned sideways. In one fluid motion, out of Arcos's view, he dropped the gun in his pocket and threw the tin of Altoids over Arcos's head. It gleamed briefly in the streetlight as it sailed into a cluster of bushes.

"Asshole!" Arcos chased after it.

Saul yanked open the driver's side door of the plain wrap, squatted, and opened the fuse box below the steering wheel. He pulled the fuse for the ignition and several others, tossed them in the backseat, then closed the door and started down the hill.

Arcos was still thrashing around in the bushes. "Where's my gun, Parker?" he screamed.

Saul fired up the Mustang. He stowed the gun in the glovebox and steered around Arcos, who ran into the road, shaking Saul's tin.

Saul buzzed down the window.

"Hand over my gun, now," Arcos said. "Or I'll take your badge with it."

"Go ahead and try. I'd like to see how you justify drawing your weapon."

"I'll bury you with my report. You're done."

Saul laughed. "Be sure to include how I disarmed you. Look, I'll call you tomorrow, okay? Right now, I've got to get to my gig at the Castle."

As Saul rolled up the hill, he heard the insubstantial clunk of the tin as it bounced off the rear window. Then it clattered behind him in the road. Ahead, the white Mercedes along with Ashley York and Wilson had slipped away in the fog.

Homecoming

After leaving Gray's, Ashley found the 101 easy enough. She shivered as she plowed up the Cahuenga Pass and into the white vapor. She should slow down, but then she'd lose sight of the taillights of the only other car ahead of her, and she'd be alone.

"But I am alone," she said to her own eyes reflected in the rearview mirror, to the empty space behind her in the backseat. She was the only car that exited on Mulholland and drove up out of the fog into the moonless night. Through Gray's eyes, everything in the distance had seemed sort of blurry, but now the rooftops and the tree limbs along the ridgeline stood out, distinct against the void above.

Mulholland snaked north. It swerved toward the overlook perched high over the San Fernando Valley where the grid of streetlights and cars stretched out for miles and miles. She drove past cliff-top mansions, bougainvillea, past weathered oaks and dry grass. As Mulholland twisted toward Laurel Canyon, a pair of headlights came on fast. She dreaded dealing with

August. But at least Sammy would be there to help her, and at least she had her body back.

The hillside dropped away to the south where an ocean of white cloud engulfed the LA basin. The three tallest downtown skyscrapers stabbed up through the white vapor and shone brightly for a moment before they too went under. Above Hollywood the clouds gave way to the hills. Lights glowed through the mist that snaked up the canyons and cast an eeriness into the otherwise stark night.

At the gate, her guard booth was empty. Sammy must have gone on his rounds. She used the gate-clicker and cruised down the drive. Andrea's car was parked by the house. Gray hadn't mentioned seeing her, and normally she'd have left by now anyway, but maybe she'd decided to stay after all Ashley had revealed this morning?

Inside, the house was filled with a vast silence.

"Andrea?" Ashley's voice echoed in the kitchen.

"Ashley!" It was August, his voice muffled from below the refrigerator parked on top of the cellar door. Now she understood the soreness in her back.

"Is that really you down there?"

"Of course it's me. What the fuck happened?"

But how could she be sure? "Where's my mole?"

"Get me out of here." He choked and started crying. "Hurry, please."

"Not until you answer me."

"What are you talking about? How did I get down here?"

"I have a mole no one knows about, but you've seen it."

"The one on your hip?"

"Which hip?"

"Your right hip." Before she could correct him, he added, "I mean my right, your left."

"What's our status?"

"What do you mean?"

"The status of our relationship."

"I don't know. We broke up. Is that what you want to hear?"

"Yeah, but who broke up with who?" This, she knew, would be hard for him to admit.

"Why does it matter?"

"It doesn't matter if you want to stay in the cellar. Fine with me."

"You said you wanted to focus on your career. But you didn't have to break it off."

"Okay. I'll call Sammy." Although she couldn't think of a good explanation to explain to Sammy why August was trapped in the cellar, she knew she could count on him. In fact, he was just about the only person she could count on.

"Don't call Sammy," August whined. "*Please*, just let me out."

Sammy to the Rescue

Sammy set his Red Bull by the window of the booth an answered as calmly as he could. Mr. Mellow. Mr. Smooth. "Ashley. What can I do for you?" He mentally kicked himself for missing her return.

"I need your help," she said. "Mind coming down here?"

The way her voice wavered told him that maybe he could do something—maybe this was his chance to finally prove himself to her. She had never invited him inside this late at night. This was it. By the time he reached the house, he'd convinced himself that maybe Ashley didn't need his help at all, that she'd called him down there under false pretenses, and maybe, just maybe, her intentions were romantic. Maybe things were about to get hot and heavy like he had fantasized.

He threw open the front door and called her name.

"August is trapped in the cellar," she shouted from the kitchen.

Sammy jogged to her. Her explanation—as if she

needed to justify herself—was that August had attacked her. She stated it matter-of-factly, as though throwing August in the cellar was self-defense 101.

Sammy was disappointed that this was why she had called him down here but at the same time amused. "I'm fine if we just keep him where he is."

Ashley shook her head. "I want him out of my house."

"Understood." Sammy rocked the fridge leaned back on its wheels. Almost the instant he rolled it off the cellar door, August burst out, threatening to sue for pain and suffering.

Sammy took him by the shoulders and steered him toward the door. "Ashley should sue you, little man. You're not even supposed to be here."

Ashley screamed, "What have you done?" She bolted down the cellar stairs.

Sammy resisted the urge to run after her because he couldn't leave August here unguarded.

August stared at his hands. "It wasn't me."

"Uh huh." Sammy wasn't even going to validate him by asking what it was. Instead, he clamped an arm around August's neck and dragged him toward the cellar.

Ashley wailed from below.

"I'm going, okay?" August said. "Let go."

Sammy eased up on the pressure and August started walking on his own. Sammy released him, pushed him forward, and followed him down the narrow steps.

At the foot of the stairs, Ashley was crouched over Andrea's body, pumping her chest.

"There's nothing you can do," August said. "She's been dead a long time."

Sammy shoved August aside and pulled Ashley off her. He lifted her into the air and tried to hug her. She balled his shirt in her fists and cried.

In the light streaming down from the kitchen, Andrea's skin was pale. Her head lay twisted and lifeless on the concrete floor, one leg bent under her.

Ashley threw off Sammy's arm and whirled on August, slapping him and punching him. "You evil asshole fucking bastard!"

He just stood there in a daze, his eyes out of focus. "It wasn't me." His voice shot up an octave, as if even he doubted even his own denial.

Sammy had been dying to smack that arrogant I-own-the-world smile off August's face, but watching Ashley do it was even better. He only pulled Ashley back because he knew she'd regret it later.

Ashley pulled out her phone, tears streaming down her cheeks.

"Hold on," August said.

Ashley held her phone up over her head in search of service.

"We have to figure things out," August said, "before we call."

Sammy leaned in real close to August and stared down into his dark narrow eyes. "What's to figure out? Why you killed her?"

"I didn't touch her." August raised his voice as Ashley started up the stairs. "If you call the police, you're going to have to answer a lot of questions. And once the media finds out, they'll never let it go. It'll ruin your life. You can think what you want, but you can't prove I had anything to do with it."

Sammy hated to admit that he might be right. Once the media got wind of a dead body at Ashley's house, a shitstorm would rain down on all of them. August, Ashley, and Sammy, too.

He followed Ashley up the stairs, a little nervous to turn his back on August. He glanced over his shoulder. August was following wearily behind, as though dragging himself up the stairs.

In the kitchen, Ashley had set her phone on the counter. She rubbed her hands over her face and through her hair. "We'll say it was an accident. That's what it was."

It was hard to imagine that an accident caused the bruises on Andrea's neck, but Sammy bit his tongue.

He scowled at August as he emerged from the cellar and stepped back from the door. He looked terrified. And it wasn't Ashley or even Sammy that he was afraid of—it was something else. Something else entirely.

"What about the little psychopath? We can't just let him go."

"What else can we do?" Ashley said. "We can't lock him in the cellar and throw away the key."

But reporting Andrea's death as an accident might even be worse for Ashley than if August confessed to killing her. Ashley was probably here when it happened. And nothing could change the fact that Andrea was dead. It was terrible, but Sammy couldn't let her death ruin Ashley's life. He had to think about the future, his future and hers.

"We can't say anything. I'll take care of this for you."

Her eyes widened.

"How?" August asked.

"None of your damn business," Sammy said. "You just keep your mouth shut. And stay away from

Ashley from now on. You got that?"

August blinked rapidly.

"What do you think's going to happen if the cops find your fingerprints are all over the cellar, and I bet they'd find your DNA on Andrea, too. Wouldn't they?"

"Doesn't mean I killed her."

"You want to roll the dice? My brother got fifteen years in San Quentin just because he ran when the cops came out shooting."

"So what do you want me to do then? Just go home?"

"For a start. If we need anything else, you'd better deliver or it's your ass, not mine." He glanced at Ashley. She was staring at her phone, but she wasn't reaching for it.

"I'll call my driver," August said.

"What did I just say? You're not calling anyone. You weren't here tonight."

"So you'll give me a ride home?"

"No. Hell no. But I'll help you up the driveway."

Sammy ushered August out to the road and watched him walk downhill into the fog as if his feet weighed one hundred pounds each.

Arcos and the Castle

"Damn fucking mother-jacker," Arcos said as he replaced the fuses Parker had removed.

Across the street, there was a trundling sound. Arcos looked up. The dude Ashley York had been hanging with was rolling a trash can down his driveway to the curb.

Since Parker had been dumb enough to say where he was going, Arcos decided he had time to question the dude, so he crossed the street and introduced himself to the man. He apologized for his earlier curtness and got the dude's name: Gray Wilson.

Gray looked around wildly, seemingly unable to focus on any one thing. "What happened to Parker?"

"Parker?" Arcos glanced back toward his Crown Vic, where Parker should have been handcuffed in the backseat but wasn't. "He's gone."

"You let him get away?"

Arcos balled his hand into a fist. Who did Wilson think he was? Arcos didn't have to explain himself to Wilson. If Carter were here, he wouldn't take any lip, but he wouldn't lose his cool either. Without Carter, Arcos was finding it harder and harder to keep his anger in check. But thinking of him helped Arcos focus. The most important thing was to clear Carter's name. This was all that mattered. Maybe he didn't have to explain anything to Wilson, but it was a good opportunity to rehearse what to put in his report. "Turns out Parker had an accomplice. I didn't get a good look at him because of the fog and my back was turned, but I got in a pretty good kick. I would have taken him out, too, but Parker got the drop on me. It was two against one."

"Why was he here?" Wilson asked.

"I was wondering that myself. I don't buy it that he wanted an autograph. How do you know Ashley York?" The fact that she had been here was more than a little suspicious.

"It's a long story," Wilson said. "You'd never believe it."

"You'd be surprised what I'll believe, after today."

Wilson took a shallow breath. He glanced around again, and then proceeded to unload the biggest pile of bullshit Arcos had ever heard, which started with a body-switch between Wilson and Ashley York, thanks to a magic charm. When Wilson got to the part about August Grant trying to kill him, Arcos clapped. "Bravo. Great performance."

"I knew you wouldn't believe me," Wilson said.

"Can you prove anything you just said?"

Wilson shook his head no.

"What about the what-did-you-call-it?"

"The Encanto. It's broken. We threw it away."

Arcos followed Wilson's gaze to the trash bin. "So it's in there?"

Wilson's eyes widened. "Along with my son's dirty diapers. Take my word for it: it's broken."

But it seemed like it was more than just diapers he was afraid of. Was he hiding something? Probably Parker hadn't set him up with a prop to back up his outlandish story. "You're going to have to show me."

Wilson glanced around but didn't move.

Arcos marched to the bin and threw open the lid. The stench assaulted him. Wilson wasn't lying about the diapers. He appeared beside Arcos, gingerly moved aside a bag, and reached slowly toward a round, white stone…but then pulled back.

"The bag leaked. Probably better not to touch it."

"Ever heard of soap?" Arcos snatched it up and shook it.

Nothing happened.

"Did Parker give this to you, or is this some old knickknack you just happened to throw out?"

"I got it from a fortune-teller."

"Which fortune-teller?"

Wilson swallowed. "I don't know her name."

Arcos shook his head. *Nice move, Parker.* He wanted to press Wilson harder to make him admit this was a diversion, and probably would have if he weren't already feeling a little guilty for taking things too far with Streeter. Besides, he knew where to find Parker. Parker was at the Magic Castle. Parker had said he was going there because he thought Arcos wouldn't believe him. An obvious fake-out.

"Tell Parker to try harder next time." Arcos threw the stone in the bin and kicked it. It scraped along the gutter. A crumpled milk carton spilled out. He kicked the carton into the road and started toward his car.

If it had been the other way around and Arcos had

been shot while supposedly jacking a car, then nothing would have stopped Carter from finding the truth. So Arcos owed it to him. He had to find Parker and make him talk this time. Whatever it took.

By the time he reached the Magic Castle, it was nearly ten. He rolled down his window and badged the valet. "Is Parker still here?"

The Latino with slicked-back hair opened Arcos's door and tried to hand him a ticket. "Yes, Officer. I take good care of it don't worry."

Arcos shook his head. "¿Está el Detective Parker aquí? Muy gordo." He motioned to his belly.

The valet stared at Arcos as if he'd spoken Latin instead of Spanish. But Arcos was fluent. The valet understood, and they both knew it.

"Fine." Arcos took the ticket and got out.

He stepped over the velvet ropes and passed the insubstantial man with a clipboard, heading for the front door.

"Excuse me, sir. Are you on the list?"

He ignored the man and entered a small room that looked like a vintage furniture shop with a velvet couch and shelves of faded hardbacks, never to be read again. Flames flickered behind a tacky gold-colored screen in a fireplace framed by dark carved wood. On the mantel was a vase of dried flowers.

Arcos turned to find the guy with the clipboard had followed him in. His tux was clean, pressed, and decades past its prime, just like the guy wearing it. "You must be Arcos."

Arcos straightened.

"Saul put you on the list."

Arcos didn't know what to say to that. Old guy had his wires crossed thinking he was on the guest list when Parker had no doubt asked for him to be banned.

"He's in the Parlor of Prestidigitation," the guy said.

"How do I get there?"

The old guy waved toward the bookshelf. "Say the magic word."

Arcos wanted to wring the guy's arrogant white neck. "Please."

The old guy raised his eyebrows. "Getting warmer."

"How about you take me to Parker or we have ourselves a problem."

"Try *abracadabra*." He winked.

Arcos slid a hand into his coat to show he meant business. The old guy didn't know his holster was empty, and lucky for him that it was. "You try."

The old guy stepped back and waved his hand. "Abracadabra." The bookshelf slid open to reveal a narrow staircase.

Before Arcos could react, a knot caught in his throat. *Carter would have loved this*. Arcos turned away and hurried down the plush carpeted stairs as the bookcase slid closed behind him.

The stairs emptied into a sitting room with chandeliers, dark varnished walls, and gaudy, gold-framed portraits of men in formal wear. Arcos and Carter had teased Parker for moonlighting at the Castle, but now he wondered if Carter might have been jealous. He had a love for geek stuff which he kept well guarded. If Arcos hadn't happened to glance through the browser history or Carter's phone, he'd never have learned that Carter spoke Klingon.

Beyond the sitting room was a dim bar and a dining area with small round tables where couples sat seemingly entranced by the theme song of some old

TV show, which Carter would no doubt have recognized, stroked out of a grand piano seemingly all on its own. *Yeah, right.*

Arcos intercepted a blonde in a tight black dress on her way to the tip jar by the piano and asked her where the Parlor of Presti-whatever was. She told him it was downstairs.

But the stairs weren't so easy to find. The Castle was a labyrinth of narrow hallways that snaked at odd angles between bars, theaters, a restaurant, and more bars.

When Arcos finally found his way down the stairs, a tall man, double-wide, appeared in the narrow hallway ahead of him. *Parker.* His back was turned, but his size was unmistakable in that awful brown suit. Who wore brown? If Carter was right about anything it was that brown suit wearers should be shot on sight.

Parker walked down the corridor as if in a hurry, unaware of Arcos. Although the carpet went out of style a century ago, at least it absorbed the sound of his shoes.

Twenty yards ahead, Parker turned a corner. By the time Arcos caught up, Parker had disappeared into a short side-hall, which led to a door beside a bust of Houdini. The door was locked. Beside it, a lit sign said "Houdini Séance."

Arcos banged on the door.

No answer.

"Parker!"

"Sir," a man's voice boomed behind him.

Arcos turned.

A pair of men in dark suits wedged themselves into the side-hall, blocking the way out and trapping Arcos into the narrow space in front of the door. The white guy was tall, too solid to call wiry yet too slight to be heavy. The Latino had the broad shoulders and chest of a bodybuilder and held his arms as if ready to pounce. If it came down to blows, Arcos could take one of them, he figured. Probably the tall guy, but not both.

"When the sign's lit," the tall guy said, "we require silence."

Arcos pulled his badge. "Look buddy, I don't mean to interrupt, but either Parker comes out or I go in."

The tall guy waved the beefy dude away. "I've got this."

The beefy dude grunted with annoyance and plodded off down the hall.

The tall guy held a finger to his lips until the beefy dude was well out of earshot then whispered, "I can get you in for fifty."

He must have known Arcos couldn't do shit without a warrant. So Arcos paid him forty, plus another empty threat.

Tall guy took the bills, folded them, and smirked. He slid them into his front pocket then brushed past Arcos and knocked softly on the door. Three long knocks, two short.

"They'll let you in once they've contacted the medium."

"How long will that take?"

The guy motioned a flattened palm toward the floor. "Keep it down. If I have to come back, you'll be leaving."

He seemed pretty confident as he walked away, as if he knew Arcos was powerless to do anything besides stand there like a dumbass beside the bust and a golden statue of a half-naked angel with her arms raised, practically mocking him.

It was as though Parker had the whole city in on his scheme to rob him from learning what really happened to Carter. And just learning wasn't going to cut it, Arcos realized. *No sir. No siree.* What did he think would happen when he cleared Carter's name? No one cared about Carter except Arcos. Arcos and no one else. Carter was the only man he'd ever loved, the only one he ever would.

Arcos inhaled through his nose in short, ragged breaths. His anger ticked up with each passing second. Damn it all. He should break down the door and make Parker pay. All that mattered now was avenging Carter's death.

Overs

Gray stood at his easel and considered the underdrawing he'd started of Charlie. Living Ashley's life had given him the distance he needed to realize something: the unspoken elephant in his marriage was him standing in his own way. He had to let Claire in on his dream of being an artist. But how?

He decided to paint Charlie in front of his house with all the Halloween decorations. The painting would be like American Gothic meets Edgar Allen Poe. Crows everywhere. Charlie's coat trailing off behind him, blending into the witches on the walkway. Gray's pulse quickened and something rose inside his chest. He felt lighter as he imagined how to paint the lines around Charlie's mouth and eyes, every detail on his haggard face.

Claire burst into the garage with an ah-ha expression on her face as if she'd caught Gray with his pants down, which she might as well have, because that's how he felt with his half-finished sketch out in plain sight.

He moved to block her view of the easel, wishing he could throw a drop cloth over it without drawing her attention.

"Where's Ashley?" she asked.

"She left."

"So what's going on?"

What could he say? The truth? He had tried that already on Detective Arcos, who, of course, believed none of it, and neither would Claire. When Gray had tried to explain to the detective how he and Ashley had switched bodies, and then how Wayob had tried to kill him because of the Encanto, it had only made him angry. Arcos only cared about Parker, who up until tonight Gray thought he'd invented in his painting.

"Did you hear me?" she asked.

"Just cleaning up."

"Looks to me like you're staring at a scribble."

This is it, Gray thought. *Now or never*. He leaned on the workbench, his fingers curled around the handle of a brush.

"What did he want with you?" Claire asked.

"Who?"

"Who? I could hear that detective yelling from inside."

"Sorry. Did it wake up Tyler?"

"Don't apologize," she said. "The guy was a jerk. He tried to bully his way into the house."

Gray wondered when, but he didn't want to get diverted from what he needed to share with her. "Listen, Claire, we need to talk, okay?"

"Damn right we do."

Gray stepped toward her. "Let's go inside."

She stiffened in the kitchen doorway. "What did

Ashley want? And don't lie. She didn't come all the way over here for your painting." She wasn't budging without answers.

Had Claire ever faced such a dilemma where the truth seemed unbelievable? Maybe she thought he'd never believe wherever she went after that big argument in college, so she just said she was driving around "all night."

But the truth was, that was in the past, and the past was over and done. He could only change the future, and the first step was to tell Claire what he wanted.

"I quit." Relief flooded through him. There it was. He had finally said it out loud. The first step was the hardest and now he'd taken it.

Claire blinked rapidly. "You quit? Quit what?"

"My job. I quit my job."

"Because of Ashley? When were you going to tell me?"

"This has nothing to do with Ashley. I didn't tell you because I wanted to get my plan together first. I… I'm going to open a bar."

She glared over his shoulder at the Scotch on the workbench.

Just two bottles. He hoped she didn't know about his stash underneath the workbench, and then there was all the booze in the kitchen. Why did he have so much booze?

"Seriously?"

"It's just the start. The bar is so I can paint. I'm going to set up a studio in the back room."

"Okay, yeah. That sounds smart. Maybe I'll open my own consulting firm with a nursery in the back so I can spend more time with the kids."

It did sound a little ridiculous when she said it like

that. But there was no point in explaining; he could tell she was too charged up to listen right now.

"You paint all the time," Claire said. "Even after everything that happened tonight, you were painting. You don't care about anything else."

"That's not true." He never had enough time to finish anything. She didn't get it. She didn't understand how much uninterrupted time he needed to focus on his craft, if he had any chance of improving, any chance of achieving anything at all.

"It costs a lot of money to open a bar," she said. "What about the mortgage and day care?"

"I did the math. We've got enough for five, maybe six months." In truth, it was more like four months, and they would have to take out a second mortgage for the down payment on the bar.

"That's our savings. Our safety net."

"And who do you think put the money in savings?"

Her jaw clenched. She inhaled sharply through her nose. "Fuck. You."

"Let's go inside. We need to sit down and be calm about this." Gray put his hand on her shoulder.

She shoved it away. "I don't want to calm down. You insisted I quit my job for the kids. You think I wanted to quit?"

"I—"

"You said it was a new phase of our marriage."

She was the one who had insisted her job was so much worse than his that he'd had to concede the point because, after all, he didn't come home with stink in his clothes. "I thought you wanted this."

"You think I like changing diapers? Stuck here all day with no adult interaction. Work was easy compared to this."

"Are you saying you want to get back into sewage treatment? Your salary wouldn't cover the mortgage, much less daycare." He regretted saying it like that, but it was true.

Her jaw twitched. The acetylene sparked in her eyes. He had crossed the line.

She leaned toward him as she spoke, her breath hot in his face. "If you don't care about us, then think about the career you're throwing away." The flame in her eyes was too intense to look at, but he had to. If he couldn't hold her gaze, then he knew she'd never listen.

He swallowed. "I care about Mindy and Tyler and you, but my career was a carrot on a string, dangled out of reach. You don't know how it felt, going in there every day."

She shook her head. "Get another job then. Why not try that first?"

"I can't think about other jobs right now." Jobs were like prison. He needed to paint. If he could just create one piece he was happy with—his masterpiece—he could endure anything. He could tolerate a shit job to support his children, and it would be worth it. He loved Mindy and Tyler, and he loved Claire too, but he needed to make a mark on the world—his mark—even if no one ever saw it like he did. And if not now, then when?

"I have to do this." Gray examined the brush in his hand, having no recollection of picking it up. A Princeton Select Black Taklon, with a blue handle and nickel ferrule.

"You don't know a thing about running a bar," she said.

"So, I'll learn. It's not about the bar anyway. I told

you—"

"You've never finished a painting."

"Yes, I have. How would you know?"

"Where?" She glanced toward the workbench, as if she knew about the unfinished paintings he'd hidden beneath it, the paintings he could have finished *if* he'd wanted to, but what was the point? When a painting failed to achieve his vision, he moved on.

"They're not good enough," he said.

"Not good enough." She nodded once, like those three words summed up his whole life.

A stone rose up in his throat. He tried to swallow it back. What if his art was an invented obsession? A way to avoid accepting his shortcomings?

He glanced at his feet. "I need some time alone. To figure things out."

Claire clenched her fists. "You mean with Ashley. You want to hook up with her."

"No. Of course not."

"Go ahead and try it. I dare you. You're a fool if you think you stand a chance." Claire opened the door to the kitchen.

"Ashley has nothing to do with this." Gray snapped the brush in half. "None of this would have happened if you weren't so obsessed with her." He had twisted the snake, true, but he never would have even thought of Ashley if it weren't for Claire.

"So now you're jealous of who I follow on Instagram?" Claire turned her back to him and marched inside.

He tossed the broken brush on the workbench and followed her. They had gone off track. He had let his anger distract him. He'd rather lose a limb than give up painting. He felt selfish for that, but money was a distraction. Money, and the job, and not dealing with Claire despite how bad they both knew things were.

Claire was at the sink, the water running. He spoke to her back. "I'll never see Ashley again. This is about me. I have to do this for myself."

She shut off the water and turned to face him. In the soft light, her face looked calm, her eyes an unfathomable blue. She ran her fingers through her hair and stepped forward.

"Why did you want to have Tyler and Mindy?" she asked, "if you're going to go off and leave?"

There it was again. He was the one who had wanted kids, and she hadn't. A fact she threw back at him every chance she could. He had hoped a child would change things, would bring them together. Claire had resisted so fiercely for two years that when she finally agreed, he'd thought maybe a part of her wanted a child too.

But when Mindy came—as much as they both loved her—she couldn't bring them any closer. No closer at all. It was a mistake to put expectations on a child.

"I'm not leaving," he said.

"Maybe you should. You're exhausting. Everything's all about you."

She had a point. Maybe he'd been ignoring her needs, like she'd been ignoring him. Belittling his art. They needed to work this out together. "Let's sit down. Let's talk."

"I can't," she said. "I'm too tired. I'm done." She turned abruptly and marched out of the kitchen, leaving a silence in her wake so cold that it froze him in place.

"Claire?" He trudged after her.

But she had locked the bedroom door. He knocked

softly, so as not to wake Tyler. "Claire?"

She didn't respond.

He returned to the kitchen, opened the pantry, and took out a bottle of Scotch. For the first time in his life, the scent did not entreat him. It smelled like industrial cleaning solution. His eyes watered. He tilted the bottle up and took a long pull of the brown liquid, forcing it back and finding no comfort from the burn in his throat.

In the living room, he navigated around the magazines and towels on the floor. He stood at the back door looking out at the fog that had settled over the yard, choking the crickets into silence. It creeped him out.

He shivered. He turned off the outside lights, and the fog was replaced by his reflection. Split by the frame of the door. He locked it.

He scratched his left butt cheek, which he realized had been bothering him for hours, and felt some sort of plastic beneath his jeans. He unbuckled, dropped trou' and turned his backside toward the mirror.

The lights suddenly brightened.

"What the hell are you doing?" Claire had appeared from the hallway. "What the hell is that?"

It was a clear plastic bandage, and beneath it was the outline of a unicorn.

She marched toward him. "You got a tattoo? Are you kidding me?"

"It's temporary," he said, although from the burning sensation he could tell it wasn't. "I thought Mindy would like it." As the words came out, he heard how dumb they sounded.

"You want Mindy to look at your butt? What the hell?"

"I…" *Dammit, Ashley.*

"You got it for Ashley, didn't you? Don't lie."

"No. She—"

"That thing's not sleeping in the bed with me. When I wake up, you'd better be gone." She turned off the lights and left the room, furious…and yet, he thought he'd caught a slight smile tracing her lips. The tattoo was just so ridiculous she didn't know how to respond. In the morning, they would talk.

He lay on the couch and closed his eyes, and as he tried to focus on what he could say, the more obvious it became that their marriage was failing. Maybe they needed some space. Maybe if they lived apart for a while they could come back together and start over.

Sometimes the only way up was all the way down. Even Monet had tried to drown himself. A sinking feeling washed over Gray, pulling his heart down like *Ophelia Drowning* by Paul Steck. He reveled in it. He wanted to feel like this forever, to live in the stillness far below the waves where the sunlight was dim and impossibly far.

With no job, there was no way he could afford his own place plus continue to support them all. Would he even be able to get a loan for a bar? Just the thought of running a bar made his head hurt. The amount of work it would take to fund his art. How could he abandon his whole life just to be an artist? What was most important?

Mindy and Tyler.

He would have to beg for his job back, and even then, Brad would only hire him if he absolutely needed him to meet all the deadlines. Meanwhile, Gray would rent whatever cheapest place he could find close to Mindy and Tyler. Anything was fine, so long as he could see the sky—just a tiny slice of blue from a basement window would be enough—and a corner where he could paint.

Where's Parker

At the kitchen counter, Hernandez scrolled through the gruesome photos on her laptop, feeling more and more defeated with each passing minute. The likelihood of solving a murder dropped exponentially after the first day, and now twenty hours had passed since the murder of Jenna Collins, and still there were no leads.

She knew Parker would have a hunch of some kind, but where was he? It had been hours since he went to Ashley York's, and still his phone was going straight to voice mail.

It was a custodian, at the Quality Inn on La Brea, who had discovered Collins's body discarded in a back-alley dumpster. Collins had been a high-end escort with a website and handler. She was leagues above the Quality Inn, and Hernandez doubted she'd been killed there. Still, Hernandez had to be thorough. So, she'd spent all day eliminating the staff and the guests, except for a retired couple, from Ohio, who had checked out before the discovery of the body. Unlikely they hired a prostitute for a three-way and then murdered her, but Hernandez asked the local police to keep an eye on them, anyway, because of Ruiz's Third Agreement—*Don't Make Assumptions*.

The Four Agreements was one of the many books she'd

discovered in her philosophy course, at USC Extension, that had expanded her world. In order to stay positive and to make sense of the terrible things she saw, she studied a few pages every night.

"Whoa," Rumi said, from behind her.

Hernandez slammed the laptop shut and turned toward her teenage son. "Why are you still up?"

"I was thirsty." His wavy hair held the imprint the headphones he wore while playing video games in his room.

"I've told you how bad all that violence is before bed."

"Like you can talk." He pointed at the laptop. "She looks like a zombie."

Hernandez hated when her job affected her personal life, and tonight it was her fault that Rumi had seen the shot of Collins laid on a bed of black trash bags, her arms sticking straight up in the air.

The medical examiner had determined that Collins died on her stomach with her arms and head hanging below her body, while her blood cooled and coagulated for hours and rigor mortis stretched her muscles into tight bands. Why wait so long to move the body? Had the sick bastard actually slept beside her? Only the Hulk could have carried her after rigor mortis set in. Yet her corpse showed no sign that it was dragged, no post death trauma at all.

"I'm sorry you saw that," Hernandez said.

"No big deal," Rumi said. "She was a hooker, right?"

"She was a person. She had right to live her life."

Rumi shrugged. He scuffed back to his bedroom, and no doubt continued his video game.

She wanted him to understand why she cared so much about Collins, a victim who could no longer help herself, but was he ready? Was he willing? Even when he listened he never seemed to hear her. He was at an age, now, where she'd to let him learn on his own.

Parker she could count on to understand that Collins deserved justice, to help in spite of his suspension, except that he was already consumed with Wayob, who she'd learned more about and she was dying to tell Parker what she'd discovered. Dying to talk to him, in general. Just to hear his voice. Except, when he made jokes about himself. There was no reason for him to be insecure, to say he was on a diet when she asked him over for dinner. Couldn't he see how attracted she was to that big brilliant brain of his? To the playful man who emerged when he practiced magic?

She texted again, then called. "Pick up. Pick up. Pick up."

But it was only his voicemail that answered. "Don't disappear on me, Parker."

Where the hell are you?

She carried her laptop to her bedroom, where tonight her king size bed seemed too much mattress for just her, alone. It practically filled the room. A ridiculous amount of bed, and she wasn't tired at all. And she knew where to find Parker. Sooner or later he'd show up at the Castle.

She knocked softly on her mom's door and when she didn't answer left a note that she was going out.

Déjà Vu

Saul parked in the lot under the Good Samaritan Hospital and took the elevator to the fifth floor.

When the doors opened, he charged out.

Tonight, the nurse at the station was a heavyset white woman. Her mouth tightened into a thin line and her shoulders tensed forward as Saul approached.

"I know it's late," he said. "But I need to see Saroyan."

"He's discharged. You forget?"

If Saul had been notified, he'd have missed it because he'd turned off his phone. "Discharged where?"

The nurse, Dana Atkins according to the name tag clipped to her collar, squinted at him. "You really don't remember? He made bail. He went home."

Saul's stomach sank. "What's his address?"

She sighed heavily. "How about you write it down this time?"

As she searched in her computer, Saul realized he already knew. Saroyan lived in Mar Vista—the stucco building—where Saul had awakened behind the wheel of his car.

He returned to Mar Vista and parked on Berryman by Saroyan's apartment, next to the same olive tree from that morning.

He lingered around at the entrance and turned off airplane mode on his phone. Scrolled through the texts. All from Hernandez. He wanted to tell her that he'd driven here, last night, in his sleep. He should tell her. If he told her that he'd dreamed of entering Saroyan's bedroom—*if* it was a dream—would she believe that it was a glimpse of his real room? First, he needed to see for himself, see if it looked anything at all like his dream. He told himself again that it would be totally different. And he knew it was a lie.

A man wearing earbuds, in his midtwenties, pushed out through the door and past Saul. Saul grabbed the handle and swung it wide.

Inside, he found Saroyan's apartment: 112. He knocked and waited…

No answer.

He knocked again. "Mr. Saroyan? It's Detective Parker, LAPD."

He carried a set of picks in his coat, but he first pulled out a handkerchief, wrapped it over the knob, and turned. It was unlocked.

Inside, the cramped room that served as a living room and kitchen was bathed by a dim fluorescent near the entrance. Saul waited for a reaction. His feeling of déjà vu, triggered when Arcos had mentioned the apartment, now morphed into dread.

"Saroyan?"

No response.

Using the handkerchief, he closed the door.

Suddenly certain his fingerprints were already on the knob. He wiped it down.

The couch was angled toward a flat-screen and buried beneath a mountain of newspapers and yellowed junk mail. Between the couch and a side table stacked with cups was an empty space the size of a wheelchair. A glass slider opened to a small patio surrounded by a wall.

There was only one other room, and Saul's stomach lurched at the thought of going in there. *Don't.* But he had to.

He used the handkerchief to push through the door —and was assaulted by the stench. On the bed, lying on his back, was Saroyan. He was not breathing, and his arms were frozen by his head as if his last living act had been to raise them in defense. Against who, Saul would rather not guess. And certainly, he did not care to read the torn paper in Saroyan's hand. The note, which Saul now realized he'd already known was here. The single sentence scrawled in black ink as if penned by a child.

He stood paralyzed at the foot of the bed. It had been him—and yet not him. But...his own hands. This morning, when he'd convinced himself that he'd driven here in his sleep, that was denial. It was worse than somnambulism. Worse than Kenneth Parks, who had driven fourteen miles to murder his mother-in-law and then to a police station before he woke up. Parks had not left a note. Sleepwalkers never left a note. This was murder.

The dream-like images drifting back to Saul were memories. He had been more than asleep. Somehow, Wayob had gained control of Saul's actions, induced Saul's muscles. Forced Saul's hands to suffocate

Saroyan with a pillow, left carelessly on the floor by the bed. Impossible.

Yet here Saul was. Standing by the corpse of a man murdered by his own hands. Murdered by Wayob.

Wayob had used Saul like a puppet. But how? Saul was not susceptible to hypnosis. This was worse than hypnosis.

From his pocket, Saul pulled out a latex glove. Size XL, but it barely squeezed onto his right hand. He lifted the torn piece of paper.

If you're reading this note, then Saul Parker murdered me.

His stomach dropped. His head throbbed. The large, black letters etched into the paper were familiar. The text arced unevenly down.

Perhaps, at one point, before he believed Wayob was real, Saul might have thought that Saroyan deserved to die. But not now. Now he knew the man was a victim, like Rydell. And Sadie.

On the back of the note was the Ford logo and a copyright notice in small font. Saul sealed the note in a plastic bag.

He thoroughly searched Saroyan's apartment. The bureau contained starched shirts folded tight, pants and underwear. When he opened the top drawer, a mound of crumpled receipts toppled out. The closet was filled with dirty clothes and more old newspapers. The note was the only thing Saul found related to the murder, aside from the body, which might remain undiscovered for days if Saul left without reporting it.

That way, he could also buy himself some much needed time to investigate on his own. But what if time wasn't enough? What if thorough forensics uncovered some clue that he'd missed? Some way to find Wayob? Saul would not take such a risk.

So he inhaled deeply, and swallowed, and called Hernandez. He needed her here first. She still had his plain wrap, which he feared contained the origin of the note.

When she answered, he heard a piano playing in the background.

"Tell me you're not at the Castle," he said.

"I was looking for you. What's the problem?"

"Arcos is there."

"So what? You don't think I can lose Arcos?"

"The problem is Wayob framed me and I need your help."

"Framed you how?"

"Saroyan's dead."

"You mean…murdered?"

"Most likely."

"Shit, Parker."

"Exactly." He gave her the address.

Sammy and Ashley

Sammy slowed as he approached the exit gate and smiled too big at Edwardo in the guard house. He'd meant to play it cool, but he'd messed it up already, because usually he only nodded to Edwardo, who ordinarily ignored him. There was too much animosity between the security employed by the Beverly Park Homeowners Association and the additional private guards, such as Sammy, hired by some residents. But Edwardo hardly glanced up as the gate arm raised. If he noticed Sammy's smile, he didn't acknowledge it or that Sammy was driving Andrea's car.

What am I doing? Security guards don't hide bodies; mobsters do. And Sammy certainly didn't. Yet here he was, turning out of Ashley's neighborhood and onto Mulholland with Andrea's body in the trunk. For his own sake as much as Ashley's, he'd kept her out of the plan. She had had nothing to do with Andrea's death. She simply couldn't be responsible for the massive bruises on Andrea's neck. Hard to believe that even August Grant could have caused them. Sammy had always hated August and would have turned him in to the police if there were any way to do so without igniting a long bitter trial by the press that would harm Ashley and everyone involved.

The problem was that there was no *right thing* to do. Not anymore. There was no reason Andrea's death should ruin Ashley and therefore Sammy's life. Maybe Ashley could hire better lawyers than his brother, CJ, had, but lawyers weren't shit when it came down to the media lowlifes who hovered around her like vultures. Andrea's death would create a frenzy. Even if Ashley were proved innocent, she might end up like OJ, her life ruined. And if the shit came down on Ashley, it would come down on Sammy too. So, he had to hide her body. It was the only way.

After this, he hoped, she'd finally see him as more than just an employee. He would take a bullet for her if he had to.

Low fog crept north across Mulholland and thinned out over the valley lights below. He slowed around a turn, pulled out his phone, and called Greta.

"Just wanted to let you know I'm going to be late."

"Yeah, I noticed," she said.

"It's going to be a couple more hours." He tried the soft sell. It was going to take a lot longer than that by the time he buried Andrea's body and stashed her car at LAX. "I've got to help Ashley."

"What are you, her only staff?" Greta asked.

"I gotta do this. I thought you wanted me to get ahead."

"You'd better make sure she appreciates it is all I'm saying. You're having a child, Sammy; your child needs a future."

At Coldwater, Sammy stopped at the light. "You're

not even pregnant."

"Maybe if you weren't at Ashley's all the time, I would be. Here I put my career on hold, which was going somewhere by the way, to have your baby, and you can't even come home and give it to me."

"I've got to go," he said.

"Well, I'm not done talking. Did you get rid of that dog?"

Sammy regretted telling her about Shera, who he'd hoped to adopt, but fat chance Greta would ever agree to that. "Working on it."

"What do you mean *working* on it? Are you keeping it in the booth? What, do you think it's your secret little pet?"

The light turned green, and Sammy sat there. "It's a she, by the way. I'm just keeping her until I find her a home."

"That's not your job, Sammy. This is what I keep telling you. You're not focused. You need Ashley to see your drive and ambition, not some dog she told you to get rid of. You'll never be shit, the way you're acting. You're going to get yourself fired again."

Headlights raked across his car. He looked suspicious just sitting there while the light was green. He turned right onto Franklin Canyon.

"Don't worry about it. I've got this."

"Don't worry about it? What about the other guards? Huh? They'll dime you out. Is that why you're staying late? You'd rather spend time with a dog than—" Her voice cracked and cut out.

"I've got to go." He hung up before she could ask where he was that he was losing reception.

The road snaked down past a cluster of houses to a steel gate that barred the entrance to Franklin Canyon

Park. It closed at dusk. Sammy shifted the car to park and hopped out. A hundred yards up, the concrete house built on the cliff might have a view of the gate, but with all the lights on, anyone inside would be oblivious. He popped the trunk. Inside, Andrea's body had shifted to the right. She was curled in the fetal position, facing away. He pulled the bolt cutters from beneath her legs, carried them to the gate, and cut the padlock that secured the chain. The gate swung open.

He drove through, closed the gate, and secured the chain with the padlock at an angle that required close inspection to see the damage.

He drove down into the fog, past a pond and a reservoir surrounded by redwoods. The road narrowed.

He backed into a dirt turnout, killed the engine, and clicked off the headlights. Darkness filled the canyon. From somewhere high above, a pack of coyotes barked and howled.

He got out. On the ridge of the canyon, the lights of Ashley's house glowed indistinctly. So close, yet a world apart from the wilderness where he stood.

He popped the trunk and killed the light but could still make out the shape of Andrea's body. The engine ticked in the stillness. He slumped her over his shoulder, grabbed the shovel, and stepped into the fog that shrouded the trail.

After a few hundred yards, the trail tapered into brush that tugged at his pant cuffs as he ascended the hillside. He whistled as he climbed, trying to ward off the feeling of being watched.

At the foot of an oak, he carefully lowered Andrea's body to the ground. He glanced around and listened hard. From one of the limbs above him, an owl hooted twice. Then another owl resounded in the distance, as if to say they were out there in the darkness, watching.

Sammy stood there for a long moment. Doubting himself. What was he doing? He reimagined his goal, working at Ashley's side with a big new title and a suit. He was done with security. It had merely been a means to get his foot in the door, and now that door had finally opened.

He dug and chopped into the dusty ground, hacking through tangles of shallow roots woven like nets into the hillside and wrapped around stones as if to squeeze out water. The shovel threw sparks as it scraped rocks. He tried in three places, but the rocks were everywhere.

He pulled off his shirt, used it to wipe sweat from his face, and then tossed it over a bush to continue digging. Andrea deserved better than this, but it was too late to stop now. He felt like an archaeologist excavating the big irregular stones by digging around them, then using the shovel as a lever to pry them from the earth. One boulder refused to be dislodged and nearly cracked the handle. So, he dug under it and left it jutting into the hole.

An eerie pinkish hue diffused through the fog. He needed to hurry. When it got brighter, he'd be easy to spot, and a Black man with a shovel had no business in Franklin Canyon.

He carried Andrea to the hole, but with the boulder in the way, he could only prop her inside it partway. He climbed down on the opposite side of the rock, grabbed her legs from underneath, and pulled. In order to gain enough leverage, he had to sit in the dirt with his back against the side of the hole and his legs braced in front of him.

The hole should have been larger, but he managed to get her body fully in and under the rock, her head propped forward with her chin on her chest. Her blue dress appeared almost silver in the dim filtered light.

He had gone too far. This was the wrong choice. If there was a way back to the point before his involvement, he'd have let Ashley call the cops, regardless of the consequences. But too late now. Now he'd look guilty. They both would.

He climbed out. The fog lingered in the canyon as if waiting for Sammy to say something. He tried to speak. "Andrea." What else could he say? She was sarcastic, sure, but he would miss her energy. Without her there would be a void in Ashley's house, a void filled with guilt.

He tried not to think about her panties, which he had found balled up in a rag beside her body in the cellar, and what that might mean.

He couldn't stand seeing her body contorted under the boulder, in that hole not fit for a grave. With the back of his hand, he wiped his eyes. He began shoveling dirt on top of her, regretting that he couldn't do better for her, and that her body was too stiff to lay in a more comfortable pose.

Dawn lit the sky but the canyon remained in shadow. As the sunlight tracked down the cliff toward Sammy, he regretted many things. More than burying a Spanish woman in the sagebrush, he regretted letting Greta push him to this point. Making him promise to try harder, day after day, making him push and push until Ashley made him some kind of big shot. He regretted that Greta's ambition was his. He'd tried to make her dream his own, but in so doing it had grown to include Ashley, and now Ashley was all he cared about.

If Greta knew about Andrea's murder, she'd insist that Sammy use it as some kind of leverage over Ashley. Which might work, if he cared about anything other than Ashley. But he wouldn't blackmail Ashley. And Greta wasn't going to say shit, because he wasn't going to tell her.

Diversion

Arcos was fed up with standing here like a turd stuck in the bowels of the Magic Castle. He didn't give a shit about whatever was happening in the séance room. And, for that matter, why did Parker care? What did he think? The spirit realm would help his unsanctioned investigation? *Ha.*

Arcos backed up three paces, ran forward, planted his heel into the door. It swung open so easily that he lost his balance—it wasn't even latched anymore—and he caught himself on his hands. The door sprang back and hit his leg.

He got up and found himself not in the séance room but another hallway. About forty yards long and dark. It led to another door.

Arcos ran down the hall and twisted the knob. The door opened. He stepped through. Inside, six upholstered accent chairs were arranged around a desk which faced a poster of *Thurston the World-Famous Magician* framed with ornate, tarnished metal. Thurston's cheeks were rouged. His lips the same bright red as the little pair of devils who sat one on each shoulder, the left one whispering in his ear as he seemed to be peering out from the poster, looking directly at Arcos.

Beethoven's Ninth pumped through speakers hidden somewhere in the ceiling. Arcos had thought he hated classical music before he met Carter, but then Carter awakened something inside him, some hidden part of himself that he never knew existed and never would have known if not for Carter and the way they had lain together and let the music wash over them.

Across the room was another door. Arcos twisted the knob. It was locked. Behind him, the door he came through closed. He ran back and tried to open it, but now it was locked as well. He was trapped here in this strange room, with Beethoven's Ninth, and Thurston, the World-Famous Magician, with his little devils and lips red as blood.

Arcos kicked the door. It hardly budged. Solid oak. "Parker!"

He sat in a chair and faced the poster. The World-Famous Magician's eyes seemed focused to the side with a look of intense determination, the way Wilson had looked away as he spouted all that bullshit about switching bodies.

Arcos sat up a little straighter. He'd assumed that Wilson had been glancing at the trash bin because Parker *hadn't* set him up with a prop to back up the ridiculous story. But the stone was there. Wilson had started to reach for it, and then pulled back, as if drawn to it yet afraid and determined to resist, and Arcos had been too pigheaded to realize it at the time. But obviously, Wilson believed it was truly powerful. He tried to recall if he'd noticed anything unusual about the stone. Maybe it had been a little lighter than a regular stone would have been. Could that mean something?

Arcos glanced down at his hands. What would Carter have believed if he heard Wilson's story? He'd probably have come up with some kind of theory, like dark energy or something, from one of those crazy podcasts he listened to at the gym.

Arcos's scalp prickled. Someone was watching him.

He glanced around, and then up at the poster. Had Thurston's eyes just moved?

Arcos marched to the poster and grabbed the metal frame with both hands, but it was mounted solidly to the wall. Behind the glass, the poster appeared to be just a cheap painting. Yet the eyes *had* moved. Arcos was sure Thurston had been looking to the side before, and now he was looking down. Down at Arcos.

He stepped back, clenched his fists, and fought back the urge to punch Thurston's goddamn, red mouth, because Carter wouldn't have bothered wasting his time with this. He would have found out why the hell Wilson was afraid of the allegedly broken Encanto.

Did Parker know?

He knew something, alright. Could be why he'd gone to Wilson's, and why he'd tricked Arcos into following him here. Arcos had fallen for yet another diversion. Yet again, he was playing the chump. Clearly, Parker wanted him out of his way. What if it was because there was some element of truth to Wilson's fairytale? Smart move making it sound so preposterous that Arcos had dismissed it. It could be related to Parker's unsanctioned investigation, which might be related to Carter's killer.

He had to get back to Wilson's.

The locks on the doors had the sort of ancient slot below the knob that required a skeleton key. He rummaged through the desk, but all he found was a deck of cards, a calligraphy pen, and three dice with sixes on all sides. Since he joined IA right out of the academy, he'd never picked a lock before, but he'd seen it plenty of times on TV. It looked easy enough.

He grabbed the pen and approached the door opposite the one he'd entered through. He shoved the tip of the pen into the keyhole and wiggled it around. Nothing gave. Nothing budged. He pried the pen against what he imagined must be the tumbler. The pen broke. Ink sprayed out onto the doorknob and all over his hand. He flung the broken pen at Thurston, the World-Famous Magician. It bounced off the wall below the poster where it left an unsatisfying black smear.

Since both doors opened inward, he could forget about kicking them in. He picked up the nearest chair. It was heavier than he'd thought. He turned it over, arched his back against the weight, and with a running start slammed it into the door. It made a satisfying thud, with an echo from beyond the door. Although the door refused to budge, he hoped the Castle bastards would respond to the noise. The overdressed customers would, no doubt, complain about the banging.

Arcos took a break. Caught his breath. Untucked his shirt and wiped his hand on the T-shirt underneath. Then lifted the chair, charged across the room, and slammed the chair into the door through which he'd entered. He tried again and again until his arms gave out. He dropped the chair and slouched against the door, catching his breath.

The opposite door was now ajar.

Arcos shouted as he ran toward it. "Hey!"

Outside the door, stairs led down into darkness, and the sound of hard soles pounded on wood. Arcos yelled again.

At the bottom of the stairs, someone pushed through a door. Dim light spilled in and flung their shadow into an emergency exit on the opposite side of the landing. Then the door swung closed, and they were gone.

Were they expecting him to follow? If so, then he wasn't going to fall for it. He wasn't going to step willingly into another trap. As he felt his way down the stairs, he wondered if the emergency exit was even real. He couldn't trust anything here. If it was real, it might be hard to get back inside the Magic Castle, but did that matter?

He found a horizontal push handle on the door and shoved it open. An alarm blared. He stepped out into moist, night air.

He was in the alley behind the Castle facing a brushy hillside. Above, a car slowed around a bend. Its headlights swept the fog and lit up the back wall of the Castle.

He hustled along the side of the building, and the alarm ceased.

As he rounded the corner, he caught sight of Detective Hernandez exiting the building.

"Hold up," Arcos yelled.

She ignored him, as though she had no idea who he was. She handed some cash to the valet and strode toward her unmarked cruiser parked near the entrance.

"Halt right there and that's an order," he said.

She turned toward Arcos, combed back her bangs, and cupped her hand to her ear, as if she couldn't hear him. She ought to know better than to fuck with IA.

"If you get in that car, I'll cite you for impeding an investigation."

She shook her head and tapped her watch. Before he could reach her, she slid into her cruiser and sparked the engine. He slapped his fist against the trunk but she put it in gear and rolled down the hill toward the exit. *Fine. Just fine.* Like he needed her to find Parker anyway. He knew what Parker was looking for, and once Arcos had the goddamn Encanto, Parker would come to him.

The valet with the slicked-back hair resumed his perch on the stool by the little stand. He gazed off into the night, as if completely unaware that anything had happened.

"I need my keys," Arcos said. "I'll fetch my car myself."

The valet held out his hand for the ticket. Arcos reached into his pocket. The ticket was gone. He'd definitely put it in his left side pocket—he was sure of it. The fucking tall guy. He must have lifted the ticket when he brushed past Arcos. Lucky for him, Arcos was in a hurry.

"Lost my ticket." Arcos smiled. He repeated in Spanish and showed his badge again.

The valet shrugged and shook his head.

"¿Hablas español?" Arcos asked.

"No, señor."

"What about English? Do you speak English?"

"No. Sorry."

"What *do* you speak?" Arcos glanced at the entrance. The front door of the Castle was unmanned.

"I don't."

Arcos wanted to punch the valet in his pockmarked face. He reached past him to the lock box with the keys, which, of course, was locked. "Key." He twisted the air.

"Sir." The valet motioned him back.

"You remember me. I know you remember me. My key is in there. My car is property of the LAPD." Arcos held out his badge again and pointed to it. "You don't want to mess with the police."

The valet blinked and shook his head.

Arcos slid back his sleeves. Time for the valet to learn respect.

The valet whistled, loud and shrill.

The broad-shouldered bodybuilder stepped out from the shadows by the entrance. "There a problem?"

"Yeah," Arcos said. "Your buddy lifted my ticket."

"We can't give you a key without a ticket."

"I'm a cop. You're obstructing my investigation."

"You'll have to talk to the manager about that."

Arcos started toward the entrance.

"He gets in at ten tomorrow."

Arcos stopped and stared at the bodybuilder.

He stared back and shrugged slightly, as if punching Arcos to a pulp would be all in a night's work. "How about I call you a cab?"

"You'll regret this when I come back tomorrow with a few of my fellow officers. We're going to question everyone and scour this dump top to bottom. Might take all day."

"Looking forward to it." The guy stepped toward Arcos.

Arcos turned and started down the drive. He should have called a uniform right then. He would, except he had no way to explain losing his car *and* his gun without becoming the laughingstock of the department. He summoned an Uber with his phone.

While waiting on the sidewalk in the fog, he considered the part of Wilson's story where August Grant became possessed and bent on killing Wilson. If there was any truth to it, then maybe August Grant had been trying to scare Wilson into giving him the Encanto. Well, he didn't scare Arcos. And if Parker and Hernandez weren't at Wilson's, then no one would be around to see him raid the man's trash. Not this late at night. He'd grab it quick and get out.

At 1:12 a.m., a black Prius with the Uber logo in the windshield rolled to the curb. The driver had pasty skin and a hipster beard. His belly sagged over the lap-belt. He mumbled a greeting as Arcos situated himself in the back.

As the Prius accelerated, Arcos leaned his head back. All the energy drained out of him. He tried not to think about the miserable look on Streeter's face when Arcos shoved it into the carpet. He should apologize. He had gone too far. Maybe with Parker too. Parker didn't kill Sadie Wu, and after everything that had happened, Arcos couldn't even recall anymore why he and Carter had been so determined to turn the screws on him. Now, Parker hardly seemed to matter.

Carter was dead. And Arcos had made it worse by lashing out.

As he drifted off, his wrongs washed over him. So many wrongs. He needed to escape. The ride to Silver Lake would take twenty minutes, at least, and twenty minutes of sleep would be a relief after the all-nighter and the worst day of his life.

Saul and Hernandez

While waiting in the Mustang outside Saroyan's apartment, Saul texted Pete at the Castle.

Saul:
I need you to hold Arcos for a few more hours.

Pete:
I was just about to text you. He's in the wind.

Saul's stomach churned uneasily. Arcos had been here this morning, and if he showed up now it would seal Saul's fate.

Saul:
When did he leave?

Pete:
A few minutes ago. We held his car at valet, but he called an Uber. When you said he was a jerk, you weren't kidding. It nearly got violent.

Saul:

Impressive you were able to hold him as long as you did. Thank Barney for being me.

Fog drifted between the streetlights. His eyelids grew heavy in spite of his fears of Arcos showing up here. Even worse was the thought that Wayob might regain control. What if he only let Saul live because was planning to force him to commit another murder?

Saul had no intention of sleeping until he learned exactly how Wayob had done it. From what he'd read about the human brain, he knew its functions were triggered by simple impulses transmitted by electrochemical signals. Science was always advancing. Who could say with any certainty that a brain, at least the motor cortex, couldn't be controlled? Not Saul.

He startled awake, surprised to find his eyes had closed. He powered the seat upright. Buzzed down the window. Tore open a new bottle of NoDoz and downed a double dose.

Headlights approached from behind and flashed in the rearview. Hernandez. *Thank god.*

She slowed as she passed in his plain wrap and parked in front of him. Saul swallowed and finally made the call to dispatch he'd been procrastinating. For the second time in twenty-four hours, he reported a murder. But he only admitted to finding the body.

Saul climbed out of the Mustang and met Hernandez. As she emerged from the car, the shock of white falling across her forehead, his heart fluttered. He engulfed her in his arms with no forethought whatsoever.

She pulled back.

His gut. He had practically pushed her back with his big stomach.

Last night at the Castle—when *she* had hugged *him*—he was leaning over such that there was a gap and his belly didn't press into her. He kept it hidden in the trench coat so she'd no idea how immense he was. Until now. He felt naked before her.

She eyed him up and down. "Looks like you waded

through a dust storm."

Was she just mentioning the dirt on his pants to cover her disgust of his belly? He probably didn't smell great either. "I made the mistake of trying to hike to Ashley York's from Franklin Canyon."

"Surprised you didn't badge your way in. She wouldn't know you're on suspension."

"She has a guard who's all full of himself." Saul tossed her the Mustang key. "Thanks for the wheels."

She pocketed the key and glanced around at the stillness, the fog, the arching limbs of the olive tree above them. "Can't believe I beat the circus."

She was right. By now, emergency response vehicles should have clotted the street. Except that he'd deliberately delayed calling in order to buy time.

He opened the door to his plain wrap and lowered himself into the driver's seat, dreading what he'd find.

"You're not leaving?" she said.

"I just need to check something," he said over his shoulder. "Call the L-T. Tell her you're on this case."

"Never going to happen," Hernandez said. "You found the body while you're on suspension. We'll be lucky if IA doesn't get involved."

"You're first on the scene," Saul said. This gave them temporary control, and if Levy had any say at all, she'd keep this out of IA, if not for Saul's sake then for her own, because they should have had an officer watching Saroyan's apartment.

Hernandez crossed her arms. "This is the part where you tell me what the hell is going on."

He searched his pocket for a glove. "One second."

"We've been partners for how long?" she asked.

"Two and a half years." He found one.

"Three in January."

"I thought you started in July?" As he stretched the glove over his fat hand, the latex ripped.

"No," she said. "You always forget. It was January when I got the transfer to Homicide Special. Remember how cold it was?"

He tossed the glove into the floor well. Maybe he didn't remember the month, exactly, but he remembered the first time he saw her. It was cemented in his mind. The way she strode into Homicide Special. Tight leather jacket, broad hips, and not-entirely-white-yet bangs, which she had brushed back from over her right eye before shaking his hand. His hand already sweating as she shook it.

"I thought it was hot," he said.

She sighed. "I bet you're always hot in that coat. My point is, I've always had your back, haven't I?"

Saul found another glove and inched it onto his hand. "I'm not holding out on you. I'm just still trying to figure this out myself." He leaned across the center console and opened the glovebox. Removed the manual.

He turned it over.

Déjà vu.

He opened the back cover. The next to last page was half missing.

Now he knew for sure.

From his pocket, he retrieved the plastic bag containing the note and held it against the manual for her to see. "Perfect match." He handed her the note.

She smoothed the plastic over it and angled it to the streetlight. "Shit, Parker."

"You need to get this to forensics tonight," Saul said. "Compare it to my handwriting."

Her eyes grew wide. Her brows ratcheted down, creating furrows across her nose. She held the note further from her face. "You didn't write this."

But Saul knew now that he had, or rather, his hand had. He heaved himself out of the car and shut the door. "Wayob's framing me. That's how I wrote when I was a kid."

"So why not copy Saroyan's handwriting?"

"That's his mistake. And I hope it's enough. Check for fingerprints."

"Fingerprints won't clear you." She patted his gloved hand. "I wish they could."

"I know. I'm afraid the prints you'll find are mine."

"Wait. What are you saying?"

"I think…somehow…Wayob got control of my body while I was sleeping."

"Whoa. You think Wayob hypnotized *you* into killing Saroyan?"

Saul shook his head. "Worse. I read all about hypnosis. You can't compel someone to act against their belief system."

Hernandez stepped back. "You mean…like a demon?"

"It seems impossible, I know. But if I wrote that note—"

"I'm getting worried about you, Parker. You look like a wreck. You could use some sleep."

"I can't sleep. Not until I stop Wayob."

Hernandez shook her head slowly.

From the distance, the sound of sirens approached. Saul had said this wasn't a code three, but of course they hadn't listened. He had three, maybe four, minutes to convince her. "Listen…" As he stepped toward her, she stepped back.

If she was freaked out, he couldn't blame her. But at this point, all he had was the truth. So he gave her some space. He leaned against the car and told her everything. How he'd woken up here this morning with no memory of driving here, the flashes of dream fragments that turned out to be memories—of his hands shoving the pillow over Saroyan's face, of Saroyan slapping and clawing. Then falling still.

As he rambled on with no explanation for how what he described could have happened, Hernandez stood there in the mist. Behind her a firetruck careened onto the street. She turned and hurried toward it, as if relieved by its arrival.

The firetruck's red strobes flashed, out of sync with the blue from a squad car behind it, creating a chaos of frantic lights slashing the fog.

Hernandez motioned for the firetruck to pull aside and marched toward the squad car. Saul followed. He rubbed his sleeve over the scratches on his forearm—the scratches he'd been avoiding all day. They were from Saroyan.

A pair of uniforms leaped out from the squad car. Young and fresh, hungry for action. Saul ordered them to cordon off Saroyan's apartment. They rushed toward the building, unaware of his suspension.

"You want to see the body?" Saul asked Hernandez.

She gazed down the street. More blue strobes approached through the mist. "We better steer clear until we know who's in charge." She whirled to face him so suddenly he almost gasped. "Occam's Razor. Saroyan wasn't a young guy. He probably died from a stroke or a heart attack or something."

"I wish," Saul said. "But the evidence will show foul play. The obvious explanation is that I killed him. But think about it. Why would I leave a note lying around like that?"

Hernandez bit her lip. "You weren't there."

Saul appreciated her willingness to believe that he hadn't been involved, but the theory didn't work. "The note alone would fry me. So, why make it look like I wrote it?"

Hernandez shrugged. "It doesn't make sense. But regardless of who wrote the note, it's a setup. No other explanation."

The note was a setup, she was right about that, but there *was* one other explanation. One she was not ready to believe. Saul wondered if his own belief was influenced by his conviction that Sadie did not commit suicide. If Wayob could control someone's body, it explained Saroyan's change from Friday night to Saturday. It explained almost everything.

But how was Wayob doing it? Until he could explain how, no one would believe it. It seemed impossible to him too, except that it *had* happened. He had experienced it himself.

The second squad car rolled up, followed by a plain wrap driven by Garcia, another detective in Homicide Special except he reported to Lieutenant Delrawn instead of Levy.

He parked and unfolded himself from the car. His suit was wrinkled and his gray hair tousled like he'd climbed out of bed and left in a hurry. He nodded gruffly to Hernandez, turned to the squad car, and spoke to the officers through the window.

"Shit," Hernandez said. "This might be worse than IA."

"At least he's a real detective." Saul hoped he'd remain

impartial. Saul's freedom might depend on it.

As the squad car reversed back to Washington to block the intersection, Garcia approached Saul and Hernandez.

"So, Parker, what brought you here in the middle of the night?"

"The victim was our suspect," Saul said. "We'll take the case if you don't want it."

"Wish you could," Garcia said. "But from what I understand, you're on suspension."

"Hernandez isn't."

"I suggested that, too, but Delrawn says it's out of her league."

Saul crossed his arms. "Yeah? Levy might say the same thing about you."

Garcia shrugged. "But not to my face though, right?"

Saul exchanged a glance with Hernandez. She mouthed, *Chickenshit*. Garcia was right about Levy.

Garcia motioned toward his plain wrap. "Mind stepping into my office?"

"We're good standing," Hernandez said.

Saul's knees were tired of holding his weight and he *did* feel like sitting, just not with Garcia. He glanced toward his own plain wrap, which he shouldn't be driving on suspension.

"Who found the body?" Garcia asked.

"That would be me." Saul described the scene, without mentioning the note or Wayob or his fear that Wayob had used his hands to do the killing.

"What makes you think it was murder?" Garcia asked.

Hernandez looked away, and Saul followed her gaze. Above the street, a turbulence spiraled through the fog. An eerie texture to the darkness between the intervals of light.

"Check for yourself," he said.

"Your suspects have an unusually high mortality rate, don't they?"

Saul squared him in the eye, but before he could speak, Hernandez said, "Saroyan bludgeoned a guy to death in plain daylight. No one's going to mourn the bastard."

Garcia grumbled. "Why are you even here, Detective

Hernandez?"

"I called her," Saul said. "Saroyan was ours, like I said."

"*Was*," Garcia said. "So, I'll ask again, what brought you here tonight? Don't expect me to believe you just came to check on his wellbeing."

No way Saul could tell Garcia his theory about Wayob. "I found out that Arcos and Carter had followed me here, and I had a bad feeling. You ever get a feeling in your gut?"

Garcia frowned. "I've got one right now. You think this is related to Carter's death?"

Saul shrugged. "Arcos sure seemed panicked. Something was off." If Garcia found evidence that Carter had entered Saroyan's apartment, he might tie Saroyan's murder to Carter. Which would buy Saul some much needed time to find out how Wayob did this.

Garcia turned to Hernandez. "What do you think?"

"About Arcos and Carter?"

"Who else?"

"Hard to say." She glanced at Saul. "*The heart of another is a dark forest.*"

Not exactly backing his diversion, but at least she wasn't contradicting him. And she wasn't mentioning the note. And for this, he owed her. Big time. She had put her career on the line.

Garcia turned toward the apartment. One of the uniforms Saul had sent to cordon it off had stationed himself by the entrance. "Alright, I'm going in for a look." He glanced back at Saul. "Stick around where I can find you."

Saul held his palms up defensively.

Garcia cut across the lawn toward the building.

"Thanks," Saul said to Hernandez.

She tilted her head toward the Mustang. "Get in. You have to hear what I learned about Wayob."

She slid behind the wheel, and he eased himself into the passenger seat. His weight sunk the car. As he closed the door, it scraped the curb.

He grimaced and pretended to focus out the window. Garcia was at the entrance to the apartment speaking with a uniform, who nodded and scowled toward the car where

Saul sat.

"Saul!" Hernandez slid her seat forward and levered it straight up.

"The curb is too high," he said. "I'll call Public Works."

"Forget it," she said. But he knew how much she cared about the car.

She swiped her phone and showed him a black-and-white photo of a familiar-looking Latino in a dark uniform. Saul had seen this photo before. No doubt about it. Same proud nose. Same cleft chin. Same sun-shaped insignia on his lapels.

"His name was Miguel Arredondo Sosa," Hernandez said. "He was the chief of police for Guatemala City back in the nineties. And he was investigating Wayob himself."

"Luis Luna's father?" Saul felt a charge in his gut.

"Exactly. How did you know?"

"She has the same photo in her apartment. How did he die?"

"Shot by the Guatemalan army for attempting to assassinate their president, allegedly."

"It was Wayob," Saul said. "Wayob forced him to do it. Don't ask me how."

"It is suspicious. I'll give you that. The chief of police, who is investigating Wayob, suddenly tries to kill the president, and with seemingly no motive? I'm wondering if Wayob is a CIA codename. The CIA orchestrated the Guatemalan coup in the 1950s. Who says they stopped there? Maybe they brainwashed Sosa into the assassination, like in *the Manchurian Candidate*."

"Wayob confessed to killing an officer decades ago. Dollars to donuts it was Sosa."

"That confession was over the phone, right?"

"Right. It was Aleman's voice, but he was channeling Wayob. I just don't get why he'd confess at all?"

"Maybe it was to throw you off course," Hernandez said. "The CIA could have faked the whole phone call with some kind of voice-matching software. That's why Aleman denied it. He never actually called you."

But she hadn't seen the conflicted emotions that played

across Aleman's face when Saul questioned him, the way his throat constricted and turned red. Probably recalling dream-like memories of whatever Wayob made him do the night he walked off his shift at the MDC.

Saul buzzed down the window and inhaled. He felt light-headed, like the fog had choked all the oxygen from the night air.

If Sosa had been the fall guy for a conspiracy, then why involve Aleman? The theory was too complicated. Plus, Saul had experienced Wayob's ability firsthand. Wayob had forced him to murder Saroyan.

"What happened to the president?" Saul asked. "Did he die?"

Hernandez shook her head. "A year later, his own Minister of Defense overthrew him in a coup. He spent the rest of his life in prison awaiting trial for crimes against humanity."

"That certainly supports your conspiracy theory," Saul said, "but then why wait so long to off Luis Luna?"

She combed back her shock of white. "I don't know. Maybe the two deaths are unrelated."

But Saul couldn't stomach the coincidence. "The son of the man who was killed while investigating Wayob is himself killed by a man who, at the time, claimed to be Wayob. These two events must be related."

She pressed her lips together. "So maybe it took them this long to find him?"

"Why bother? After so much time, how could he be a threat?"

"I don't know. But Rosa's grandmother went back to her maiden name when they came to the US. Her real name is Gloria Sosa, and the army claimed she robbed the National Palace. So, maybe she *did* take something. That's why she had to leave Guatemala. An article I read actually blamed the army for her murder."

Saul rubbed his forehead. He recalled Gloria Luna's warning, spoken in measured English: *Leave it alone.* Her milky eyes had glanced down and to the right. What was she hiding? Maybe now, with this information about her husband, they could pry it out of her. "We should talk to her again. She might be the key to this whole thing."

Hernandez held up a finger. "On this, we agree."

"Want to drive?"

"We can't go now. It's the middle of the night. Plus, you're on suspension."

"Hasn't stopped me so far."

Hernandez shook her head. "We have to be careful. If Wayob's CIA or something, we might stir up a nest of hornets and still never get close to the truth. I'm wondering if we should leave it alone."

A chill shot through Saul's stomach. Leaving it alone was not an option. Not now, not for him. "Let Wayob go free? Is that what you want?"

"No, but..." She gazed at him intently. "I'm worried about you, Parker, from the bottom of my heart."

"I appreciate that. I do. But we can't afford to wait." He wanted to reach across and turn the key himself. While they were sitting here talking, Wayob could be claiming his next victim. "Remember at the death notification, how Mrs. Luna said it was her fault?"

Hernandez nodded. "That was weird. She said it three times. But Saroyan killed her son. We've got video."

"That's how it appeared. Wayob deceived us with our very own eyes. He used Saroyan to kill Luis Luna, and I think Mrs. Luna knew. You saw how she acted. She was hiding something."

Hernandez's eyes widened. "So now you believe Saroyan's *confession*?"

Saul's fingerprints were almost certainly on the note, and the note was in his handwriting. He needed Hernandez to believe what he knew in his gut to be true: Wayob had written the note with Saul's hand, probably after it had killed Saroyan.

"Most of it," he said. "Let's see what Mrs. Luna says." Maybe if Hernandez heard it from the elderly Luna, she'd believe.

"She's sick and blind, and you're too wound up. You'll spook her. Let's just go in the morning."

Saul said nothing. With or without Hernandez, he had to go, and he had to go now. He had to learn what Gloria Luna knew.

From his coat, he removed the plastic bag with the hair. If Hernandez wasn't going with him, at least she could get it analyzed discreetly. "I found this in Sadie's bed. We need a DNA test."

Hernandez shone her phone on the bag. She puffed her cheeks and exhaled. "How about a little quid pro quo?"

He didn't have time, but what could he say? Every victim deserved justice. "Sure thing."

She swiped to an image on her phone and handed it to Saul. "That's how we found her."

Saul stared at the screen frozen with disbelief.

Impossible.

He blinked but the image remained.

He held the phone closer... The girl. It was the girl from his nightmare. Except with all the color drained from her face. Her dark hair dull and tangled. She was on her back on a bed of black plastic bags at the bottom of a dumpster. Arms above her torso, sticking straight up.

Saul should have told Hernandez, right then and there, how in his dream, in the hallway at the Roosevelt, Jenna Collins had smiled as she approached him. How she'd whispered in his ear. The words. What had she said? All he could recall was the way her breath tickled his ear lobe, the way her lips brushed his neck.

His stomach twisted.

Had his body been used by Wayob to murder Collins as well?

Saul hoped not. He hoped with every fiber of his being.

Hernandez was staring at him, her mouth half-open.

His mind was reeling. He had to say something, but what? He stated the obvious. "Looks like she was moved after rigor mortis set in."

A frown flickered briefly across her face and was gone. "She wasn't robbed, and there was no recent sexual activity. So, what's the motive?"

"How was she killed?"

"Strangled. There is some minor bruising on her neck, but besides that, there's not a mark on her. Want to take a look at the murder book?"

He had wanted to, at Langer's, earlier. But now...he felt nauseous. He stared out the windshield at the flashing lights in the fog. "Can't imagine I'll find anything you missed."

"I'd consider it a favor."

Saul was torn. He was curious, yet at the same time he wished to block Collins out of his mind. The less he knew, the better. "Levy will freak," he said, which was what Hernandez had said when he asked at lunch.

"She'll never know. I have it on my laptop, at home."

Saul blinked. He tried to focus on the fog. But the strobes, the discordant chaos of light.

"You can sleep over," Hernandez was saying. "Save yourself a trip to Hollywood and back. We'll go to the Lunas' first thing in the morning."

Saul stared at her. Was she really inviting him over? After he'd fantasized for so long.

But, not like this. Not while he was a bloated whale. Not when he might lose control of his own body.

"I'll keep an eye on you," she said, "if you're worried about becoming Wayob or whatever."

She means her bed. How could he say no? He swallowed. "Not a good idea."

She crossed her arms. "I can handle myself. If it'll make you feel better, I'll cuff you to the bed." Her lips twitched.

She had smiled, almost. Or had he imagined it? Was she joking or was she flirting with him? "Oh, I know you can handle yourself," he said. "That's what I'm afraid of. Might set a bad example for Rumi, though, if he finds out you've got a crazed fatso cuffed to your headboard." He forced himself to laugh.

Hernandez closed her eyes and pressed her lips together. It wasn't funny. "Nothing's going to happen," she said. "Don't worry."

He felt his ears flush. What was he thinking? Presuming *her* bed?

"I should stick around. Might be dawn before Garcia's

done with me." But they both knew Garcia would order Saul to vacate the scene as soon as he got a handle on it.

Hernandez nodded. She pressed a hand to his arm. "Want me to stay?"

"Nothing you can do here." He cracked the door and tried to wedge himself out through the gap without scraping the door on the curb again. And failed.

Hernandez glanced away from the harsh grating of the metal on concrete as if she hadn't heard it. She might not be so kind when she discovered the scratches on her rims.

Before closing the door, he leaned down and waved goodbye.

"Parker." She leaned toward him across the seat. "Promise me you won't harass the Lunas in the middle of the night."

"You got it." He glanced right. The roots of the olive tree had shattered the sidewalk. Without Hernandez, communicating with the elderly Luna was going to be difficult, but what choice did he have? Lives were at stake.

He shut the door, and Hernandez looked up at him through the window, her brows rippled with sorrow. Her mouth opened and closed. As she brushed back her shock of white, her face went blank. And Saul wasn't sure if he'd seen anything at all.

He straightened, knocked twice on the roof, and stepped back onto the sidewalk.

She looked straight ahead, clenching the wheel with both hands. She k-turned, eased around the squad car at the end of the block, and turned right. Her taillights faded away, drowned by the strobes of the firetruck, ambulance, and squad cars. Drowned by the fog. And the night.

More than any other moment in his life, Saul wished he could change the one he had just lived. Let someone else worry about Wayob. Go home with Hernandez—to *her* bed —wrap her in his arms, close his eyes, and just feel. The warmth of her body against his.

He crammed himself into the plain wrap. Downed a double of NoDoz. Checked his face in the mirror. His eyes were bloodshot from the combination of sleep deprivation and caffeine. His hair was solid gray. No more pretending that in dim light it looked brown. He pulled back the wattle under his chin and flattened his cheeks.

He looked ridiculous.

He angled the mirror away from his face toward the VW van parked behind him, and the blue lights spinning through the fog.

He sparked the ignition and yawned. Across the street, limbs reached into the mist that drifted in the streetlight. In spite of the NoDoz, he felt drowsy, and he needed his mind sharp now more than ever.

Ashley in the Mirror

Ashley curled into a ball on her bed and tried not to think about where Sammy was and what he was doing. She turned the lights up as bright as they would go, but it wasn't enough to ward off the awful image of Andrea at the bottom of the stairs, one leg twisted under her body at an impossible angle, the purple bruises on her neck, the wrong paleness of her skin, eyes glazed over and bulging as if in disbelief.

Ashley was going to go crazy if she didn't talk to someone. Where the hell was her phone? It wasn't in the bedroom. She wandered out to the stairs and looked down into an impossible darkness. *Maybe check the guest room first.*

And that's where she found it. Right there on the nightstand. *Weird.* Gray must have been sleeping in the guest bed.

There were like twenty texts from Don, which she ignored. She unlocked her phone and called her dad. It was the middle of the night, but he always answered her.

Not this time.

She left a message saying to forget the message Gray had left this morning. He should just call her at her number as soon as he could, no matter how late.

She played the voicemail from Don. He was basically yelling at her for leaving the screen test. Apparently, because of all the drama, they had cast someone else into what would have been the breakout role of her career, and now the opportunity was dead, as dead as Andrea at the bottom of the stairs.

Don's texts were a blur. As she blinked away her tears, she saw the one from August.

August:
You home? We're coming over.

August would have known he wasn't welcome, so why announce he was coming? Unless he was Wayob, and Wayob was crazy, but then who was *we*?

She gazed out the window. Beyond the fence at the edge her lawn, fog roiled in the canyon. It glowed from all the lights of LA. Somewhere out there in the fog, Sammy was hiding Andrea's body.

She shivered and stepped back from the window. How had it come to this? Sammy had nothing to do with Andrea's death. She should have kept him out of it somehow. She had tried to, but he'd taken charge, as if she wasn't thinking clearly. And she hadn't been at the time—he was right about that—but now he'd implicated himself in a crime. Why would he do that?

She returned to her bedroom, locked the door, and changed into her softest PJs, the ones covered with stars and moons. They reminded her of Mindy's bedroom in the nightlight. Ashley lay on her bed with the lights still on and closed her eyes.

She had felt something special with Mindy. Of course, to Mindy she would have seemed like her father, but Ashley still felt the connection—a real human connection. That's what was missing in her life. Connection. She wanted someone who truly cared about her. Someone like…Sammy.

The idea struck her so suddenly that her whole body shook. He obviously cared about her more than she had realized before, and maybe it went deeper than work. It wasn't just that she felt safer with him on duty, she felt comfortable around him. And the way his white shirts clung to his muscles made her drool. She'd always had the feeling that it would be so yummy to get physical with him, and now she wondered if maybe they could be something more.

With each passing minute, she grew more awake. And she had the feeling that someone was watching her, that Wayob was peering down through the walls of her house, and that she might wake up with him here in the room with her.

She sat up. The room was empty. And she knew in her rational mind that her house was empty too, but she'd never stop worrying until she talked to someone.

Why wasn't her dad responding? Strange that she hadn't heard from him since Friday.

She had no idea what Sammy would believe, and she wasn't ready to go there with him. Not yet. *One step at a time.* So, the only person left she could talk to about this was the last one she wanted to call. Maybe Gray had traded bodies with her by accident the first time, but not the second. Yet she kept right on talking to him in her mind, so fuck it.

She'd smashed his phone while in his body, so she dialed the number of the disposable smartphone she'd bought. It rang and rang. *He's not going to answer.* But then just when she was on the verge of breaking down, he answered.

"Thanks for the tattoo," he whispered. "If Claire finds out I'm talking to you—"

"Andrea's dead," she blurted out. "Wayob killed her."

Gray went quiet. And she could almost feel the weight of the news sinking into him.

When he finally spoke, his voice trembled. "Maybe if I had called 911—"

"No. Wayob probably killed her before he came at you. Her body was in the cellar. There was nothing you could have done."

"So, what did you tell the police?" Gray asked.

"Nothing. Sammy's hiding the body."

"Oh my god." Gray sounded panicked.

Shouldn't have told him. "We had no choice. Like you said, it was Wayob in August's body. He's a jerk, okay, but not a murderer. If you had seen the body…" Her throat tightened. She couldn't speak.

"I'm so sorry," Gray said. "I guess no one would believe the truth. August is *August* now though, right?"

Ashley recalled how August had lost all his usual self-confidence. He wasn't sure what had happened and was obviously freaked out. She almost wished that he had been responsible. At least then she wouldn't have to worry about who Wayob was now, and they could have called the police instead of going down this dark, dark road from which there was no coming back.

"Yeah." Ashley lay back on the bed and twisted her hair through her fingers. "It's him, alright. He threatened to sue."

"For what?"

"Locking him in the cellar."

Gray groaned.

"What if he's still out there?"

Gray sighed heavily. "You mean Wayob? He's trapped in the Encanto, I think."

"You think?"

"That's what he was afraid of. Getting trapped in there when we switched back to our own bodies."

A chill ran down her spine. "But you don't know for sure?"

"He was trying to kill me," Gray said. "I didn't exactly have time to ask questions."

"I don't know why I thought you'd know anyway. It's been a rough day."

"Yeah. Claire and I are splitting up."

"Oh man." Ashley got out of bed and went to the mirror. "Because of me?"

"No. It's been a long time coming."

"Did you tell her we switched bodies?"

"How could I?"

"Good point."

"Let's get some sleep, okay?" he said. "Tomorrow I'll come help you."

"I don't need your help. I just want to make sure we're safe from Wayob."

"Me too. I think the fortuneteller who gave me the Encanto knew about Wayob. I'll go talk to her tomorrow. She had a girl with her who speaks English."

Ashley glanced at the window. The solid gray mass

of fog pressed against the other side looked about ready to burst through. The image of Andrea's contorted body at the bottom of the cellar stairs flashed in her mind, and her throat tightened again.

"Promise?" was about all she could say without crying.

"I promise," Gray said.

Ashley ended the call, fell back on her bed, and gave in to the tears. Andrea was dead. Nothing Ashley could do would change that, still the tears came anyway. Andrea had been more than an employee—maybe not a friend, yet—but they were getting there.

After the tears stopped, Ashley wiped her face with the sleeve of her nightshirt and tried texting Sammy again...

Her texts still refused to go through. Nothing else she could do. Things would be better in the morning.

She turned out the lights, climbed under the covers, and closed her eyes. She tried to focus on something else, anything else. The breakout role she'd lost in the Kaufman-Penn project. She should be furious about missing her chance—she totally could have played the crazy girlfriend—so why did she feel relieved?

She had wasted so much time rehearsing, trying to overcome the queasiness in her stomach that always built up to the point of vomiting. And for what? So she could pour her heart out for the critics and the haters to shit on? She felt nauseous thinking about all the lunches, the schmoozing, and the screen tests, which, in the best case, would only lead to a long road of tedious rehearsals and publicity.

Acting just didn't seem worth all that. If she tried something else, the haters would no doubt say she failed, but who cares? Why waste her life worrying about their opinions? How had pretending to be someone else become the basis for her self-esteem when she could be helping others, when her money could do so much good? She could open a charity to provide support for victims of violence, and she could name it after Andrea... Not that it would make up for her tragic death, but it would be a start.

—

At 3:13 a.m., Ashley was no closer to sleep and still had no word from Sammy. She got out of bed. Dim light oozed through the blinds she'd left open. She found the glass of water on the dresser.

As she drank, something tickled her lip—one of her hairs must have fallen in. *Gross.* But she was too thirsty to fish it out in the dark. As she gulped, a whole clump brushed her lip and wiggled.

She turned on the lights. In her glass, an upside-down brown spider was struggling not to drown. She dropped the glass, which shattered on the floor, throwing water everywhere.

She stared at the shards of glass around her feet. No sign of the spider. It would be hard to spot against the wood grain, unless it moved.

She stepped carefully back from the spill, stripped off her shirt. She picked up the larger shards of glass and used her shirt to mop up the water, the smaller pieces of glass, and hopefully the dead spider. Gingerly, she carried the glass and the wet ball to the bathroom and threw them away.

In the mirror, her hair was tangled, her eyes bloodshot and dry. Her skin looked blank and unlived in. After all the treatments for eczema, all her struggles to banish the blackheads, the pimples, the deep pores and imperfections, she had lost sight of her life.

Behind her, a creepy shadow stood in the shower. She marched to the line of switches and banished the shadow and all its brethren. The lights were too bright for this hour, but she needed to rid herself of this eerie feeling that someone or something was watching her, that her big, empty house wasn't quite as empty as it should be, and for this she needed a little help.

From the medicine cabinet she snatched the big bottle of quick-release Ambien, which she opened on her way back to the bedroom. She took two, closed the electric blinds, and checked the alarm. No doors or windows had been opened since Sammy left with Andrea's body at 11:38.

Sammy was going way out on a limb, and she knew August had nothing to do with it—he was doing it for her. How could she ever repay him? He was far too charismatic to be wasting his days in her security booth. He deserved better.

Leaving the lights on, she climbed under the covers. Her pillowy bed seemed too big for just one person. She flopped around until finally she felt the dulling effect of the Ambien pulling her to sleep, and, gladly, she gave in to it.

Charlie Goes Down

Lying in bed, Charlie's aching back refuses to let him sleep. It feels like Vietnam. Like he's still humping the boonies outside the wire, with the M79 and extra grenades in his pack and all his false bravado as his squad eggs him on: *Hulk, Hulk, Hulk!*

Despite all the Oxycontin that the crazy degraded Charlie into licking from the carpet, his thoughts return again to the after-midnight pharmacy—the one he heard about in Glendale where they have an on-site doctor who writes prescriptions no questions asked, and they supposedly take Medicare.

Like all the beds and the sofa here in his daughter's house, the mattress sags and pinches his spine. No better than a pile of bricks. He counts to a hundred, and then to a thousand, as a dim line of moonlight flickers along the wall.

He hears a noise outside. The sound of glass bottles stirred together. What kind of crazy recycles this late at night? One more interruption, and that's it: he'll go to the pharmacy.

Something smacks. Bottles rattle. He groans as he sits up.

He gingerly gets to his feet and shuffles to the window. He cracks the curtains and peers out. Across the street, some kind of crazy—blurred by the fog washing over the hill—is rummaging through the Wilsons' bin. Doesn't he know removing items from the trash is against the law? Can he not read the clear English spelled out in not one but two places on the bin?

Charlie works his way downstairs using the banister for support. He checks out the front window. The crazy is still there, digging through the trash. Don't the Wilsons know that if you allow even one crazy in the neighborhood, you might as well invite the whole horde? Do they want crazies clogging the street with their dilapidated carts full of junk? Of course not, but they'd rather lie in bed and let someone else take responsibility. Like Charlie has nothing better to do. He ought to let it happen, see how the neighborhood likes it once they have the crazies camped up and down the street using their lawns as toilets.

The crazy has emptied the garbage bin into the street and is studying some object he's found. It's more than Charlie can stand. It really is. No one gives a damn about anything anymore. They probably won't even care when their street becomes another Skid Row.

"That's how it is," he says to himself. "Yet again, all up to Charlie."

He hurries out the front door, not quite running but shuffling quickly. Fast as a man his age can be expected to move.

The crazy is on his knees, peering into a pile of

scattered trash with his face close like a dog about to devour it.

"Hey," he yells, "you can't do that!"

The crazy snatches up some small object and presses it against whatever he has in his hand.

Charlie shuffles across the lawn, the grass cold and wet on his bare feet. It soaks his pajama bottoms. The crazy is wearing a suit and has a bald pate that Charlie would recognize anywhere. The crazy is not just some vagabond; Arcos is back.

Arcos stands, his face twisted with deranged anger. Whatever regrets he'd mumbled earlier when he left Charlie's house are all gone now. His eyes seem out of focus, like they don't see Charlie at all. And there's something familiar about them. Something in his eyes that wasn't there before. If he wasn't completely and utterly crazy then, he is now.

He screams and drops whatever he was holding: a baseball-sized stone, and something smaller. They land on a half-opened plastic bag.

"It stabbed me," Arcos says.

"Serves you right." Charlie balls his hands into fists, still high on the Oxycontin—he's fearless.

He swings.

Arcos ducks. "Don't touch me!" He reels back, slips on a dirty diaper, and falls backward.

Charlie forces his aching back to bend enough for him to pick up what the crazy had been holding: the white stone and a small black snake.

"Clean this mess up and get out of here," Charlie says.

Arcos struggles to his feet, his arms rigid. Ready to strike. His fierce eyes bore into Charlie as if gazing straight through to his soul.

"Give it back to me, and you may live."

Mucus runs from Arcos's nose. He does not wipe it away. Just like the officer who bludgeoned the bum on Halloween and scared him out in front of Charlie's car.

"I know you, old man," Arcos says.

Terror seizes Charlie. *It cannot be.* Yet somehow… this is no longer just Arcos.

Behind his crazy, out-of-focus eyes, Charlie also sees the crazy officer.

Charlie's muscles refuse to act, as if the crazy's stare has reached in and frozen his blood all the way down to his heart. Very slowly, Charlie offers the round, white stone. The crazy reaches for it with trembling hands, stubby fingers stained with dirt. Just before they reach the stone, Charlie tosses it into the road.

Anyone who knows anything about anything knows better than to give to a crazy, or the crazy will take and take until you have nothing left.

The stone clacks on the pavement and rolls down the hill under Gray's car, with the crazy chasing after it. He crouches down by the rear tire, then springs to his feet and bolts to the next car down the hill, where he falls to his knees and reaches under it.

Charlie scurries toward the house. Not that he's running away; Charlie never runs from a fight and he's not about to start now. He's not afraid of some trash thief who can't even wipe his runny nose, but Charlie means to have the upper hand. He means to have some sort of weapon by the time the crazy realizes that Charlie still has the snake in his fist.

Despite the flood of adrenaline, Charlie can't move any faster. The pavement chafes the brittle skin of his feet. The wet grass will be a relief, he thinks, but when he steps over the curb, his feet nearly slide out from under him.

"Where is it?" The crazy growls.

Charlie glances back. The crazy is squatting down in the dim streetlight over the trash. He examines a diaper and the plastic bag that the stone fell on. Then, he places them back in the bin.

"Ha," Charlie chuckles to himself. *Cleaning up, just like I asked. The Wilsons should thank me.* Too bad they'll never know.

As the crazy runs his hands chaotically over the pavement, Charlie realizes that he doesn't have time to take the safer route up the street to the front walk. So, spreading his arms for balance, he makes his way diagonally across the wet lawn to the front door.

"You took it," the crazy says, much closer behind Charlie than he expected.

Charlie focuses on the front door, which he left half-open. His feet smack the steps. If he could just make it inside…

He crosses the threshold, and he shoves the door shut behind him. But instead of the satisfying latch click he longs to hear, the door smacks the crazy's fingers. The crazy howls.

Charlie doubles down on his luck and throws all of his one hundred and thirty pounds against the door. It crunches the crazy's fingers against the frame. This time, he retracts his hand and screams.

Charlie shuts the door and locks it. "That'll teach you," he says. "Now get out of here."

But Charlie knows better than to expect the crazy trash digger to give up so easily. As he hurries through the parlor, his chafed feet streak the carpet with blood.

In the kitchen, Charlie yanks the largest knife from

the wood block. Its steel blade tapers to a deadly point. He grips the oak handle firmly in his palm and swipes the air. "This will teach him."

Glass shatters and breaks, and a heavy object crashes through the living room window. Charlie reconsiders his plan. Anyone who knows anything knows it's better to live to fight another day.

Hurrying into the garage, he ignores the pain as the concrete floor scuffs his feet. He throws open his car door, tosses the knife onto the passenger seat, and falls in behind the wheel. He turns the key. As the engine starts, he glances in the mirror. He was in such a hurry that he forgot to open the garage door, and the door opener is…right where it belongs, of course: clipped to the visor of his son-in-law's car, which Charlie moved to the street in order to hide his own dented car.

Charlie climbs out of the car. Before he can make it to the button by the kitchen door, the crazy bursts through, shoving him back. Charlie falls on his butt. A bone snaps. Sharp pain in his hip.

The crazy stands over him. "I remember you."

If Charlie could get to the knife on the passenger seat… He scoots backward. Hits his head on the driver's side door.

"I looked a bit different." The crazy steps forward and leans over him. He stinks like baby shit. "This is the same car, isn't it?" He runs his hand over the dent in the fender. "I had to finish him off, thanks to you. A mercy kill, you understand?"

Charlie is mesmerized by the crazy's eyes, by the stream of mucus running from his nose. It takes all Charlie's effort to turn away. Coughing on exhaust, he clutches the door handle to pull himself up, ignoring the pain in his hip, the dizziness. If he could just get up higher, get better air.

"I believe you have taken a piece of the Encanto."

Charlie glances through the window to the knife on the passenger seat.

The crazy grabs him by the shirt and shoves him down. He hits Charlie in the face, then slams him against the fender, right below the dent where he hit the bum.

Charlie slumps down against the tire, light-headed and sick. Blood oozes from his nose into his mouth. Charlie spits, but more fills his mouth, and all he can do is watch the crazy lean into the car where the knife is sitting right there in plain sight.

Now the crazy is standing over him. Charlie realizes that he must have blacked out.

"Thanks for this." The crazy wields the knife. "Now, I expect you'll cooperate."

"I'd rather die," Charlie hears himself say.

"Is that so?" As the crazy leans down, he sways, seeming to lose his balance.

Charlie tries to scoot away, but the crazy's hand slams into Charlie's chest, pinning him against the tire.

The crazy leans forward and presses the razor-sharp knife against Charlie's throat. But giving in now would be like giving in to all the crazies who ever were. If Charlie hands over the little snake this crazy seems obsessed with, he'd be no better than a crazy himself. If he gives in now, then it might as well have been Charlie bludgeoned by the officer and mowed down in the road.

Clutching the snake in his palm, he hides his hand in his pocket. He inhales. The pressure of the knife blade against his skin perhaps weakens, ever so slightly.

"I'd rather not hurt you, but I will." The crazy stares at him, his breathing deep and irregular. The intensity of his eyes, still malicious but fading, as if he's unable to maintain his evil train of thought.

The exhaust, Charlie realizes. The car is poisoning the air. Charlie laughs, or he tries to. At least if he's going out, he's taking the crazy down with him.

Charlie can no longer move. Even without the blade against his throat and the reeking crazy pressing against his chest, he couldn't get up now.

The knife pressure lessens, this time for sure, and the crazy's eyelids flutter half-closed. He's saying something, speaking in gibberish, or at least that's how Charlie hears it.

He drops the knife and slaps himself lethargically, his face now purple and swollen. His mouth hangs open and drool slimes down his chin.

He slumps sideways. His head lolls against Charlie's chest. The white stone rolls out into Charlie's lap.

Charlie pulls his hand from his pocket, but it falls uselessly to the floor. He can no longer feel the shape of the snake in his palm.

He turns his head toward the kitchen. He could still survive, maybe, if he could get out from under the crazy...but he can't even see to the door. Beyond the dented fender, everything blurs and swims.

Charlie never should have abandoned that bum on Halloween, leaving him behind like roadkill. He should have stopped. He should have called for help. He should have plowed his car into the crazy officer, who is somehow now here, in Arcos's body, pinning Charlie against the fender just below the dent left by the bum's body.

Charlie's eyes are closing, and he knows the last thing he sees will be that dented fender. He cannot bear it. He tries to scream, but the sound is trapped in his throat. He summons all his will. And more. And manages, just barely, to tilt his gaze. Miles away, on the floor beside him, the black snake, which he had to go and get himself killed for, slithers into shadow in the palm of his hand. He tries to focus on the white stone in his lap. On the roundness...

It fades to black.

Driving To A Dead End

At three in the morning, Saul was speeding east from downtown on the 10, Hernandez's words reverberating in his head: *Nothing's going to happen.* He slapped the steering wheel. That was the problem. Nothing would ever happen. He grabbed hold of a fat roll and squeezed. Not with this belly.

He should have told her that he recognized Collins from his nightmare, but what if she didn't believe that it was just a dream? And…what if it wasn't?

He had to tell her. But first he'd question Mrs. Luna. Maybe now, with what they had learned about her past, now that he was prepared to believe, she'd tell him whatever it was she was hiding. And it would help him make some kind of sense out of all this. It would explain how Wayob had forced Saul's own hands to end Saroyan's life. And possibly Collins's.

Hungry.

Nothing to eat. No time to stop. He listened to a podcast about weight loss through meditation. A soothing British voice instructed Saul to concentrate on his breathing, which he did, for eight minutes, while keeping his eyes on the road.

When the voice returned, Saul did feel less famished. But now his chest hurt, and his heart hammered against it. Now he realized what he'd been avoiding: the true reason he'd shut down his phone. It wasn't that Arcos and Carter might track him; it was the awful image. The photo on his phone that he'd unconsciously avoided when he showed Claire Wilson the photo of Aleman.

Behind him, a car honked. It took him a moment to realize that it was at him, that his foot had slipped off the accelerator.

He had to delete the photo. Which meant acknowledging its existence. But there was no denying it now. He held up his phone so he could glance at the screen and still see the road. He opened the photos app... His stomach lurched. It was worse than he feared. He tapped the trash can icon, but the image remained. He pressed harder. His phone seemed to insist that he take it all in: Jenna Collins, on a gold bedspread that matched the one in his room at the Roosevelt. Her eyes open. Seeing nothing. Lifeless. His badge on her chest. Bruises on her neck. From his hands.

Saul had, of course, fought against it desperately. This much he remembered clearly now—like he was in a free fall trying to rise against gravity, being forced to not only witness her murder but to feel her body go limp.

Finally, the awful image vanished, replaced by a photo he'd taken at the Castle, of the Disappearing Woman trick.

He blacked the screen and tried to think of

something else. The elderly Luna. He prayed she was home. He prayed she wouldn't hold back. Prayed she'd know how to prove his innocence. How to stop Wayob.

His phone buzzed in the cup holder. It was Hernandez. She would know if he ignored her.

He swallowed. Had to answer.

"You're in the car," she said. Not a question, an accusation, and her assumption was correct: he was breaking his promise to her by going to the Lunas.

"Put yourself in my shoes."

"Not possible," she said with a harshness in her voice that jolted his head back in the seat. Through the phone, he heard the sound of keys, a door closing. Footsteps on stairs. "Forget the Lunas," she said. "Meet me at the PAB. We've got some new evidence you're going to want to see for yourself."

His stomach twisted. He wasn't allowed at the PAB while on suspension, and they both knew it. "Evidence on who?"

Through the phone, he heard the door chime of her car, then a guitar chord ripped in his ear and abruptly went silent. Her engine turned over. "You were at the Roosevelt last night, right?"

"For a few hours," he said.

"You didn't spend the night?"

"I went to bed after I checked in. But evidently, at some point, I went to Saroyan's."

"You don't know when?"

If Collins's murder had occurred at the Roosevelt the way Saul now recalled it, then why did Wayob move the body?

"I'm almost at the Lunas," he said. "I'll call you afterward."

"No, wait for me. You'll need help translating."

Time was running out. He had to prove what had happened before Hernandez arrived, and he had a bad feeling about this new evidence. Almost certainly, it implicated him in the crime.

"Promise me," she said, "you'll wait outside."

"Sure thing," he lied.

A cloud slithered across the moon.

He ended the call and exited onto Loma Avenue. He sped between shadowy warehouses, their fences topped with razor wire.

The road dead-ended into the lot for the Lunas' building. A faded red Civic with a dented bumper and a patch of rust by the plate was parked beside a brand-new-black Tesla sports car with dealer tags. It was probably worth more than the whole building.

Saul parked by the Tesla. He unfolded himself from his car. Above the lot, tires hissed along the freeway. The clouds had thickened up and all but erased the moon.

As he climbed the stairs to the second floor, they shook under his weight, and the rusted rail offered little support. The whole upper porch sloped away from the building.

He knocked on the Lunas' faded-blue door.

No response.

He knocked again.

"Not a good time," said a voice behind the door. A man's voice.

Saul held his badge to the peephole. "It's urgent. I need to speak with Gloria Luna."

The door cracked an inch. A sliver of face peeked through the slit. An eye, a cheek, and a chin—a white man, familiar, his silver hair moussed up and trimmed neat.

"Abuela passed."

Saul Goes Down

As the door opened wider, Saul staggered back a half step. Light flickered behind the man in the doorway. His tailored suit fit snug on his broad shoulders. Spry energy seemed coiled in his posture. His lip twitched.

Saul steadied himself. "When?"

"Yesterday," the man said.

"How?"

"Cancer."

"May I come in?"

"Now's not a good time."

"I need to speak with Rosa. It's urgent."

"It's almost four in the morning."

"Could be a matter of life and death."

"Let him in," Rosa said from behind the half-open door, her voice flat and defeated.

The man looked toward her. He held the door firmly and pleaded with her in fluent Spanish.

Rosa, who had lost her father and now her grandmother, both in less than a week, raised her voice to the older white man who had answered her door like he owned the place.

Saul stuck his foot in the doorway and leaned closer.

The man stepped back. Rosa pulled the door open. She wore a long black dress. Her eyes were bloodshot and teary.

"I'm so sorry for your loss," Saul said.

She pressed her lips together and nodded, then abruptly turned and led them into the apartment.

Candlelight trembled on the ceiling and walls from a host of prayer candles on the kitchen counter and on the shelf by the window. There, a photo of Gloria Luna had been added beside the one of her son. Only one ceramic owl remained of the collection that had been on the shelf beside the couch. Strewn about the floor were a half dozen half-packed boxes.

Saul navigated through the boxes and faced the man. "I didn't catch your name."

"Evan." His voice shot up an octave, as if trying out how his name sounded. "York."

Impossible. But it was him. Saul recognized him now from the news, and from googling Ashley York.

Evan York stood there fidgeting like his hands felt wrong. No sign of his characteristic charisma. If anything, this man with a billion-dollar net worth looked almost ashamed.

The odds of encountering both Ashley York and her father on the same night in separate locations were slim, but possible. But the odds of finding him here, at the Lunas, were implausibly low. Wayob must have something to do with his presence, though Saul couldn't fathom what the connection could be.

He tried to sound calm as he asked, "So, how do you two know each other?"

She looked at York as she carried a wooden chair from the table and planted it beside her grandmother's empty recliner.

"I help people out," Evan York said.

"A philanthropist," Saul said. "Very kind." It sounded fishy, although he wished it was true. York's limitless resources could provide a bright future for Rosa.

Rosa sat in the wooden chair and motioned Saul to the sofa.

He took a step toward it and paused. There were thousands in Rosa's situation or worse just in LA alone. And why come here in person? Was it something Evan York couldn't trust to any one of the countless people in his employment?

He glanced at York. "Why Rosa?"

"I help a lot of—" Evan York's brow roached. "Many people."

Saul held his gaze. "That's great. Really great. Surprised I haven't read about it. You must have reporters lining up for an exclusive."

York studied his empty palm as if it suddenly contained something important to consider. "I keep a low profile. For security reasons."

Saul nodded. "I would have pegged you for the generous donation sort of man, but why the personal touch?"

"It's, uh, like family. The people I help." York looked down and to his right. "It's rewarding, you know?"

Saul nodded, keeping his face neutral.

Rosa, in her little chair, had gazed off toward the shrine by the window, where the marigolds and candles surrounded her grandmother's photo now instead of her father's.

Saul sank into the cushion across from her and leaned forward. "Can we speak alone?"

"I need him here," she said.

Behind her, the narrow hallway led to a bedroom illuminated by a floor lamp. On the bed was a suitcase and a modest stack of clothes.

"Are you moving?" Saul asked.

Yet again, Evan York answered for her. "She needs to be closer to school." He took the last ceramic owl from the shelf and crossed the room. "She has to take a bus and two trains from here, twice a day." He stood behind Rosa, clutching the owl to his chest with one hand while gripping her chair with the other.

Rosa flicked her eyes up at him. "It's not that bad."

"It's too much. I'm so glad you're moving."

Saul's phone buzzed in his pocket. He reached in and squeezed the button on the side to silence the call. Hernandez, probably. She would be here soon.

Evan York kneeled, tore some bubble wrap beside one of the boxes, and began wrapping the owl. An unsavory scent hung in the air.

Saul placed his hands on his knees and focused on Rosa. "Have you heard of a man who calls himself Wayob?"

Rosa glanced at York, who seemed consumed with fitting the owl into a box.

"Your grandmother might have known him," Saul said, "or known about him."

Rosa pulled her hair over her shoulder and smoothed it through her hands. "He hurt someone." Not a question. A statement.

"Who is he?"

Rosa lowered her voice. "Wayob is an evil spirit."

Saul shook his head slowly. A spirit was like no explanation at all. Spirits and ghosts were illusions he'd seen conjured from backstage by actors and projected onto smoke. Houdini had made a career of debunking spiritualists, and Saul agreed: they were a hoax. Although he did not understand Wayob's ability —so far—Wayob was still a man. Had to be. No other option.

A logical explanation had to exist, Saul was quite certain. Like the ghost of Irma at the Castle, who had to be a person in another room playing the piano remotely through some secret mechanism Saul had not yet discovered.

"Wayob is more than a spirit," he said. "He's responsible for multiple homicides. Including your father."

Rosa's eyes darted to Evan York. He sat back and froze.

"How do I find him?" Saul asked.

"Find the man who has the Encanto," Rosa said. "Wayob will kill him, if he hasn't already."

"What's the Encanto?"

"It's like a compass made from white stone, and the dial is carved black glass in the shape of an evil-looking snake. It traps Wayob." Rosa's eyes seemed to stare past Saul.

On the floor beside the armchair, York gazed up at Rosa, his brows bunched up forlornly.

"How does it work?" Saul asked.

"I have no idea," she said. "Abuela told the man to destroy it."

"What man?"

"She had to give it to him. We were in danger—"

A burst of knocks rattled the door. "Policía. Parker,

open up."

He couldn't let Hernandez in. Not yet. Not until he understood the truth behind this fairytale, enough to convince her of his innocence.

"That's just my partner," he said. "Before we let her in, you have to tell me how the Encanto traps Wayob."

Rosa glanced toward the doorway. Sat forward. "I don't know."

"Why give it away?"

"Abuela knew somehow that Wayob was coming to kill us. By gifting the Encanto, she drew Wayob's spirit inside, somehow, and trapped him there. If Wayob is free, then that man did not destroy it. He must have used it."

"For what?"

Rosa inhaled. "To switch bodies."

Saul would have laughed—he wanted to laugh— except Rosa appeared dead serious. She believed this. York's face went pale, his lips tightened to a grim line.

"Mrs. Luna," Hernandez knocked again. "I need you to let me in. Parker is dangerous."

Evan York leaped to his feet and looked from Saul to the door.

"How about you go stall her while I talk to Rosa," Saul said.

"I'm not leaving you alone with her. No way."

Saul held up his palms. "Wayob's got me in a real tight spot here. He's framing me. What I'm giving you is a chance to explain yourself. It's more than a little suspicious finding you here with Rosa the night after her grandmother died. I'm trying to reserve judgment, but my partner is not going to like it. She'll find this inappropriate."

The doorknob rattled. "At the count of ten, I'm

going to break down the door."

York sat straighter and tensed his shoulders. His head swiveled from Rosa to the door to Saul. Stalling was a sign of guilt.

Maybe Hernandez would believe Saul's innocence if she listened to Rosa. At this point, it was the best he could do. He heaved himself up off the couch. "When I let her in, you have to tell her what you know, both of you. Tell us everything."

He shouted toward the door. "Stand down. I'm coming."

What could he say? He had rushed here seeking answers, but so far he had none. Maybe if she saw the sincerity in Rosa's eyes, that would be enough for Hernandez to at least question the evidence that she must have found that linked Saul to Collins. And Evan York, whatever his reason for being here, seemed to agree with Rosa's story.

Saul opened the door and motioned her in. "You have to hear this for yourself."

Hernandez stood there, her chin tilted up, her chest puffed. "*He who fights with monsters should see to it that he himself does not become a monster.*"

"Nietzsche, right? What's the part about the abyss?"

She combed back her shock of white. "*When you gaze long into the abyss, the abyss gazes also into you.*"

"That's about the size of it."

"Hands behind your head," she said. "You know the drill."

"Please, you have to listen to Rosa. And get this, Evan York is here. Evan-fucking-York!"

Her eyes hardened. She stepped back to the porch rail. Hand to her weapon.

"Cuff me if you want, but just listen for ten minutes.

Please, Rhonda."

"This isn't a negotiation, *Barker*." She had flattened the *P*. He was back to Barker now. "You're under arrest."

He held her gaze. Stepped out onto the porch. Did not ask what for or who. Could be Saroyan or Collins or both. Both dead by his hands. By Wayob using Saul's body.

"I need your weapon. Nice and steady."

He held his coat open and slowly pulled his pistol from the shoulder holster. He passed her his pistol, the barrel pointed toward his chest.

She checked the safety and slid it into her pocket. "I need your phone too."

"Why?" Saul asked but he knew why. She had found out, somehow, about that awful image, which, thank goodness, he'd deleted.

She stood legs apart, gripped the Glock holstered to her hip. "That's an order."

She wouldn't shoot him. Would she? If he was going to make a move, now was the time to do it. But what could he do? Without Hernandez he had nothing. He had to appeal to her sense of reason. He had to convince her that he wasn't responsible, but how?

Very slowly, he slid his phone from his pocket and held it out toward her.

She refused to take it. "Unlock it."

He didn't have to. The Fifth Amendment protected him, but if he refused, she'd assume the worst. He pressed his thumb to the screen and handed it over.

She scrolled through the photos.

Saul's legs felt like giving out. "What are you looking for?" He tried to sound innocent, but his voice cracked and he couldn't quite meet her eyes.

The tension in her cheeks was almost unbearable.

She frowned. Tapped. Swiped. Tapped and swiped. Her eyes widened. She stepped back as if he'd struck her, and he felt like he had. She nearly dropped the phone but recovered it with her other hand. She gripped it gingerly at the edges, fingers extended, as though it were scalding hot, and turned the screen toward him.

It was the photo. Collins. Her lifeless eyes boring into him.

Saul looked away. His vision blurred. He couldn't speak.

"Just because you deleted it," Hernandez said, "doesn't mean it's gone."

Did he know that? He should have.

"You disgust me," she said. "I trusted you."

It took all his strength just to stay on his feet. He reached toward her. "Hernandez—"

"Hands on your head." She shoved his phone into her pocket and reached for her weapon.

He wanted to fall on his knees and beg her to believe him, but begging wasn't going to get him anywhere. "Think about it. Why would I have a photo like that?"

"I have thought about it. I thought about it the whole way here. How I had a partner who was holding back, keeping me out of the loop. Your reaction when I showed you a photo of her corpse. And now I get it." She drew her gun. "I said hands on your head!"

He complied. "I didn't remember. Not at first. It just came back in a haze, like a dream. That's what I thought it was, just a dream. I sound crazy—I know I do—but there is an explanation. Maybe it was my hands, but Wayob did the killing."

"Sounds like you've got a real good defense. I was willing to believe that you were framed for Saroyan, but I don't buy that you were possessed. People kill people. Not demons." She snapped the cuffs off her belt. "You know the drill."

If he didn't cooperate now, she'd never listen to him again. He held out his arms. "Wayob framed me. If you won't believe me, listen to Rosa. Wayob is still out there. We need to stop him before he kills again."

She shook her head and snapped the cuffs tight on his wrists. As she marched him down the rickety stairs, she kept a safe distance behind him.

"How did you know about the photo?" he asked.

"Anonymous call."

"Nine times out of ten, anonymous tips with real information come from the perp."

"Guess this is one of those rare times, then, unless you called in the tip on yourself?"

"That would make about as much sense as staging that photo with someone watching."

"Well, I doubt you told anyone about it. Ergo, he saw you do Collins. We found fibers under her nails that match for the carpet at the Roosevelt."

"You talk to the staff?"

"They didn't see shit, and there's nothing on the security footage. If you're suggesting a conspiracy, then what's the motive? Collins has no connection to Guatemala or the Lunas. It's too complicated. Plus, the way she was murdered—it was personal. What did she do? Laugh at you?"

Saul shook his head. "I don't know what triggered Wayob. When time did the call come in?"

"This morning, but you know how many phony tips we have to sift through on something like this."

"Collins's murder wasn't reported until noon."

"Exactly—he saw you. Occam's Razor."

Nice play, Wayob. He took two more steps down and turned to face her. She raised her gun. For the millionth time, he wished he'd accepted her invitation. If he'd slept at her place instead of coming here, she probably wouldn't have stayed up working the Collins case. Wouldn't have reviewed the tip log or the forensics. But all that could have been was no good to him now.

"Were you able to confirm his story?" he asked.

"We're working on it." She waved her gun barrel toward the lot. Her Mustang was parked behind his plain wrap, blocking him in.

At the bottom of the stairs, Saul paused again. "How about I drive to the PAB? Save the man hours on the boot who'll have to fetch my car. You can follow me the whole way."

Hernandez snorted and opened the rear door of her Mustang, her weapon stiff by her side.

Saul obeyed her unspoken order. He tried to make eye contact, but she refused to look up at his face. He eased himself into the backseat. The shocks groaned from his weight.

"Think about it," he said. "Evan York here, in the middle of the night, with a girl less than half his age. A young girl who just lost her whole family."

Hernandez slammed the door in his face. Threw open the driver's door. Sat decisively and jammed her key in the ignition.

He thought about what Rosa had said.

He watched Hernandez's reflection in the rearview.

When she finally glanced up at him, he asked, "Do you believe in ghosts?"

Acknowledgements

Thanks to my amazing editor Marissa Van Uden for reading so carefully and paying attention to every detail. Sharpening this work was no easy feat. Thanks to Robin Samuels for such thorough proofreading. Thanks to Donn Marlou Ramirez for the amazing cover design. Thanks to the Writers of Sherman Oaks for the two years of critiquing LA FOG, especially Scott Coon who read every single entry. Thanks to Ted Boyke, Ryan Vinroot, and Seth Freedman. Thanks to Matt Marcy for giving me a glimpse into the life of a magician. If you have the opportunity, check out his show. Thanks to Damien Chazelle, James Lee Burke, Michael Connelly, and thank you, dear readers, for taking the time and supporting my work.

CPSIA information can be obtained
at www.ICGtesting.com
Printed in the USA
BVHW071443170522
637235BV00006B/407